ARTHUR QUINN

AND THE
FENRIS WOLF

Book 2
The Father of Lies Chronicles

ALAN EARLY

MERCIER PRESS
Irish Publisher – Irish Story

MERCIER PRESS
Cork
www.mercierpress.ie

© Alan Early, 2012

ISBN: 978 1 85635 998 6

10 9 8 7 6 5 4 3 2 1

A CIP record for this title is available from the British Library

Printed and bound in the EU.

Praise for *Arthur Quinn and the World Serpent*

Shortlisted for the Best Children's Book, Senior, in the 2011 Bord Gáis Energy Irish Book Awards and chosen as the featured book in the first UNESCO Dublin City of Literature 'Children Save Dublin' Project

'A brilliant creation … fast-paced and thrilling.' – Eoin Colfer, author of *Artemis Fowl*

'A clever blend of fantasy and the every day. It's like Harry Potter, Dublin style.' – *Irish Examiner*

'A gripping yarn that races along towards its epic finale on the streets of the capital … This is bound to be a sure-fire hit and in the Potter, Jackson, Quinn death match, I'll be shouting for the boy in green!' – *Inis Magazine*

'A truly superb book … with several real surprise twists built into the plot, this book was an amazing read … a must read for fans of fantasy and mythology … simply wonderful.' – Mary Esther Judy, *The Bookbag*

'This original and gripping story skilfully draws out the threads linking modern-day Dublin to its darker Viking past by bringing Viking mythology vibrantly to life. A sure-fire hit with adventure lovers.' – *Bookfest*

'A mystical world of mythological characters comes alive, time stops, the unimaginable occurs, and the excitement is full blast from beginning to end.' – *VOYA, Voices of Youth Advocates*

Dedicated to my parents, Luke and Ann, and my brother Paul. I couldn't have written these books without their constant support.

PROLOGUE

The last wolf in Ireland was slaughtered over two hundred years ago. In times before that, they freely roamed the Irish countryside. They slept and hid during the day and prowled the land at night, feeding on livestock and men too weak or stupid to escape them. But man fought back. And by the late 1700s, all wolves were eradicated from Irish soil.

So if someone had wandered through a certain Irish forest in the early twenty-first century, they might have been surprised to find a wild wolf lapping at water from a stream.

The glow of the near-full moon hanging over the forest highlighted the tall, bare trees. Fresh frost glistened on the hard and mossy ground, while sheer ice formed at the stream's edge. The wolf was covered in grey fur, matted around the legs with caked mud. He was a young wolf, no larger than an average Labrador, but with lean muscles in his shoulders bobbing up and down as he drank up the cool water.

He had been on his own for three nights now, heading north, heading home. Nothing felt better than leaving the rest of the pack for a few days once a year, for time by himself, time to think, time to run, time to hunt. But food was scarce in this part of the country. He'd devoured a hedgehog on the first night but had found nothing since. His stomach rumbled, paining him. He wasn't drinking the water out of thirst but rather to fill his stomach.

He was so grateful for the water that he didn't hear or smell the wolf on the opposite side of the stream.

The second wolf was unquestionably larger and broader than the first. It didn't have the same malnourished look as the grey one, but appeared sturdy and well fed. Its fur was golden blond – lustrous and thick – with a black stripe running down its back. It stood on a rock by the stream, not drinking, barely breathing, merely watching the grey wolf.

The water felt good on the grey wolf's tongue, though it was so cold it stung the nerves of his teeth. If the weather continued as cold as it had been, the stream would be frozen over in another night or two. The ice at the edge was sure to spread. As he slurped up the water, he studied it for the first time, noticing thin icicles dipping along on the stream. No doubt these had broken off from the branches of trees further upriver. It was while watching one of these icicles that he spotted the golden wolf's reflection.

Without even chancing a look at the wolf on the other side of the stream, the grey wolf bolted in the opposite direction. He'd just reached the cover of the undergrowth when he heard the golden wolf follow, splashing in and out of the stream in one fluid motion.

The grey wolf knew it would do no good to hide. If the other wolf could smell him as well as he could now smell it, then his only option was to outrun it. He raced through the undergrowth, diving headfirst into the darkness with briars and branches swatting him in the face and tearing at his coat. And all the while, the golden wolf pursued.

As he plunged deeper into the forest, the grey wolf recognised some landmarks: a certain mossy stone, a gnarled branch, a tree that had been split by lightning. He'd come this way only minutes beforehand, when he was searching for the stream. He quickly formed a plan. If he turned off course fast enough, then he might trick the golden wolf into following the scent he'd left on the track earlier, and this would give him enough time to escape.

He took a deep breath and broke off to the left as swiftly as he could. He was moving so fast now he couldn't hear if he'd shaken the other wolf. The muscles in his legs were burning by the time he came upon a felled tree stump. The stump was lying on its side. It was hollow and large enough for him to crouch down inside. He crawled in on his belly, held his breath and listened to the woods around him.

Silence. Not so much as a breeze rustled the dead leaves on the ground. Total silence.

The wolf stayed there and watched the moon until it had moved what he judged to be a good distance across the sky. Then he cautiously emerged.

Suddenly something was on him, turning him around and pinning him down on his back. He looked up to see the golden wolf there, fangs bared and growling.

The grey wolf started to struggle, but it was no use. A green light unexpectedly flowed out of his captor's eyes. The radiance covered him entirely, obscuring the other animal. It was momentarily so bright that the grey wolf was forced to close his eyes, then suddenly it faded away. The golden wolf was gone now. There was a man in its place, his hand locked on the wolf's throat. His hair was platinum blond and his nose was long and stately. His facial hair had been shaved into a neat, modern beard. He wore a three-piece suit underneath a black coat that reached down to his shins.

Terrified, the grey wolf yapped and whined. The man just smiled. The grin went from ear to ear, exposing two rows of sparkling white teeth.

'Who am I?' the man said, as if in response to the wolf's whimpering. 'I am the Trickster Lord, the God of Mischief, the Father of Lies. I am Loki.' He leaned forward, tightening his grip on the wolf. 'Now it's your turn to answer me. Where are the others?'

CHAPTER ONE

'Where are the others?' Arthur Quinn asked when he returned from the bathroom.

'Just gone to get some drinks and stuff,' his dad, Joe, answered.

The bowling alley was alive with noise: coins being dropped into slot machines, pinballs bouncing off bells, video games buzzing and whirring and firing, pins being knocked down and replaced in the alley itself; and over it all pumping pop music from the 1980s. It was Sunday evening, the last day of Joe's Christmas break, and he had brought them here for one final treat before the January drudgery began.

Arthur ran his hand through his short hair – he'd gotten his once shaggy mane cut just before Christmas – and sat next to Joe, who was busy putting names into the electronic bowling scoreboard. Arthur studied his reflection in the screen. He had the same blue-green eyes as his father but his freckles were a gift from his mother. At the thought of her, he instinctively looked down at the pale gold ribbon tied around his wrist. It had been hers. Before she'd died.

At the time he'd thought that her death was the worst thing that could happen to him. But since then he'd been through a lot of craziness. Looking at Joe, he mused that he wasn't the only one. Only a few months ago his father had been viciously attacked by the Norse god of mischief, Loki. Joe had been seriously injured and for a time Arthur wasn't sure if he'd survive. Even now, his right leg hadn't healed properly and Joe still had to use a stick in order to move around. Apart from that, things were starting to get back to normal for Joe. He worked as head engineer of the Dublin Metro tunnel-drilling team, overseeing the massive excavation job under the Liffey – and it had all been going smoothly of late. Arthur was pleased for him.

Of course, Joe had only a fragmented recollection of his attacker and he certainly didn't suspect that it had been a Norse god. But then, apart from Arthur and his friends, Ash and Max, no one else in the world knew about their tangle with Loki. The god had gotten close to them by posing as Will, a shrewd and personable boy who turned out to be just one of the forms the Trickster God was able to assume. He had fooled them into helping him free the Jormungand – a giant flying snake also known as the World Serpent, who was Loki's oldest child. Loki's plan had been to use the Jormungand to destroy the world, and he would probably have succeeded had it not been for Arthur, his friends and a resurrected army of dead Vikings.

'Here they come now,' Joe said, looking up from the scoreboard. Their neighbours, Ash, Max and Stace Barry, were approaching, each one loaded down with boxes of popcorn, hotdogs dripping with ketchup, and drinks. At twelve, Ash – short for Ashling – was the same age as Arthur. She usually tied her auburn hair up in a ponytail, but this evening it hung free around her face. Stace was seventeen and in her last year of school before going to college. She looked just like an older version of Ash. Max, their younger brother, was an excitable seven-year-old who had had a difficult couple of months. Arthur was pleased to see Max back to his old self. During the incident with Loki, Max had been held hostage by the Trickster God. For several weeks after, Max had suffered terrible nightmares. He would wake up sweating and screaming and only Ash's cuddle could calm him back to sleep. During the day, he would be jittery and paranoid, afraid to leave the house by himself. But the longer there was no sign of Loki, the more the nightmares faded, until finally, a couple of weeks ago, they had stopped completely. Max was now almost back to that same boy who, even when Arthur had just arrived in Dublin, constantly pleaded with him to play football in all weathers. He, Arthur and Ash were the only people Loki had allowed to retain their memories of his devastating attack on Dublin, and even though it was over two months since the attack, Arthur knew that all three of them thought of it frequently, although they rarely spoke about it.

Arthur shook away all thoughts of Loki and got up to help the Barry siblings with the snack food.

'What took you so long?' he chided with a smile.

'Some*body* had to fix their make-up!' Ash said with a sideways glare at her sister.

'It wasn't me!' shouted Max with a mouth full of popcorn, simultaneously trying to take a sip of Coke.

'You can't really blame me,' Stace said as she handed a hotdog to Joe. 'There are some good-looking guys around here.' She surveyed the bowling alley, fluttering her eyelashes, then turned back to Ash. 'Don't worry. You'll understand one day when you get interested in boys.'

Ash's face flushed. She glanced at Arthur, hoping he hadn't noticed. But he was too busy helping Max unload his armfuls of food and drinks. He looked up, catching her gaze.

'Sorry,' he said, 'I missed that. Did you say something?'

'Nope!' Ash said hurriedly before Stace could butt in. 'Nothing! So, are we ready to play?'

'All set!' exclaimed Joe, hitting the Enter key one last time on the scoreboard. 'You're up first, Max.'

Across the city, in the cobblestone square of Smithfield, was the Viking Experience. Surrounded by a high wall covered in murals depicting ancient life and legends, it was a recreated Viking village, chock-a-block with small plywood houses topped off with thatched roofs. Among all the laneways and streets, there was even a market area and a short bridge over a shallow moat. It promised to give visitors a chance to 'See how the Vikings really lived in ancient Dublin!'

It was after eight o'clock on a frosty Sunday evening

so, of course, it was shut. In fact, as it was the off-season, it had been shut since mid-November and wasn't due to open again until the end of February. During the days that it was open, actors played the parts of the inhabitants of the village, while worn mannequins represented other Vikings at work in the small houses. Except that they weren't all really mannequins.

Following the incident with Loki, Arthur was faced with the prospect of hiding almost one hundred dead Viking soldiers who had been resurrected to help him fight the Jormungand. He came up with the plan of sneaking them into the Viking Experience. Here they could mingle with the flaking mannequins and no one would question their dark, leathery faces. It suited them perfectly. They'd feel at home and yet they'd still be hidden, in plain sight. As long as they didn't move much during the days while there were visitors, the nights were theirs to do what they pleased. And on this night they'd lit a bonfire in the centre of the market.

The army had been hidden under the earth for over a thousand years. And yet it seemed like mere minutes from the time they'd all died silently to the time they awoke last October. They'd given their lives to protect the world – each one taking a potion to stop his heart, only for it start up again if, or when, the Jormungand was to escape – and the world would never know it.

Bjorn, the leader of the soldiers and Arthur's second-in-command, sat closest to the fire on a papier mâché throne they'd borrowed from the prop room. Even though they were dead and the cold didn't bother them, Bjorn was still glad to be reclining in this seat of honour. It felt good to pretend that they still needed a fire to keep warm. He looked around at his army. A handful of his men had been destroyed by the Jormungand, but most had survived. They all wore the same dusty tunics they'd put on the day they were sent to guard the World Serpent's lair. They could have exchanged them for cleaner, more comfortable clothes from the costume room, but they didn't want to. It was nice to still have that link to the past, to their families, to their wives and children who'd died centuries ago.

Bjorn smiled to himself as he watched his men. They were joking and laughing – although, in the grunts that were all their dried-up voice boxes could manage, the chuckles came out as wheezing, throaty sounds accompanied by shoulder-shakes. A couple were even attempting to sing songs from their homeland in high-pitched snorts. They were happy. But for how long? He had assumed that once the Jormungand was defeated they would finally have been granted a peaceful death. And yet, here they were, still alive in a strange place and a strange time.

Suddenly a shiver ran up his spine.

This was unexpected. He hadn't felt the sensations of hot, cold or pain since he'd awoken, and yet what had just happened was unmistakable. A cold shiver, rising from the base of his spine, had shot upwards to his neck.

A nearby Viking grunted to him. It roughly translated as, 'What was that?' From the fearful expression on all of their faces Bjorn knew that they'd all experienced the same thing.

'I don't know,' Bjorn grunted back, 'but I fear that dark times are coming.'

※※※※※

In another part of Dublin, a few miles from where the bowling was now well under way, in Arthur's empty bedroom something equally strange was happening.

It was almost totally silent in the Quinn household. The flat-screen TV downstairs was on standby, the buzzing of its tiny red light barely audible. The large refrigerator in the kitchen hummed faintly. The numbers on the alarm clock that had been a birthday gift from Arthur's mother to Joe a few years ago blinked softly in the dark. The light was on in the downstairs hallway to dissuade potential burglars. Abruptly all of these things and every other electrical item in the house simultaneously switched off, as all electrical power was drained within a two-mile radius of the Quinn home, plunging the area into darkness. Mobile phones turned themselves off, MP3 players stopped playing, laptop computers ceased to run. Even cars were stopped in their tracks, their electronics failing instantaneously.

There was only one glimmer of light in the entire blackout area, but nobody was around to see it. It was in Arthur's room, emanating from under his bed. It was a steady and pulsing green glow coming from a mysterious object: a hammer with an iron head, curved at the top. There were runes – ancient letters – carved into the head, while fine rope was wrapped around the short handle. Arthur had found it in the Jormungand's lair with the Vikings. He'd used it to defeat Loki and then, unsure of what it was or what to do with it, but sure it might come in handy at a later date, he'd stashed it under his bed. And now it was glowing vividly.

It was Arthur's third turn to bowl. After the second round, Stace was in the lead, which surprised even her. Arthur stepped up to their lane – to cheers of encouragement from the others behind him – and concentrated on the pins at the far end. He squinted and lined up his ball. When he was happy with his aim, he took two steps backwards.

With one last look to make sure his aim was dead centre, he ran forward, crouching slightly with his arm back to launch his ball. He swung forward to release it, but just as his fingers slipped out of the holes, a sharp and searing pain burned into his chest. The ball thumped onto the glossy floor, wobbled slowly forward for a bit and then slid into one of the gutters as Arthur clutched his chest and fell backwards to the floor.

The pain was gone as quickly as it had started. Arthur watched the ball roll down the gutter towards the pins. Only they weren't pins any more. They were teeth: huge razor-sharp fangs. He recognised them instantly. A forked tongue flicked out between them, globs of spit landing on the waxed floor. It was the mouth of the Jormungand! It was back. Somehow, it had returned and it was making its terrible screeching sound.

Arthur scrambled backwards in a panic, looking around

to see if anyone else had noticed the transformation, but everyone was acting normally, laughing, bowling and chatting with their friends. When he looked back at the end of the lane, the mouth was gone. Once again it had become a set of white bowling pins, nothing more. But the words painted above the pins had changed. It had once read 'BOWLING FUN!' in a brightly coloured font. Those letters were gone now, replaced by lines and cross-hatches. He couldn't read them but he knew exactly what they were. Runes.

He got to his feet and looked around him. Every sign and poster in the bowling alley had changed. The letters were no longer from the English alphabet: they'd also been replaced by runes.

The pendant Arthur always wore around his neck had fallen out from inside his T-shirt and was lying against his chest, glowing bright green. With one swift motion, he pulled it off and stuffed it into his pocket. Instantly, the runes reverted to English words.

'You all right, son?' Joe asked. 'You took quite a spill there.' The others had gathered at the end of the lane, looking at him with worried expressions.

'I'm fine,' he uttered eventually. 'I just slipped.'

Joe smiled sympathetically as he and Stace returned to

their seats. Ash and Max waited behind with questioning faces.

'Just slipped?' Ash asked.

'No,' Arthur conceded, 'no, I didn't just slip.' He took the glowing pendant out of his pocket and showed it to them, careful not to let anyone else see it.

'What does it mean?' Max asked, his voice trembling with trepidation.

Arthur didn't want to say the words but he had to. 'I think it means it's starting again.'

CHAPTER TWO

Bang!

Arthur woke with a start to find that he had a crick in his neck. He looked around, momentarily confused, then checked the time on his phone. It was a little after seven in the morning and Joe had just left for work, slamming the door on his way out.

After arriving home from bowling the previous night – which had taken much longer than usual thanks to the fresh and treacherous layer of frost on the roads – they were surprised to find that their street had been plunged into a blackout. There was total darkness, save for the large moon hanging in the night sky.

'It's probably due to the weather,' said Joe, dropping Ash, Max and Stace off. 'Maybe the ice on the power lines became too heavy and broke them.'

The Barry siblings went into their darkened house to find that their parents had positioned flickering candles around the rooms in place of the electric lights. Mr and Mrs Barry were reading by the soft light while their granny, who had been staying with them since Christmas, was on the couch, snoring like a jackhammer.

The Quinn men returned to their quiet home. Entering it like this, so silent and lifeless, reminded Arthur of their first time in the house a few months previously. It was all very modern inside, with white walls, pale wooden floors and recessed ceiling lighting. But now those bulbs were in darkness.

Joe tried flicking the switch but to no avail. 'I think there's a torch in the car,' he said and went back out into the cold.

Arthur took his mobile phone out of his pocket to turn on the flashlight application. As he hit the key, he realised that the phone was unexpectedly off. He tried the power button, but no luck there either. With an irritated grunt, he dropped the phone back in his pocket and turned to face the darkened stairwell. His eyes had become slightly adjusted to the gloom – not by much, but enough to follow the steps upstairs.

The first-floor hallway was windowless and none of the

adjacent doors were open, which meant that there wasn't even any moonlight to penetrate the total darkness. He could just about see for a foot or two in front of his face. Arthur thought of what had happened at the bowling alley. Was the vision some kind of warning? What if Loki was hiding in the darkness?

As soon as the thought formed in his head, he regretted it.

'Don't be ridiculous,' he said to himself out loud, just to break the silence, and moved forward towards his bedroom door. He pushed the door inward, expecting to be confronted with more darkness. Instead, he was surprised to find a soft green light filling his room. It pulsated gently and reminded him of the light the pendant gave off. Only it wasn't the pendant: that had stopped glowing before they left the bowling alley and, besides, it was safely tucked away in his pocket.

The light could only be coming from one place. He ducked to the ground and reached under the bed, brushing aside a flimsy spider's web. He faintly heard its former occupant scuttling across the wooden floor. As soon as his fingertips brushed the hammer, the glowing stopped. He heard a low hum that hadn't been there seconds previously and things grew brighter. He sat up and looked out the window. The streetlights were back on, as was his desk lamp.

'Power's back!' Joe called from downstairs. 'How about some hot chocolate?'

'Yes, please!' Arthur replied. He sat back on his feet, mystified at what had just happened, then got up and went to join Joe downstairs.

When the hot chocolate was ready, and topped with a generous portion of marshmallows each, they sat sipping it together and watching *The Sound of Music* on TV for the third time this holiday season. Joe hummed along to the songs and giggled at little Gretl the same way he did every year. But Arthur barely paid attention to the singing Austrian children. The only thing on his mind was what had happened at the bowling alley. What could it possibly mean? Was Loki back? Did the Jormungand somehow survive? Were the Viking soldiers in danger? Too many questions and too few answers.

When the film was over, Joe moved to clear up the hot chocolate mugs.

'Are you finished, Arthur?' he asked as he reached for his son's half-full mug. 'You've barely touched yours.'

Arthur looked down at the drink in his hands. He'd thought he'd finished it but had been so deep in thought that he'd simply forgotten about it.

'Sorry,' he said. 'I think I'm still full from all that junk we had at bowling.'

Joe put his own mug on the coffee table and sat back down on the sofa. He awkwardly rested his arm across Arthur's shoulder.

'I'm sorry, Son,' he said.

Arthur looked him in the eye. 'For what?'

'This is our first Christmas … without her.'

'Oh. Yeah.' It was something that had been on Arthur's mind almost constantly over the holidays, only just not right at that moment.

'I'm sorry I have to go back to work tomorrow. But you'll have fun on Tuesday.'

'I know. It's fine. Honestly.' And then, because he glimpsed a look of sadness in his father's eyes, he added, 'I love you, Dad.'

'I love you too, Son.' Joe stood up, taking the mugs with him. 'Well, goodnight. Don't stay up too late.'

Arthur watched his dad go into the kitchen, limping slightly on his right leg – the one constant reminder of Loki's vicious attack. At the thought of it, Arthur was suddenly filled with rage. He clutched the pendant in his pocket. Even though it had stopped glowing, he could still feel a faint warmth from it. At that moment he swore to himself that he wouldn't allow Loki to hurt his father or his friends ever again.

He bounded upstairs, taking the steps two at a time, and stepped into his bedroom. His desk lamp was still switched on – a bad habit that Joe was always scolding him about – but he turned it off, plunging the room into darkness. After a few seconds, his eyes became accustomed to the dark, brightened slightly by the amber glow from the streetlights penetrating the darkness in the room.

He knelt down and reached under his bed, pulling out the hammer. The head of the hammer was forged from a dark and dented iron, with runes beaten into each side. The handle was half as long as the head was wide – barely long enough for an adult hand to wrap around it. The whole thing looked very heavy and Arthur knew from the way it thudded to the ground if he dropped or threw it that it was a dead weight. And yet it didn't feel heavy when he lifted it – in fact when he held it, it was like an extension of his arm and felt just right.

Shortly after the incident with Loki, he'd asked the Vikings what it was and what it meant. All he'd managed to grasp from the rather one-sided conversation was that it was very powerful and none of the soldiers wanted it. It was his now, they'd indicated. He made a mental note to try asking them again soon.

He placed the hammer on his desk. Then he took the pendant from his pocket and laid it alongside. He sat down and looked at the silent world outside. Arthur could see Ash's house across the estate. All the lights were switched off, everyone in bed, asleep. He suspected some were sleeping more peacefully than others. A warm tangerine glow flickered through the living-room window – the last embers in the fireplace burning down, no doubt. All the other houses on the street were equally undisturbed. Here and there a light was still on, but no one moved and nothing stirred. The grassy knoll in the centre of the estate – known as the green – was actually white now, painted by an ever-increasing crust of frost. The trees were leafless and the cars were lifeless. And all the while, Arthur watched.

He stayed at his desk, watching the night pass by. If Loki showed up, he'd know. Every hour on the hour he got up and paced the room to stretch his legs. At one point a light flicked on in the Barry household. He wasn't fully sure of the layout of the house but he guessed that it might have been Max's room. Moments later, the window was in darkness again. The nightmares are back, most likely, he thought grimly.

The only movement outside all night occurred just after 4 a.m. when the young couple across the estate left their house, pulling suitcases behind them. Probably off to some warmer climate on an early flight. Arthur couldn't help but feel jealous of them. They looked so happy to be leaving – exhausted but happy. They certainly didn't have the worries he did.

An hour later, as he leaned back in his chair, he found that his eyelids were getting heavier by the minute. Maybe, he thought to himself, I can close them. For just a couple of minutes. To rest them. And then I'll be able to stay awake for the rest of the night.

He allowed his eyelids to close, relishing the sweet release. The next thing he knew the downstairs door slammed as Joe left for work and it was just after 7 a.m. He shook his head, groggily cursing himself for falling asleep. Apart from Joe's Land Rover pulling out of the drive, the estate was still deserted. The sun hadn't risen properly yet, but there was a faint pink hue in the sky. By the looks of things, it was going to be another bright and clear day. Which probably also meant that it was going to be as cold as it had been the past few weeks. This cold snap had started well before Christmas and, although it

31

hadn't snowed, every outside surface was still coated with ice and frost.

He swivelled in his seat and looked at his bed. He didn't want to crack but it did look very inviting. Arthur weighed up his options. It was getting bright now and it was unlikely that Loki would appear during the day – if he was coming at all. More people would start going to work in the next hour. Loki probably wouldn't risk it.

Arthur stumbled from his chair and collapsed onto the mattress with a thwump. He was sound asleep seconds later, still in his clothes, lying on top of the blanket and snoring lightly.

Krzzzz …

Arthur blinked his eyes open and dazedly wiped away the line of drool that had formed between his mouth and the pillow. The room was awash with white winter light now and when he sat up in bed he had to squint. The noise that had awoken him so harshly sounded like a bee or else a large bluebottle. Either way, it shouldn't have been in his room in the middle of winter. Unsteadily, he swung his feet off the bed and stood up. Then he spotted the source.

His phone was vibrating noisily on his desktop. It was rattling against the iron hammer, making it louder than usual. He grabbed it and pressed the answer key as quickly as he could.

'Hello?' he croaked in a dry, hoarse voice.

'Hiya!' Ash's voice replied from the other end. 'It's just me. I'm outside. You up yet?'

'Yeah, yeah, I'm up.' He stifled a yawn then cleared his throat. 'What time is it?'

'It's eleven. Are you going to let me in or do I have to freeze to death out here?'

'I'll be down in a second.' He hung up and pulled out a fresh T-shirt and jeans from his wardrobe. He didn't have time for a shower with Ash waiting outside so he ran into the bathroom and sprayed some of Joe's Lynx under each arm. It stung so much that he hopped back into his room with his arms splayed wide. When the pain subsided, he pulled on the fresh clothes and went downstairs.

He was still rubbing the crick out of his neck as he opened the door. Ash – all bundled up in a heavy waterproof coat, scarf, hat and gloves – stepped inside. A bitingly cold gust of air followed her in. Arthur, still in his bare feet, shivered and shut the door behind her.

'What's wrong with your neck?' she asked, noticing him massaging the tender spot.

'I slept in my chair,' he explained.

'You did what?'

'Actually, I only slept there for a couple of hours. I stayed up most of the night.'

'Why would you do that?'

'A couple of reasons. I was on lookout for Loki, first of all. And then … well … I didn't want to have any more of those weird dreams.' During their first encounter with Loki, Arthur had experienced a number of strange and vivid dreams. They were visions of a place called Asgard, where the Norse gods lived. He'd learned a lot in those dreams, like why the gods banished Loki from Asgard and what they did with him, but he still didn't want to start having them again. If that happened, it would leave little doubt that Loki really was active once more.

'Oh,' said Ash. 'And did you see anything?'

'Nothing. No sign of Loki and no dreams.'

'Well that's good. Maybe it was a false alarm.'

'Maybe. Hopefully. Max had another nightmare, though, didn't he?'

She nodded. 'Same as before. He's flying over the city on the World Serpent and then he slips off. And Loki just lets him fall. He woke up screaming.'

'I saw the light.' He paused, reluctant to suggest what he was about to say. 'Ash, I think we should go and see the Vikings today. Before we go to Westmeath.'

Every year after Christmas, the Barry siblings went to visit their cousin in Westmeath for a few days and this year they'd invited Arthur to join them. When they'd suggested it to his dad, Joe was thrilled at the prospect of Arthur having something to occupy him during the remaining days of the Christmas break while he was at work. They were getting the train the following morning.

'Well, I'm free now if you want to go?'

Arthur looked down at his feet. 'Just give me a couple of minutes to put on some shoes.'

※※※※※

After pulling on two thick pairs of socks, a warm, fleece-lined coat, a woolly hat with flaps that covered his ears and a matching scarf and gloves set, Arthur hid the hammer back under the bed and left the house with Ash. As they walked gingerly towards the bus stop, treading carefully to avoid slipping on the ice, he checked a couple of times to make sure he'd remembered to bring the pendant.

Without it, he wouldn't be able to communicate with the Vikings, although a couple of the younger men seemed to be picking up some English. The pendant acted as a sort of translator and let them understand him even if he couldn't always understand their answering grunts.

As they turned the corner onto the main road, they spotted a bus hurtling towards the stop. They realised they wouldn't make it walking so broke into an awkward sprint. Arthur could feel the soles of his shoes sliding along the icy path as he ran. The waiting crowd were boarding the bus quickly and Arthur and Ash were still only halfway there, but then they had a stroke of luck as one of the passengers dropped her coins on the ground. She took her time retrieving them, delaying the bus long enough for Arthur and Ash to glide the last few feet along the ice before the driver closed the door. They scrambled on, both out of breath, and the bus pulled off towards the city centre.

Christmas lights were still strung across the main streets of Dublin, twinkling merrily and swaying in a light breeze. Council workers in high-visibility yellow jackets were sprinkling a mixture of grit and salt on the pavements and roads to combat the ice. For a Monday morning, especially after the crowds over Christmas,

Dublin city centre was surprisingly quiet. Even though most people should have been back to work that day, it seemed as if many had decided to stay at home, keeping nice and cosy, watching family films or repeats of Christmas specials. Part of Arthur wished that he had that option. But part of him was also looking forward to seeing the Vikings. He hadn't visited them since before the start of the Christmas break and he did kind of miss them.

As the bus drove through the city streets, Arthur filled Ash in on what had happened with the hammer and how touching it had brought back the electricity.

'What does it mean?'

'I haven't a clue.'

They got off the bus at Wood Quay – not far from where Joe was working at the Dublin Metro site at Usher's Quay – and walked across the bridge to Smithfield. The high-rise apartment buildings made strange companions for the ancient cobblestone pavements, but the Viking Experience fitted right in. Arthur and Ash were very familiar with the plywood wall around the recreated village and the murals of Vikings from times past. They were also very familiar with the fire door on the south-facing wall, also covered in murals. Arthur knocked twice fast, then once, then twice fast again on the emergency exit. Moments later, the door swung open.

The dead Viking who stood on the other side was tall, with blond hair cut uncharacteristically short. Unlike most of the others, his face was fuller and fleshier and, although his skin had turned the same dark brown during death, it hadn't turned wrinkly like old leather. His name was Eirik. He had been the youngest of the soldiers, only eighteen when he pledged his life to protect the world. Arthur thought that perhaps his age had helped his skin retain some freshness. He was also the Viking who'd learned the most English. While he still couldn't speak it, he could understand most of what Arthur or Ash said without the assistance of the magical pendant.

'Hello, Eirik,' Ash said.

The dead soldier grunted in reply, displaying his blackened teeth in a crooked grin. He stepped aside to let them enter the small dark corridor. The walls were painted black and there were doors along either side: one was labelled *Office*, another *Props*, another *Costumes*.

'We want to talk to Bjorn,' Arthur told Eirik as he pulled the emergency exit shut with a clang.

Eirik nodded at them grimly. Arthur read the expression in an instant. He knows something's up, he thought.

The Viking led them along the corridor. It wound around to the left and they came to another door. He pushed it and they found themselves in the open air again; only this time they emerged into the imitation Viking village.

Bjorn was still seated in his throne in the centre of the market yard. With his high, sharp cheekbones and protruding brow, he was a sight to behold. There wasn't much hair left in his beard, although he'd recently tied the loose strands into a single braid that fell to his chest. The hair on the top of his head was just as sparse, but right now he was wearing a bronze helmet to hide it. Arthur knew he only wore the helmet for battle.

Usually all the others soldiers would be milling around, talking, singing or even honing their fighting skills. But this time they were all gathered around Bjorn – all ninety-one remaining Viking soldiers standing in front of their leader, watching Arthur and Ash.

'They've been waiting for us,' Arthur whispered to Ash under his breath.

'Why?'

'We'll soon find out.' He walked forward through a corridor that formed between the assembled Vikings. As he passed them, they all dropped to one knee, bowing their heads in respect. They had never done this before and it made Arthur feel vaguely uncomfortable. These were men he thought of as his friends. He didn't want them bowing to him. He stopped in front of Bjorn, who lowered his head.

'Don't bow to me, Bjorn,' he said and then turned. 'All of you, stand up. There's no need to bow!'

For a moment, the Vikings looked from one to another. Bjorn grunted a command and they stood.

Arthur turned back to the man he thought of as his second-in-command. 'Something happened, didn't it?'

Bjorn nodded and snorted.

'Loki's up to something, isn't he?'

Bjorn dipped his head sombrely.

'Something really bad?'

Bjorn's head bobbed affirmatively.

'Do you know what it is?'

The dead Viking shook his head.

'But you're scared? You're all really scared?'

Bjorn looked at the ground, avoiding Arthur's gaze.

'Bjorn?' he asked again.

Eventually Bjorn raised his head and met Arthur's eyes. Then he simply nodded.

CHAPTER THREE

The Trickster God never enjoyed being in this four-legged wolf form. He much preferred to stand as a man, tall and broad with a nose that couldn't smell the stinking earth around him. But being a wolf did have its benefits. He liked to run his coarse tongue along his piercing fangs and he could feel the great strength in his jaws even when his mouth was relaxed. Plus, being a wolf made it easier to follow the grey wolf.

They ran north all through the first night, leaping over hedges, bounding through briars and spooking sheep. They avoided towns and villages and crept past farmhouses only if necessary. The rolling Irish countryside was enduring sub-zero conditions, but they sprinted too fast to feel the cold. The grey wolf had given up any thought of escape. He was resigned to the fact that he had to lead the god to the others. As the sun rose in the east, bringing little warmth with it, the grey wolf idled to a stop. He looked back at Loki, whose golden wolf fur was almost glowing in the morning light, and scratched a paw into the hard earth.

Loki understood the gesture and, though he wasn't pleased, he saw the sense in the grey wolf's suggestion. It was time to stop, time to rest. The daytime was not a good time for a wolf to be out.

Too far from any caves, forests or mountainsides, they huddled together in a ditch at the side of a meadow, away from any possible prying eyes. The grey wolf slept through the day, rolling in his sleep and snoring with his great tongue lolling out. Loki didn't need sleep so simply lay quietly. He was patient. It was something he'd learned in a thousand years of captivity. Good things come to those who wait. Or, in his case, evil things.

As the day came to an end and dusk approached, he took a chance and crawled out of their little ditch. He'd heard something across the meadow and wanted to investigate. Moments later he returned to the grey wolf, carrying a dead hedgehog in his chops, dripping blood. He dropped it at the snout of the wolf, startling him into waking. The grey wolf looked at Loki then back at the hedgehog. It was so temptingly juicy, he couldn't resist. He devoured it in three bites, belching back up the skull and bones. Loki was pleased. The grey wolf wasn't like him and he would need the energy for the journey ahead.

They set off once more, heading in a north-easterly direction now. A full moon hovered in the sky, a bright white disc against silky black. Loki liked the moon. He had been present when it was created all those millennia ago. Some liked it because it was the only light in a sea of darkness; truly a gift of the gods to humanity. But Loki liked it because man generally feared it. It was a symbol of cold times, of nightfall, and humans foolishly feared the superstitions they passed on to each other. Although not all the superstitions were untrue, he knew.

The grey wolf seemed even more determined on the second night than he did on the first. He just concentrated on their destination and getting there as quickly as possible.

The flat lands in the centre of the country were easier to pass through than the hilly fields of the night before, although this brought its own problems. While on the previous night they could run for miles through hills without the risk of being spotted, here they had to stop and hide on several occasions. At one stage they had to cross a motorway, a huge man-made road of concrete and tarmac. Traffic was sparse but fast and the two wolves watched from behind a fence as cars and lorries sped by at reckless speeds. Eventually they had their chance to cross. Only one car approached in the distance but was too far away for the driver to see that there were wolves crossing. As soon as the wolves reached the other side of the motorway, they continued on their journey.

The moon was low in the sky and the sun was close to rising when they reached their destination. They'd come to a large forest and the grey wolf stopped by a gnarled oak tree. Its trunk was as thick as a car and twisted. The branches were bare, save for a few dangerous-looking icicles that hung glittering along their length.

Loki-wolf could smell the magic from the tree. The grey wolf grinned – as much as a wolf could be said to grin – clearly relishing the moment. Then he barked three times quickly.

Suddenly a large chunk of bark at the base of the tree slid aside, revealing a hollow interior. The grey wolf bounded inside and Loki followed just as the bark slid back into place, shutting them in.

It was completely dark inside and, even with his wolf eyesight, Loki couldn't see a thing. He could hear the grey wolf perfectly though – the sound of his footsteps padding away, going deeper into the ground. Loki trailed after him, finding himself in a tunnel just large enough for him to fit through. He could feel dry, hard earth below and above him.

The grey wolf dashed further down the tunnel, bounding ahead, eager to get home. Loki could hear his claws digging up dirt as he went.

As Loki loped down the tunnel, he saw a pinpoint of soft yellow light in the distance. The pinpoint grew larger and the light became brighter as he approached the end of the tunnel. After so much darkness, the light was almost blinding. He could hear a cacophony of noises beyond the tunnel: music and talking, laughing and singing, some growling.

Loki sped up towards the sound, towards the light and the warmth, relishing his moment of triumph. As he took the final leap out of the darkness, he transformed back into his man-form with an ooze of green light.

He found himself in a great circular hall. Heavy curtains hung on the walls alongside ancient and shedding tapestries depicting great battles of long ago. Large fireplaces stood every few feet around the hall, with blazing fires in each, giving Loki his first touch of warmth in days. A chandelier hung from the high ceiling, with its candles flickering brightly and the light reflecting off its hundreds of tiny crystals. A wind-up gramophone was placed on a side table, playing an old vinyl record – some crackly recording of a ragtime classic.

The hall was full of people of every age, gender and race. Loki guessed there must be somewhere between two and three hundred individuals in the hall. Most of the men were wearing suits in a variety of colours, although shades of cream and navy appeared the most popular choice. A couple wore stiff straw hats. The women favoured long dresses, layers of silk that flowed when they moved their legs, and wore wide-brimmed hats on their perfect, not-a-strand-out-of-place hairstyles. The few children were mostly in pastel colours: the boys in striped short pants and matching blazers, the girls dressed like miniature versions of the women. Some of the people had been swaying along to the music from the gramophone; others were seated at the long dining tables arranged throughout the room, eating meals of rare steak with no vegetable sides and sipping glasses of wine or tumblers of brandy; still more were lounging on couches and chaise longues, reading, chatting and joking with each other. There were wolves in the hall, too. Not as many as there were people, but still a significant number. Many of these were eating large chunks of uncooked meat on the bone or gnawing at chicken carcasses. Most of the wolves had placed themselves in front of the fireplaces.

As the people became aware of Loki's presence, the conversation died, until the only sound was the crackling tune coming from the gramophone. One by one the people turned to stare at him. The wolves too stopped their feeding and regarded the new figure warily.

Loki spotted the grey wolf, his travelling companion, now lounging by a fireplace and greedily gobbling down a hunk of meat. His eyes were on the Trickster God too.

The old music that was playing clicked to a stop and the needle lifted off the record. Taking that as his cue, Loki spread his arms as wide as he could, the rustling fabric of his heavy coat the only sound apart from the crackling of the fires.

'Honey,' he exclaimed gleefully, 'I'm home!'

⁂

'How was work?' Arthur called when he heard Joe arrive in, dropping the car keys on the hallway table.

'It was all right,' Joe answered, coming into the living-room to find his son with his feet up in front of the forty-six-inch TV. He collapsed into the adjacent armchair with a sigh. 'Things are finally running smoothly. A lot better than when we got here first. You never know – we might be able to move back to Kerry sooner than we thought. Maybe by April.'

'What?!' The plan had always been to stay in Dublin for less than a year, moving back to Kerry in August so Arthur could start secondary school with his old friends. He'd been hesitant to move to Dublin in the first place, but now he had settled in and made friends.

'Don't you want to go home?' queried Joe.

'Of course I do. It's just … so soon? It's kind of unexpected.'

'Well, it's just a possibility. It's nothing definite. Anyway, I thought you didn't like Dublin?'

'I don't. Well, I do. Never mind.'

Joe took the hint and dropped the subject. They sat in silence, watching a quiz show on the television. Eventually, Joe spoke again.

'Get up to anything today?'

'Not much. Just went into town with Ash.' As usual, he chose not to mention the Vikings.

Following their short discussion about Loki's return,

48

Bjorn had grunted something and waved some of his soldiers over. Eirik and another warrior called Gunnar approached them, carrying a bow and arrow and a longsword. The iron blade of the sword was as long as one of Eirik's lanky legs. The hilt was also iron but wrapped in a fragile, age-worn strap of leather that was stained a dark green, with runes and swirls hammered into the large, round pommel. Patches of crumbly rust clung here and there, but overall it was in great condition considering it had been hidden under the city for a thousand years. The tips of the arrows – also iron – hadn't fared as well, but they still looked sharp enough to do an enemy serious damage. The shafts were long sticks of ash, and the feathers at the end (which Arthur had read once were called the fletching) were pure white, flaked at the top with black. Eirik handed the accompanying bow to Ash – it was almost as tall as her.

'What do they want us to do?' Ash asked Arthur as Gunnar offered the longsword to him.

'I think they want us to take them,' he replied. He shook his head politely to Gunnar then turned to Bjorn. 'We can't use these. They're dangerous.'

Bjorn rumbled a response. Eirik grunted at Ash, getting her attention. He mimed that he had a bow and arrow in his grip. He pulled back the imaginary elastic string then let the make-believe arrow fly. He nodded urgently to Ash, pushing the real bow into her hands.

'They want to teach us,' she realised.

'No,' Arthur said to Bjorn, aghast. 'We can't do that. You can't teach us.'

'Why not?' Ash asked, slightly annoyed and still holding the bow. 'Just because I'm a girl doesn't mean I can't–'

'It's nothing to do with that, Ash.'

'What is it then?' She sounded like she doubted him.

'I don't want … I don't want anything happening to you. Or Max. Not like last time. And if we start messing around with swords and arrows …'

'Someone could get hurt,' Ash finished. She thought for a second then handed the bow back to Eirik. 'You're right.'

They left shortly after, letting the Vikings know that they were going away for a few days but that they'd visit when they were back in the city.

'Looking forward to your trip tomorrow?' Joe's voice brought Arthur out of his thoughts.

'Yeah,' he said, 'it should be fun.' And it was true. Arthur was looking forward to it. After what had happened the previous night, he was delighted to be going away. Maybe it would take his mind off Loki, the World Serpent and everything else.

'Now …' Loki continued. He walked through the hall, looking from one face to the next. Some had fear ingrained deep into their expressions, others appeared more defiant while some, Loki was delighted to see, looked glad to see him. 'Where is the forgotten middle child? My warrior. Where is Fenrir?'

For a moment, everything was still. Then a voice spoke up.

'I'm here.' The man who stepped out of the crowd was taller than all the rest – over seven foot at least – and Loki was surprised he hadn't noticed him before. The perfect warrior, thought the god, knows how to hide in the crowd. The man's beard and hair were black and he wore them both long and wavy. He had broad shoulders and muscled arms that hung low against his slim, athletic waist and he was wearing a navy pin-striped suit. There was a red handkerchief in his breast pocket and a cane in his hand. His eyes were golden and, even from this distance, they were a sight to behold.

'It's me,' the man said, walking towards him. 'I am Fenrir, Loki Wolf-father.' He came to a stop right in front of the Trickster God.

The man towered over him but Loki studied his face closely, noting every detail. The once-familiar visage had aged since he'd last seen it, but not as much as might be expected, considering a thousand years had passed since they had last looked on one another. He looked like a mortal man in his sixties, with tough, wrinkled skin. Loki smiled and wrapped his arms around the man in a tight hug.

'Fenrir, my son!' he bellowed. 'So good to see you again!'

'And you, Wolf-father,' Fenrir said when Loki let him go. At the embrace, the tension in the hall lessened, although the occupants remained silent. They were still unsure of what would happen. When Loki pulled back from the man, they saw that his face was serious.

'You weren't expecting me,' he said, matter-of-factly.

'No, we weren't.'

'I told you, though. Didn't I tell you I'd return!' His lips pulled back in a forced grin but his eyes remained cold.

'You did, Wolf-father.'

'It only took a thousand years but I made it.'

'You did, Wolf-father.'

Loki took a step back from Fenrir, studying his face. He was growing quite sick of the monosyllabic responses.

'Liven up, boy,' he goaded. 'It's like you're scared of me or something.'

For a split second, Fenrir looked away and then Loki knew for sure. He was indeed afraid of him. The grin melted from Loki's face. He walked around Fenrir in a tight circle and continued to talk.

'We'll take over the world together. You and I. I said that would happen, didn't I?'

'You did, Wolf-father.'

'So tell me, Fenrir.' He stopped pacing and looked the man square in the face. 'Where were you?'

Fenrir looked away again. Beads of sweat broke out on his forehead. He spluttered, but couldn't get any words out.

'Hmm?' Bubbles of spit foamed at Loki's grimacing lips. 'I expected you to be waiting for me when I broke free. Where were you? And, more to the point, where are the rest?'

'The rest, Wolf-father?'

'My army.' Loki started pacing the circle again. 'By my estimation there's, what, two, three hundred here. Maybe a little more. Are the others sleeping in some deeper part of this hideaway?'

'There are no more, Wolf-father.'

'What exactly are you saying, Fenrir? Tell me. This is no time for lies. *What are you saying*?' The last words burst out of him in a tremendous roar. When the echo died down, Fenrir answered.

'This is your army.'

There was a split-second pause and then Loki slammed his fist into Fenrir's chest, sending the gargantuan man flying backwards through the air. The people sitting at a nearby dining table scattered out of the way just as Fenrir crashed through the fine wooden top. Plates and cutlery clattered to the stone floor and splinters and dust filled the air. A couple of bystanders whimpered nervously. Loki strode forward furiously, seeming to grow in stature as he did so.

'You had a thousand years, Fenrir! A millennium while I was locked away under the earth. I expected an army of thousands on my return. And you give me this? These fools!' He stormed around the crowd, sneering at them, kicking and shoving some of the slower ones out of the way. 'Women, children and fat, lazy drunkards! This isn't an army worthy of a god!'

People and wolves alike huddled together along the walls, quivering with fear.

'Get out!' Loki screamed. 'All of you – get out!'

There was a scramble of bodies as everyone but Fenrir fought to reach the exits behind the heavy drapes and escape the furious god. He could hear the traces of their footsteps running down concealed tunnels, echoing back into the hall.

Fenrir, meanwhile, struggled into a sitting position. He shook his head, clearly dazed.

Loki took a deep breath to calm himself and turned to him. 'Do you remember, Fenrir? Do you remember what I commanded you to do the night before the gods captured me?'

Fenrir nodded silently.

'Tell me,' said Loki.

'You said to make you an army. You said that the Jormungand would help you conquer the world and that an army would help you keep it.'

'Your brother is gone now,' Loki said, remembering how the World Serpent had vanished when vanquished during his last fight in Dublin. 'And you weren't even there when he died.' He paused, shaking with rage. 'I need an army now more than ever. But it looks like my second child has also failed me. I gave you all the best of me and you fail. You fail!' He swung out a hand and struck Fenrir on the jaw. A red welt rose up on the man's cheek almost instantly and he cringed backwards, away from the god.

'I'll have to take over this task myself,' Loki said, putting out his open palm to Fenrir. 'Give me Hati's Bite.'

Fenrir looked the god in the eye but could not hold his gaze and turned nervously away. A trickle of sweat ran slowly down his face, his neck was red and blotchy and he was breathing heavily.

'I'll say it one more time,' said Loki, in a low, menacing tone. 'Give me Hati's Bite.'

'It's … it's gone.'

'Gone?' Loki took a menacing step towards Fenrir. The man slid involuntarily backwards on the stone floor. He looked around him, searching for an escape, but he knew that, as fast as he was, he could never hope to out-run a god.

'Lost!' he said. 'I mean, it's lost.'

'You fool!' Loki took another couple of steps forward, forcing Fenrir to slide further back along the floor. They were like two magnets of the same polarity, one pushing the other with invisible arms. Fenrir's fingers clawed at the ground, trying to stay in place, but the force of what-ever magic Loki was using was unstoppable and his skin caught on grooves in the stone, bloodying his hands.

'I trusted you with it and you lost it?' Loki walked ever

faster and Fenrir continued to slide, feeling a growing heat at his back. He jerked his head around to see that he was rapidly approaching one of the blazing fireplaces.

'Please, Wolf-father,' Fenrir pleaded. Sweat from the heat and fear soaked his clothing. But Loki ignored him, taking step after resolute step.

Closer, closer. Hotter, hotter.

'Please!'

Loki walked on.

As Fenrir slid involuntarily across hot coals, the flames licked up his broad back, igniting his jacket in seconds and blistering his skin. He could feel the blood almost boiling in his body and could smell the acrid stench of his long locks singeing.

This is it, was all he could think. This is how I die. I burn. In this moment, in the fire. My skin will melt and I'll choke on the smoke it makes. I won't be able to breathe and I'll die.

And then Loki stepped back. Fenrir collapsed out of the fireplace in a heap on the floor. The back of his jacket had burned away and his skin there had broken out in pus-filled red blisters. Apart from that – and the searing pain he felt – he was all right.

'That will be the last time you disappoint me,' spat

Loki. 'Now, where is your sister?'

Breathless, and still in agonising pain, Fenrir muttered something inaudible.

Loki crouched and took Fenrir's head in his strong hands, forcing him to look up into his eyes. 'Louder.' He spoke slowly and evenly, pronouncing each syllable. 'Where is your sister?'

'She's … she's dead.'

Loki rocked backwards on his haunches, letting go of Fenrir. He was taken aback by this news and for a moment his confidence faltered. He'd believed that once he'd found the wolf victory would swiftly follow, but now it seemed like it was once again slipping out of his grasp.

He stared at the smoking heap by the fire. Fenrir, the great disappointment. Fenrir, who should have achieved so much. Fenrir, whom he would have to punish for this terrible failure.

As he squatted there, watching the man fall unconscious with pain and contemplating what to do next, he heard the swish of a curtain behind him.

'Loki Wolf-father?' A voice he didn't recognise spoke. A girl's voice.

'What is it?' he snarled, in no mood to be disturbed.

'I think I can help you. I know where Hati's Bite is.'

CHAPTER FOUR

Connolly Station was alive with activity. Commuters in suits, carrying laptop cases, speed-walked in all directions. Shoppers strolled off the platforms at a much more leisurely pace, many heading straight for the public toilets. Security guards in intimidating black uniforms milled around, watching everyone like hawks. And in the middle of all the hustle and bustle stood Arthur, Ash, Max and Stace, clutching their bags and looking at the departure times.

Joe had dropped them at the station on his way to work, shouting 'Have fun!' from the driver's seat as he pulled away.

They saw from the departure board that they were an hour early thanks to the lift, and decided to have a quick breakfast in the small café in the station. Arthur and Ash both had cereal, Stace opted for a croissant and Max insisted on a packet of salt and vinegar crisps.

Max had been quiet all morning. He'd had yet another nightmare – the same one of him falling through the Dublin sky, plummeting to his death. Stace couldn't understand why he was so upset about the dream.

'Everyone has nightmares where they fall,' she'd said in the car. 'The key is to wake up before you hit the ground.'

When they were finished breakfast, Stace stayed in the café, sipping her coffee and listening for departure announcements, while the others stocked up on sweets and drinks for the journey in the nearby newsagents.

'The 8.35 train from Dublin Connolly to Mullingar is now boarding at Platform 4,' a voice echoed over the Tannoy system, prompting Stace to gather up the other three and lead them through the departure gate.

The train was new and modern, with comfortable reclining chairs and electric doors as standard. It wasn't too packed at this time of the morning and they easily found a table with two pairs of seats facing each other. Minutes later the train rolled out of the station. Stace was already on her phone, checking her Facebook page, while Max was fixated on a comic book he'd bought back in the little shop. From the way his eyes moved across the page,

Arthur could tell that he was reading the words but not really taking them in.

Arthur turned and watched the city pass by the window in silence. They travelled on high bridges and tracks, over the red-slated roofs of Dublin's northside. Pigeons roosting in chimney stacks and sheltering from the cold scattered and flew as the noisy train rattled past. A cat prowling over a garden wall slipped on an icy patch and fell to the ground, landing on its paws with a thud. Smoke puffed from some of the chimneys, and trampolines given as Christmas gifts sat idle out in the cold. Most of the streets were quiet at this early hour of the morning. As they passed the mammoth construction of Croke Park – all they could see was a large wall blocking their view – Arthur turned to Ash.

'So tell me more about this Cousin Maggie of yours,' he said.

'Well, she's technically not a cousin for starters.'

'Huh?'

'She's my grandmother's sister. But she's actually closer in age to my mom than my granny. So Mom always just called her Cousin Maggie. She's really her aunt, which makes her my grandaunt.'

Arthur raised one eyebrow at her.

'Don't look so confused,' she said. 'It's simple: she's my grandaunt but we call her Cousin Maggie.'

'Uh … okaaaay.'

Ash playfully punched his shoulder before going on. 'She's so cool, though. She lives in this big farmhouse and she's got chickens and goats and a couple of pigs and she's an artist.'

'You really like her, don't you?'

'Yeah, I do. And she makes the best rhubarb crumble. Wait till you try it.'

'I don't usually like rhubarb.'

'You haven't tried Cousin Maggie's crumble yet!'

Once the train had left the city it picked up speed and, as Arthur gazed out the window, the landscape flashed past. The train stopped several times during the journey, allowing new passengers to board in quiet villages en route. About an hour had passed when the train plunged into a corridor of dense trees and bushes, which blocked out most of the sunlight. When it emerged into the light again, the sudden glare forced Arthur to squint.

On the left-hand side of the train was a main road, cars falling behind as they passed. But on the right-hand side, through the window Arthur was looking out of, an expansive lake ran right alongside the train track. The lake spread almost as far as he could see. In the far distance he could make out the opposite shore – green fields and woodland. The water was still and totally frozen over – a great, white vastness. A basic-looking rowboat was frozen in place next to a tiny pier. A small island nestled in the centre of the lake. It was overgrown, covered in bushes, with lush green pines scattered here and there; clearly nobody lived there now, although somebody had at one time. Looming over the treetops from the hub of the island was a round tower. It was a tall cylinder made of grey stone, with a small battlement on the flat roof. Arthur could see three narrow windows cut into the wall up the tower. He'd seen lots of pictures of round towers in history books, and even a few in person back in Kerry, but he'd never seen any that were as enormous or impressive as this one, or had a roof like that.

Arthur turned to Ash to ask her about the island when suddenly the train plunged through another thick covering of trees, obstructing their view.

'Not far now,' Ash commented, smiling at him.

'Cousin Maggie!' Max cried excitedly, running with

outstretched arms along the Mullingar platform towards a woman in her early fifties. Cousin Maggie was a tall, rotund lady with unkempt auburn hair falling to her shoulders in curls. There were streaks of grey at each temple. She was wearing blue dungarees, a pink shirt, a cream Aran sweater and a long brown coat that looked like it might have been designed for a man. All were stained with spots of paint here and there; the dungarees were particularly bad. Two pairs of glasses hung around her neck, each on a little gold chain.

'Mighty Max!' she shouted back, catching the boy in her arms and squeezing him tightly. When she was done, she stood back to take a full appraisal of him. 'Look at you. You're so tall. You're all getting so big now!'

'Hi, Cousin Maggie,' Stace said.

'You're all grown up, Stace!' her grandaunt said, admiring her skinny jeans and big handbag. 'Or should I say "m'lady Stacy"?' She curtsied with a cheeky grin.

'Don't, Cousin Maggie!' Stace pleaded, watching a couple of boys she'd had her eye on earlier pass by. 'You're embarrassing me.'

Maggie stood back to her full height with a grunt and turned to Ash.

'Look at you, Ash,' she said. 'You're the image of your

mother. And twice as smart, she tells me!'

Ash blushed. 'Hi, Cousin Maggie.' She turned to indicate Arthur. 'And this is–'

'You must be Arthur,' Maggie cut her off.

'Nice to meet you, Miss … uh … Missus–' Arthur stuttered before Maggie interceded.

'There's no "Miss" or "Missus" here,' she said. 'That was my sister and my mother. You can call me Maggie. Or Cousin Maggie. Everyone does.'

'Nice to meet you, Cousin Maggie.' He offered his hand for a shake but she grabbed him in a tight hug. When she let him go, she noticed that he'd gone red.

'I like to hug,' she explained. 'I should have mentioned that. No place for handshakes or formalities around here. This isn't Buckingham Palace. Now!' She turned on one foot, military-like, and marched briskly away. 'This way. To the Maggie-mobile!'

The boxy brown Volvo that was the Maggie-mobile was parked just outside the station. Some of the paintwork had flaked off years ago at the edges of the doors, and the radio aerial was just a clothes hanger taped in place. They dumped their bags in the creaking boot and climbed in: Stace in the passenger seat, the others squeezed into the back. The car stank of animals and Arthur noticed long white hairs stuck to the worn upholstery.

'Oh, that's from Bessie,' Cousin Maggie said, noticing him picking up one such hair. 'She's shedding.'

'Who's Bessie?' he whispered to Ash as Maggie started the car.

'One of the goats.'

The Maggie-mobile coughed into life with a splutter and pulled away from the station. Mullingar was a large, busy town, but Maggie was able to manoeuvre around the hectic traffic with ease and they were out in the open countryside in a few minutes. When they'd left the town behind them, Maggie popped a cassette tape into the slot and pressed Play. Opera music filled the car. The powerful voice of a soprano boomed out of the speakers set in the doors. Maggie sang along. She knew every word, even though it was sung in Italian, but she was horribly out of tune. Max stuck a finger in each ear and Stace looked out the window, trying to ignore the noise but too polite to copy Max. Ash just chuckled happily, while Arthur did his best to keep a straight face.

A few miles outside the town, Maggie turned the Volvo down a narrow, winding road. There was just enough space for one car on this laneway and twigs scratched at the windows and doors. They emerged into a wide open space, the car bouncing along on slippery cobblestones. The farmhouse stood on top of a slight hill, looking warm and inviting. It was an old building, two storeys high and with walls that must have been repainted white countless times in the past hundred years. Smoke floated out of a pair of chimneys and little lights twinkled cheerfully on a real Christmas tree in a downstairs window. Arthur could just make out a couple of barns and sheds behind the house and there was a small chicken coop leaning against one gable side. To the left of the house was a meadow – white with frost and currently unused – and to the right was woodland sloping downwards.

'That forest leads to the lake you saw from the train,' Ash said when she noticed him looking at the trees. 'We should go explore tomorrow.'

'Here we are!' boomed Cousin Maggie as she put on the parking brake. 'Chez Maggie! Also known as Maggie's Farm. You know that Bob Dylan wrote the song about me?'

'Really?' Arthur whispered in Ash's ear. She shook her head with a smile.

He unbuckled his seatbelt then turned to get out.

'Argh!' Arthur cried. Something was staring at him through the car window – a stretched, grey face with a long black beard hanging from its chin. A pair of wide brown eyes gazed from the sides of the face and gigantic ears drooped down by the cheeks. Two ghastly looking horns twisted out of the crown of the skull. The beast snorted angrily in response to Arthur's cry.

'Are you scared of goats, Arthur?' Max asked from behind him.

'What?' The scary face bleated and Arthur realised that it was just a goat looking at him, not a wicked demon as he'd thought at first. Embarrassed, he flushed and then laughed nervously. 'Oh. Not afraid, no. It just gave me a shock, that's all.' The goat moved back from the door and Arthur pushed it open.

'Hello, Bessie,' he said, stepping out into the cold air.

'That's not Bessie,' Cousin Maggie said as she came around the car to shoo the goat off. 'That's Nessie. Because of the long neck. See?' Arthur did notice that the goat's neck seemed rather long now that she'd pointed it out. 'Just like the Loch Ness Monster. He's the billy goat. There's Bessie over there.' She pointed to the side of the house where a smaller goat peeped around the corner. Its coat was white and its horns weren't as big as the first goat's. 'Bessie's a little shyer than Nessie.'

The billy goat trotted over to Bessie and the two of

them darted off behind the house.

After that, Maggie brought her guests on a tour of the farm, mainly for Arthur's benefit. She first herded the goats back into their pen, pointing out that they were both very much in love even if they didn't know it. Then she led the visitors around the farmhouse to a barn where two large black pigs were snoring loudly on soft mounds of hay. They were brothers called Knick and Knack and she'd bought them from a farmer a few years back. She didn't intend to slaughter them – as she didn't any of her animals – she just liked the company. Next she showed them the chicken coop where three hens and one cockerel clucked at them warily.

'That's Charlotte, Emily and Anne,' she pointed out. 'And that grumpy looking cockerel is called Byron. If we're lucky, we might have some fresh eggs for breakfast.'

She promptly led them indoors where the mere smell of the wood-burning fireplace made Arthur feel instantly warm. Time-worn floral wallpaper covered the walls and the carpet had seen better days, but the house still felt very cosy.

'In here,' she said, opening a downstairs door, 'is my studio.' The room was almost totally bare, save for the artist's easel in the centre. A half-finished painting was balanced on it. Bright colours and stark geometric shapes formed the portrait of an old, smiling man. More canvases in varying degrees of completion leaned against every wall and a large picture window looked out on the driveway.

She brought them upstairs to show them their rooms.

'One for the boys and one for the girls.'

The bedrooms were identical, with a pair of single beds in each. The old radiators were on and the rooms were roasting already. Then Cousin Maggie led them all back downstairs.

'And finally,' she said, as she turned one last doorknob, 'the living-room.'

She pushed the door open to reveal the room where Arthur had seen the Christmas tree earlier. A fire roared and crackled in a tall fireplace and a set of plush armchairs were placed around it. A long dining table sat in the centre of the room, set for a meal.

'Lunch will be served in five minutes,' Cousin Maggie announced, heading for a door at the back of the room. 'I left it all in the oven before I picked you up so it should still be hot. Take a seat, the lot of ye.'

Arthur didn't think he was hungry until he saw all the food that Maggie carried in moments later: pizza and chips and fried chicken and mini burgers and hot dogs and, thankfully, not a piece of turkey or Brussels sprout in sight! All through the meal they talked and joked. Maggie told them stories of her crazy travels around the world – there were few countries she hadn't been to – and asked how they'd been in the past few months. Arthur chuckled to himself, thinking of the amazing story he could tell her, but he knew that it would be better not to. Dessert was Cousin Maggie's famous rhubarb crumble and even Arthur had to admit that it was delicious. It wasn't bitter like the rhubarb he'd tasted in the past, but rather sweet and flavoursome.

After they ate, she presented them with a large gift-wrapped box. It was almost as tall as Max, who set about opening it, pulling off the paper in shreds. Inside were lots of different-sized boxes: board games, and lots of them.

'I thought we could play some games today and take it easy,' Maggie said over the delighted cheers and thank yous.

Cousin Maggie kept them well fed throughout the day with mini sausage rolls, small triangular sandwiches and mince pies. They became so wrapped up in playing the games that time passed without them even noticing. Before Arthur knew it, it was pitch-black outside and the ticking clock over the fireplace was donging eleven times. Together, they crept up the groaning stairs to bed.

Arthur put his pendant on the bedside locker, snuggled down into the soft, warm blankets and smiled. This had been a good day, he mused, and somehow he had barely thought about Loki at all.

Everyone slept soundly inside Cousin Maggie's comfortable house, and in the barns and pens the animals couldn't have been more peaceful. Even Max, who had forgotten about Loki thanks to the fun distractions of the day, managed to sleep soundly, twisting in his bed to nightmares he wouldn't remember in the morning but never waking. Then, in the darkest part of the night, a shadowy figure stepped out of the wooded area to the right of the house. He walked towards the house, keeping to the shadows, but not unduly worried about stepping into the moonlight. He wouldn't be seen. He could sense that the occupants were all fast asleep.

With every step, Loki could feel the power of the pendant. And he could see the faint green glow emanating from one of the upstairs bedrooms as it reacted to his presence. He'd sensed it earlier in the day, the pendant drawing closer and closer. When it had finally stopped moving he had traced it to this house. It seemed that somehow Arthur had tracked him down. Or maybe it was all a coincidence. But Loki knew there was no such thing as pure coincidence.

His arch-enemy was so close. Sleeping peacefully. If not for the pendant protecting the house, Loki could have entered and finished the boy off once and for all. The boy who had defeated him once, who had killed his first child and ruined all his plans. But it wouldn't happen again, he silently vowed. *This time I'll succeed and have my revenge on this interfering brat at the same time.*

He turned and crept silently back into the forest. He had a plan.

Back in Dublin, the Vikings woke suddenly from their sleep. The pendant had been the key to the chamber that had hidden them and the Jormungand. They were linked to it and could sense it even from this distance. They felt a fluctuation in its power and as one they realised what had happened. The surge of magic could mean only one thing. The Father of Lies had been close to the pendant and, since the pendant was always with Arthur, that meant that Loki had also been close to him.

Bjorn rose from where he lay and summoned the rest of the army to him. After a few moments they agreed that Arthur needed to be warned of the danger and protected from the god as well. Luckily, in the months since Loki's last appearance, Bjorn had formed a plan for this eventuality. Eirik immediately headed for the costume room and the commander quickly joined him there. Eirik had already started painting his face as they'd practised on several occasions. The commander grunted at him.

Hurry, he ordered, the boy and his friends could be in trouble.

CHAPTER FIVE

Beams of bright morning sun penetrated the curtains, falling on Arthur's eyelids. He shut his eyes tighter, hoping to block out the light, but to no avail, so with a groan he opened them and peered around the room. The guest room was pretty basic, with peeling striped wallpaper and bare wooden floors. One of Cousin Maggie's smaller paintings hung over his bed, a surreal vision of the landscape outside the window, and a large round rug was placed between the two beds. Her cacti collection, of which she was very proud, was arranged in one corner, catching the morning light. Max's bed had been vacated and, before Arthur could wonder where he was, the scents of cooking wafted up from downstairs. He hurriedly put on some clothes, hung the pendant around his neck and ran down to join the others in the kitchen.

Cousin Maggie was hunched over the hob. She smiled at him and added a couple more slices of bacon to the already heaving frying pan. A rich, smoky smell filled the kitchen as she did. Max, Ash and Stace were already sitting around the breakfast table slurping milky tea or fresh orange juice.

'Sleep well?' Maggie asked as Arthur sat next to the Barrys.

'Great, thanks,' he said. He was surprised by how late he'd managed to sleep and was glad that he hadn't suffered any Loki-inspired nightmares.

Minutes later, Maggie served up their breakfasts. Each plate was piled high with three strips of smoky bacon, as many sausages, both black and white pudding, fried tomato halves and a fried egg. As well as all that, they had as much tea, coffee, juice and buttery toast soldiers as they could manage. When they were finished, they leaned back in their seats, almost stuffed to bursting.

'I'm going into town today,' Cousin Maggie told them, rubbing her own bloated belly. 'The farmer's market is on and I have some eggs to sell. Plus I need some groceries anyway. You lot ate me out of house and home yesterday! If you want, you can come in with me. Or you can stay here and explore the great wide yonder.'

Max and Stace decided to go into Mullingar with Maggie while Arthur and Ash chose the latter option. It didn't take them long to clean up the breakfast mess together. When they were done, they set about feeding the animals. The pigs, Knick and Knack, plunged their snouts into the buckets of grain and leftovers from the night before that Cousin Maggie had mixed up for them. Brave Nessie and timid Bessie chewed on crunchy hay while the chickens pecked at the grain that Max poured from a bucket onto the ground. Then the five of them dressed in warm clothes, wrapping scarves and heavy coats around themselves, and were soon all set for the day.

Before she left for town, Cousin Maggie gave Arthur and Ash each a sketchpad and a piece of charcoal. Art was their favourite subject at school so they were both thrilled with the gifts.

'Draw everything,' she suggested. 'You never know what might become a great painting.'

The Maggie-mobile drove off with Max waving frantically back at them.

'So where to first?' Ash asked of Arthur, watching the car chug away.

'Let's have a look at that lake we passed.'

'OK. This way,' said Ash and they headed off through the woods.

※※※※

Eirik dismounted from his horse and surveyed the land. He was on top of a low hill overlooking a wide road. Loud metal carriages like the ones he'd seen in Dublin travelled along the road at speeds he barely thought possible. It would be difficult to navigate here. Then he spotted a tall bridge that crossed the road. There were fewer of the carriages there so he'd be able to pass that way easily enough.

Upon waking the night before, he had rushed straight into the room marked *Costumes* to put Bjorn's plan into motion. The army had laid everything out well in advance, just in case. Although the actors weren't working in the Viking Experience during these quiet and cold months, they had left all their tools there. Eirik had often hidden in the costumes room, posing as one of the peeling mannequins leaning against the wall. He'd watched the actors, taking in their skills. They had little tubes filled with a flesh-coloured tincture which they squeezed onto their hands. Then they rubbed the cream into their faces, covering any blemishes or marks on their skin. After that, they opened a small pot of powder and, using a little cushion, patted the dust over the cream, taking away any unnatural shine. While watching them, Eirik first had the seeds of an idea which he brought to Bjorn. The commander saw what a useful plan it was and, together, they worked out the finer points.

When he ran to the room, Eirik sat in front of the mirrored glass and studied his dead face. It was not the face he remembered from his lifetime. Though his skin had not wrinkled or shed quite as badly as that of the others, it was still a fright to behold. He squeezed some of the flesh-tinted ointment onto his hand and smeared it all over his frightening face. Just one coat made a huge difference. He let the first layer dry and then added more. Once that had become tacky to the touch, he patted on the powder. Bjorn had entered behind him as he worked and together they gazed at the face in the mirror. The plan had worked. Though Eirik still had too-high, sharp cheekbones and a drawn, skinny face, the skin-tone was perfect. He looked positively glowing.

They worked on the finer points of his appearance for the next hour, painting his blackened teeth with a little bottle of white paint that Bjorn had observed the actors using to correct writing mistakes, and adding a blond wig that covered the loose strands that Eirik was left with for hair. He put on thick layers of modern clothing that the actors had also left behind: a couple of woollen sweaters, a coat, three pairs of jeans – all to build up his over-slim frame – as well as a pair of thick gloves. When he was done, he stood in front of the soldiers. They all agreed that he was ready to go into the outside world now, where no one was likely to give him a second look.

With grunts of encouragement, Eirik left the army behind him and stepped out onto the streets of Dublin.

Standing in the middle of Smithfield, he suddenly felt anxious. He was in a strange land in a strange time. But he knew he had an important task. He had to get to Arthur before Loki did. He could hear the pendant singing out to him from far away. Too far to travel by foot.

It was early morning by now – the sun would rise in a couple of hours – and the city was mostly quiet. Eirik didn't know which way to go when, all of a sudden, a loud voice broke the silence. The sound was coming from around a corner, past a tall apartment building. Cautiously he approached the noise. He had a longsword strapped to his back and partially hidden under his coat, but he didn't want to use it unless absolutely necessary.

As well as being home to the Viking Experience, Smithfield had hosted a monthly horse fair for generations. Breeders travelled from all over the country to trade and sell their horses. It was a hugely competitive and important fair but space in the square was limited, forcing traders to arrive early. First come, first sold.

Eirik peeped around the corner to find that a handful of horse trucks had already arrived and breeders were busy getting their beasts into the temporary stalls set up for the occasion. One such trader was huffing and grunting as he tugged at a stallion's reins. He cursed at the horse and Eirik instantly recognised his as the voice he'd heard.

'Move it!' urged the breeder. 'Move it, ya bleedin' eejit!' The stallion held firm, whinnying loudly. Eirik didn't know much about horses. Although he adored riding them – the feel of the strong beast galloping over the land, the wind whistling in his ears – he had never had many chances to do so. Back home, only Bjorn and the other leaders had owned their own horses. But watching the stubborn and cranky stallion, there was no doubt in Eirik's mind that this horse wasn't happy to be here so early on a winter's morning.

'Come on, will ya!' puffed the breeder, his face turning beetroot. Just then, he slipped on an icy patch of cobblestone. His backside plopped into a fresh and steaming pile of horse manure. 'Euugghh!' he exclaimed, getting to his feet and surveying the damage to his pants. He quickly wrapped the reins around a stall gate and stormed off in the direction of the open truck, leaving the horse where it was.

Cautiously, Eirik stepped towards the stallion. A pair of bright, black eyes watched him approach with curiosity. The Viking raised a hand to the horse's face and rubbed it under the jaw. He could feel the tension oozing out of the animal as the breeder grunted in agitation in the truck.

Eirik spotted his chance. Without a moment's hesitation, he hastily uncoiled the reins from the gate and pulled himself up onto the stallion's back. The horse even lowered itself a fraction to make it easier for the Viking.

'Hey!' shouted the breeder from the truck, who was now clutching a metal rod with a pair of crackling prods on one end. 'Get off there!' But Eirik wheeled the horse's head around and dug his heels into its flanks. The horse sprang forward, too quickly for the breeder to stop it, and Eirik was gone, following the song of the pendant.

He'd ridden through the dawn, quickly leaving the quiet streets of the city and cutting across country, taking little notice when the sun rose over the landscape. Despite the importance of the mission it felt good to be free from the confines of the village. Now, standing on a hilltop near a major road, he knew he was getting close. He climbed back onto the stallion and cantered off once more.

Arthur and Ash made their way slowly through the forest. The land sloped downwards, away from Cousin Maggie's house and towards the lake. The trees were lofty and mostly bare, although a few evergreens sprouted up here and there. The ground beneath was frost-bitten and hard, and icy leaves crunched under their feet as they walked. They didn't see or hear much wildlife, but at one stage Ash did spot a squirrel, although she was too slow to sketch it.

They stopped every few minutes on their walk, usually to take charcoal rubbings of some interesting-looking tree bark. They were able to follow a trail through the trees, which was lucky, because without it they could easily have gotten lost. Ash had always loved exploring the forest with Cousin Maggie as a toddler, usually perched on her grandaunt's shoulders, but she didn't know her way around well enough to stray off the path.

They said very little as they strolled, something Arthur was glad of. If they started talking, the conversation would inevitably turn to Loki and that was something he didn't want to think about right then.

Eventually they reached a clearing by the shore. The lake stretched out before them – still frozen solid and reflecting the cloudless sky above – and the round tower stood stoic and vacant on the little island. If they followed the shore around to the right, Arthur could see that they would reach the train track. To the left was just more dense woodland.

Arthur was surprised to see that the ground leading from the forest down to the shore was red. There was no grass or stones, just mud that had been frozen solid, and the earth was a deep terracotta colour. It reminded him of science-fiction films he'd seen of trips to Mars and seemed totally out of place here in Westmeath by the side of a lake. Now that he noticed it, he could see that the bright red stretched the whole way around the shore, almost like the lake was bleeding.

'What's with the ground?' he asked Ash.

'It's weird, isn't it?' she said. 'Apparently it's something to do with the amount of oxygen in the soil here. I'm not sure. Cousin Maggie explains it better. It's the only place in Ireland with earth like this. It's a pity it's frozen solid, though.'

'Why?'

'It's really sticky and gooey usually, especially when it mixes with the water from the lake. When I was small we used to come down here in the summers and make mud-men. You know – snowmen but with mud.'

'Cool!'

'Yeah, it really is. We should come here again this summer. You're still going to be in Dublin, right?'

Arthur really didn't want to tell her that he might be moving home sooner than they'd thought. 'Eh ...'

Luckily for him, Ash cut him off.

'Wait!' she said, looking out onto the lake. 'What's that?'

Arthur followed her gaze. Roughly halfway between the shore and the island, something was out on the ice. He squinted to try to see better. The thing looked about the size of a small backpack; it was dark brown and was moving slightly. It looked like a–

'Dog!' Ash exclaimed, shocked. 'It's a dog, isn't it?'

'Looks more like a pup to me.'

Ash handed Arthur her sketchpad and charcoal. 'Hold these for me.'

'Wait – what are you doing?'

'I'm going to save that pup,' she answered, like it was the most reasonable thing in the world.

'You can't!' he protested. 'The ice could–'

'It won't break,' she said. She put one foot on the edge of the frozen lake, leaning all her weight on it. It didn't so much as crack. 'See? Nice and solid! Listen to the dog, Arthur. It's too scared to move.'

Arthur heard it now that she pointed it out. Over the slight breeze in the air, he heard the dog whining softly. There was no denying that it was stranded out there.

'I'll be fine, Arthur,' Ash assured him again, seeing the worried look on his face. 'I'll just take it slowly.'

Ash turned away from him, trying to look more confident than she felt, and walked further out onto the ice.

'Careful!' he exclaimed as her foot slipped out from under her. She stopped, nodded back to him, then proceeded even slower and with more caution.

The going was tough and the muscles in her legs were straining before she was even midway out to the pup. She kept her eyes on her feet but couldn't see the water below the surface. Despite this, as she moved further out the ice started to groan under her weight and she worried that Arthur had been right. But she was too far gone now and couldn't bear the thought of leaving the little dog out there by itself.

Finally, she reached the pup. Its coat was mostly brown with grey streaks. Its snout was long and narrow and it had pointed ears that stood to attention when Ash approached. It looked up at her with sad black eyes.

'Hello, puppy,' Ash said, then patted her legs, stepping backwards. 'Come on. Follow me.'

The pup tilted its head as if listening to her. Then it pulled itself forward on its front paws, its hind legs dragging behind it as if something was wrong with them.

'Can't you move your legs?'

The pup whined in response. Ash took another tentative step forward, to more groaning of the ice. She was so focused on the pup that she didn't even notice the crack.

As she leant forward to pick up the pup, the ice finally gave way. There was another loud crack and Ash plummeted into the frozen lake.

CHAPTER SIX

'*Ash!*' Arthur yelled as he slid across the slippery surface of the lake, concentrating hard on keeping his balance. He ignored the angry groans and creaks of the ice below him.

He slowed down as he approached the hole, wary of the cracks spreading out from its edge. The pup was still whining in a high pitch, looking from him to the breach and back again. He heard a train pass nearby, but all his attention was fixed on the break in the ice. Where Ash had fallen through, he could see that the ice was about three inches thick. It seemed strong but was clearly not strong enough, as it continued to groan under his feet. The water was deep and dark, rippling lightly.

Ash was floating under that water, her eyes shut, her long hair and coat flowing around her like some sort of mystical mermaid.

Arthur fell to his knees and the ice gave another loud crack. '*Ash*! *Ashling*!'

There was no response from her. He could see tiny air bubbles escaping from her mouth and nostrils. She still had air in her lungs, at least, but for how long? He plunged his arm into the water, reaching for his friend, but she was sinking too quickly and was beyond his reach. The cold ate through his flesh and he quickly withdrew his arm, pain lancing through it.

He realised that the only way he could reach Ash was to enter the water himself. Before his courage failed him, and realising that every second would count for Ash, Arthur quickly stood up, kicked off his shoes and pulled off his heavy coat. He dropped it to the icy surface, followed by his fleece-lined hoodie. Now just in a T-shirt and jeans, he shivered with the cold as he took the pendant off his neck and tied it in a tight double-knot around his wrist. It wouldn't do anyone any good to lose that. Taking one last deep breath, he leaped into the water, feet first.

The water was so cold it knocked the wind out of him completely and he gasped in shock, his mouth filling up. He'd never experienced a temperature so low and his fingers and toes were numb within seconds. Choking, he returned to the surface, took another deep breath, then dived back under the water.

The singing of the pendant had steadily increased in Eirik's dead ears, its urgency transmitting itself to him. He knew he was close as he crested a small hill. Below him a long metallic snake sped down a track cut through a wood. He pushed the horse into a trot down the hill and crossed the metal tracks, pulling up beside a frozen lake. He knew from the intensity of the pendant's signal that he should be able to see Arthur, but all he could see was a pile of clothes and some sort of animal beside a large hole in the ice. The pendant was clearly there, but where was Arthur? Eirik swung himself down from the horse, looking around uncertainly. He had been sent to protect the boy, but it looked like he might already be too late.

Back in Dublin, under Arthur's bed, the hammer started to glow.

Arthur found it hard to move his limbs under the water. Or, rather, he found it hard to know if they were moving. He couldn't feel anything. But somehow he reached Ash. He shook her shoulder but she didn't open her eyes. He shook more furiously, gripping her biceps a little too tightly. Suddenly her eyelids shot up and she opened her mouth to scream, bubbles flowing out of her mouth and taking her remaining oxygen with them. Arthur quickly clamped his hand over her lips, forcing her to stop. He pointed urgently upwards.

She looked at him with wide-eyed terror, then nodded quickly. Together they kicked hard, pushing themselves towards the surface. Arthur would never forget the physical strain it took to kick his legs and swim upwards under that lake.

They reached the top of the water and hit the bottom of the ice. Arthur scanned the ice around him. He didn't think they could be that far from the hole, but in the murkiness he couldn't see it anywhere nearby and there was no shaft of light to indicate where it might be. They were lost under the lake and, from her expression, Ash had also just realised it.

They could just about see the faint glow of the sun through the thick ice. With no other obvious escape option, Arthur started pounding his fists against it in a desperate attempt to break through but, with his strength failing him, he made little impact and the white wall above them remained solid.

The hammer flew out from underneath Arthur's bed, radiating green light. It smashed through his bedroom window and soared over the city of Dublin at an impossible speed. A handful of people noticed the tiny trail of light disappear across the sky. Most assumed it had been a trick of their eye – only one man was certain that aliens were invading.

Arthur felt the air seeping out of his lungs with the exertion of knocking on the ice. Ash would soon be completely out of oxygen, followed closely by himself. They were done for. This was it. They would die under the lake. They probably wouldn't be discovered for days. Days in which Joe and Cousin Maggie and everyone else who cared for them would be tearing their hair out in frustration. Days in which Loki could enact some evil plan without Arthur around to stop it. He couldn't die under here. He wouldn't.

Ash's eyes fluttered shut once more, her whole body starved of precious oxygen. Arthur shook her again with the little energy he had left, but to no avail. Her arms drifted lifelessly at her sides as Arthur studied her face. She looked asleep, peaceful. Her body was losing the fight to stay alive.

Then a movement behind her caught his eye. Something had plunged into the depths of the water, with a white plume of bubbles marking its path. But it quickly stopped its descent and started racing towards them. For a moment Arthur wondered what new disaster was about to hit them, but then he realised the object was glowing and the glow was a familiar green colour. His heart leapt.

As it drew rapidly closer, the item came into focus. An iron top, a small handle covered in rope: it was his hammer!

It didn't even slow as it approached him. Arthur swiftly wrapped one arm around Ash and stretched the other one out, his palm open. The hammer slammed into his hand and he curled his fingers tightly around the handle. It kept moving, dragging them through the water at breakneck speed.

The hammer dived deeper, taking them with it, then turned towards the surface once more. It paused for a split second before shooting rapidly upwards again. Arthur ducked his head and shut his eyes as it broke through the ice and soared skyward.

As Arthur clung on for dear life, the hammer flew him and Ash high over the lake. It hovered there for a moment and Arthur could see a man standing on the shore with a horse by his side. Then they sailed back down to earth, landing softly on the hard ground. Arthur dropped the hammer and laid the unconscious Ash on the ground.

'Eirik?' Arthur asked, totally bewildered as to how the Viking came to be there and why he was wearing bad make-up. 'Never mind. You can explain later. Help me with Ash!'

Unexpectedly, he heard a siren in the near distance. He looked in the direction of the sound to see firefighters, paramedics and Gardaí clambering over the train tracks towards them from the main road. Some were carrying stretchers, others clutched warm blankets.

Arthur turned urgently to Eirik and pushed the hammer into his arms. 'Hide!' The Viking disappeared as the emergency services struggled over the train tracks.

The first of the paramedics to reach them raced straight to Ash. He pushed Arthur out of the way, fell to his knees and put his ear to her chest.

'Was she under long?' he asked, quickly taking her pulse.

'A few minutes,' Arthur panted.

'OK, give me space.' Arthur didn't budge, frozen with terror. 'Move away!'

Arthur took a step back as the other paramedics arrived on the scene.

'Will she be all right?' he asked as they piled around his friend, blocking her from view. 'Will she be all right?' No one would answer his question. One firefighter wrapped a couple of blankets around him. Arthur could make out the shoulders of the first paramedic bobbing up and down as he tried to pump the water out of Ash's lungs.

'Come on, come on!' Arthur pleaded, clutching the blankets and feeling heat start to seep back into his flesh, not daring to take his eyes from the backs of the paramedics working on Ash.

Come on.

Suddenly he heard a spluttering cough. The first paramedic sat back on his heels, while another rolled Ash onto her side to help her hack up the water from her lungs. Eventually she stopped coughing and, with a little help, sat up. Tears were streaming down her cheeks. Then she saw Arthur through the crowd and managed a weak smile.

Chapter Seven

The news reporter strode across the red shore with the frozen lake behind her, her hair flawlessly coiffed, wearing a long lambswool coat and matching scarf. Her leather gloves were wrapped around the microphone like it was the most vital and powerful piece of machinery in the entire world. She walked awkwardly, with her torso turned towards the camera. Her breath condensed in front of her dark-red lips as she spoke.

'All was quiet here at Lough Faol, just outside Mullingar, County Westmeath, this morning,' she enunciated in an even and unaccented tone. 'Until that silence was broken when twelve-year-old Ashling Barry …'

The camera operator zoomed right in on Ash so the picture shook slightly. She was sitting inside an ambulance parked on the verge beside the main road, wrapped tightly in a couple of blankets and sipping a plastic cup of steaming soup. One paramedic was listening to her lungs with a stethoscope. The reporter continued over the shot.

'… of Ranelagh, Dublin – seen here – fell through the ice and into the freezing waters below.'

The cameraman zoomed in on the hole where Ash had fallen through, taking care not to step too close to the edge of the shore.

'The shock of the chilly temperatures knocked Ashling unconscious and chances are she would have perished underneath the ice were it not for the quick thinking of her friend, twelve-year-old Arthur Quinn, also of Ranelagh.'

Arthur was now standing next to the reporter, with a couple of blankets still wrapped around his shoulders. His hair was no longer wet but one of the paramedics had given him a warm beanie hat to wear anyway.

'It was colder than anything I've ever felt,' Arthur said into the microphone that the reporter was holding to his mouth. 'And it was really dark down there. But I found her and we got out.'

'And how did you manage to find your way back out, Arthur?'

'Em … well, we lost the first hole, but we were lucky and found a second one.'

The camera now panned around the busy scene, then back to the lake. Some paramedics fussed over Ash, while a little dog lay on the ground nearby, snuggling into its own brown blanket. A firefighter was leading a red-faced and flustered-looking older woman over to the rescued girl, accompanied by a young boy and teenage girl. A tall blond man was standing just beyond the edge of the woodland, patting a horse and watching the others intently.

'Ashling and Arthur were incredibly lucky,' the reporter went on over the image. 'A passenger on a passing train spotted Arthur dive into the lake after his friend and called the emergency services, who arrived on the scene mere seconds after the children emerged from the water.

'Paramedics revived Ashling and have found no major injuries. The Garda Síochána have stated that ice on lakes and rivers is unpredictable and that members of the public should not, under any circumstances, take the risk of stepping onto a frozen lake. This is Karen Kilfoyle, reporting for RTÉ News.'

And with that, the camera blinked off.

'Oh my God!' cried Cousin Maggie. 'You poor things!' She bundled Arthur and Ash into a constricting hug while Stace and Max looked on worriedly. Arthur and Ash had changed out of their dripping clothes into some too-large T-shirts and pants the paramedics had on standby and each of them was wrapped in a couple of blankets.

Eventually Cousin Maggie let them go, allowing them to breathe freely again.

'We're all right,' Ash said. Her voice was hoarse and dry after almost choking on the lake water. 'Honestly.'

'You don't sound all right to me.' Cousin Maggie turned anxiously to the nearest paramedic. 'How is she, really?'

'No major damage that we can find,' he answered. 'No concussion. They both have a bit of a sniffle. But there are no symptoms of hypothermia, which is good.'

'So I can take them home with me?'

'Of course,' he chuckled. 'But at the first sign of their colds getting any worse, you have to bring them straight to a doctor.'

'Don't worry about that. I won't let them out of bed for the next day, let alone outside. And my chicken soup has been known to work miracles.'

'Sounds great. Let me just get their clothes and you

can be on your way.' He went off, calling after one of the other paramedics. For the first time Cousin Maggie looked down and noticed the pup at Ash's feet. Its fur was still damp, despite Ash's attempts to dry it with the coarse blanket. The pup gazed up at Maggie with watery black eyes.

After Ash had been resuscitated, a couple of fire-fighters had set about rescuing the pup from the ice. Ordinarily they would have used a helicopter, but since time was tight (and since the rescuee was a dog) they had to come up with another method of saving the puppy without walking onto the ice themselves. Using a special hitch system, they were able to crank a rope out over the lake to the dog. One end of the rope had a grappling hook attached and once they had cranked it far enough out they dropped the hook around the far side of the pup, allowing the firefighters to crank it back in. Ash was thrilled to have the dog finally safe in her arms.

'And who's this?' Maggie asked, crouching to pet the dog. Max, who had also just spotted the pup, did likewise, rubbing it behind the ears excitedly. Stace didn't pet it but made cooing noises at it instead as Ash filled them in on how they'd discovered the pup on the frozen lake.

'Can we keep it?' asked Ash, finishing her tale.

'Oh, I don't know, Ash,' said Maggie. 'That's up to your parents.' She ran her hands over the pup's ribs and looked at its teeth and eyes. Ash mentioned that the pup hadn't been able to walk out on the ice so Maggie also felt its legs. The front two seemed fine and healthy; but the hind pair were a different story. They were thinner than they should have been, slightly malformed with very little muscle definition.

'It's a female and she seems healthy enough apart from those back legs; she's not particularly fat but she's not malnourished. Judging by her unclipped, dirty coat, she hasn't been that well cared for. Her hind legs are lame, poor thing. That's why she couldn't walk to you, Ash. She was probably dumped by her owner because of her condition.'

The pup licked the side of Maggie's wrist. For a stray, she certainly seemed calm and amiable enough.

'That's terrible!' Ash knelt next to the pup and patted her head. 'I wonder how she got out on the ice.'

'Somebody must have slid her out there.'

'Why?' Arthur asked.

'To die,' Cousin Maggie told him sadly. 'People can be really awful sometimes.'

The paramedic arrived back at that point with their clothes in a plastic bag each, which he handed to Maggie. When he was gone, she looked down at the pup with sympathy.

'We'll take her,' she said to whoops of joy from the children. 'She can stay at mine for the time being. I'll put up some Lost Dog signs in town tomorrow, although I doubt we'll get much response, given that she was abandoned here deliberately. Also I think I have just the thing for her lame legs.'

Maggie picked up the lame pup and carried her towards her Volvo. The others followed, with Stace and Max questioning Ash furiously about all that had happened. Arthur excused himself, pretending that he'd dropped his mobile phone on the shore.

'Maybe Ash can fix it,' he claimed, running back over the track and down towards the forest. His legs were feeling shaky, which wasn't a surprise considering the strain he'd put them through under the water.

Eirik was standing by the edge of the woodland, soothing his borrowed horse by stroking its soft neck. He smiled at Arthur when he saw him approaching, his painted white teeth glinting in the winter sun.

'Is that all make-up from the actors?' Arthur inquired

when he got close enough to see it properly. It wasn't too bad, actually. The flesh-tinted foundation made Eirik's face look almost normal and, although it didn't cover all of his wrinkles, it did hide most of the crustiness. Overall, Arthur had to admit that it was a pretty good attempt. The Viking grinned and nodded with a bashful shrug.

'Good plan,' said Arthur. 'How did you know something was going to happen? Or even how to find us?'

Eirik leaned forward and tapped the pendant tied around Arthur's wrist.

Arthur understood the meaning instantly. 'Ah, of course. You have something of mine?'

Eirik nodded once more. He ducked behind a tree and emerged with the hammer. Arthur took it, hiding it under one of his blankets.

'Thanks. I guess you'd better be off now.' Arthur patted the horse and scratched behind its ear. 'Let the horse rest up for a couple of hours then return him to wherever you got him.' Eirik looked slightly forlorn at this but eventually grunted his agreement. Then he looked over Arthur's shoulder with wide eyes.

'Hello there,' said a voice behind Arthur. He turned to find Stace standing there. 'Arthur, aren't you going to introduce me to your friend?'

'Uh … well … Stace, this is … uh … Eirik. He's … um … my cousin.'

'Your cousin?' Stace seemed surprised but still took a few steps forward. 'Your cousin lives in Mullingar too?'

'Well, no. You see … he, uh …' Arthur's mind went blank. He cursed himself inwardly and tried to climb out of the hole he'd dug. He couldn't see a way out of this, but then he spotted the ambulance on the main road, packing up to leave.

'He works for the emergency services.'

'He does?'

'Yeah. They call him in if they can't reach the injured with an ambulance.' Arthur was cringing inside as he said this – no one in their right mind would buy the idea of a mounted paramedic, but it was the best he could come up with at short notice. However, Stace wasn't really listening to Arthur. Instead she was staring dreamily at Eirik, with what Arthur considered a very soppy look on her face. With a burst of confidence, Arthur continued, 'Yeah, we were just lucky that he was doing some training nearby.'

Stace actually looked impressed now as she stared at Eirik.

'Wow,' she said coyly. 'So what do they call you?'

'He's a mounted paramedic,' Arthur stuttered.

'That's cool,' Stace said. She seemed not to notice that Arthur had answered, and hadn't taken her eyes off Eirik. She put out her hand. 'Nice to meet you, Eirik.'

Eirik looked down at the gloved hand, perplexed. No one had ever shaken his hand before and he didn't quite know what to do, so he simply put his own hand out mirroring Stace. Their fingertips just about touched each other. Before it got any weirder, Arthur took Stace by the shoulders and led her away.

'Come on, Stace! Cousin Maggie will be waiting and Eirik's in a hurry.'

As Arthur herded her off, she reached around and waved at Eirik.

'Goodbye!' she called. 'Hope to meet you again soon, Eirik!' The Viking was simply standing there, staring at her with a bemused expression. He waved back, then showed off his pearly whites again in a broad smile.

'Arthur,' said Stace as she shuffled up the verge to the main road. 'He's so cute! You have to bring him around some time!'

'Uh … yeah, we'll see!'

As Eirik set off with the horse through the trees to find some grazing, a pair of icy blue eyes watched them go from the other side of the woodland. Things hadn't gone exactly as Loki had anticipated. In fact, he smiled to himself, they'd gone better.

As soon as they arrived back at Cousin Maggie's house, they piled out of the car and followed her to Knick and Knack's barn. In her arms, Maggie was carrying the pup, who was looking curiously at her new surroundings. She didn't even yap at the goats or the pigs as they passed. They went in the back door of the barn and the stink of manure was almost overwhelming. Shelves and wooden crates full of tools and old junk that Maggie had accumulated over the years were piled in one corner near the door. The pigs stayed outside in their pen, watching lazily.

Maggie handed the pup to Stace and started rooting through the heaps of clutter. She knocked empty paint cans aside and threw blunted garden tools over her shoulders. It was clear that Cousin Maggie was a bit of a hoarder, keeping stuff for years that she had no intention of ever using again.

'Ah!' she exclaimed joyfully when she finally found what she wanted. She took the pup from Stace, laid her carefully on the ground and unwrapped her from the blanket. Then she turned her back to them and started to get to work properly on the little dog. The pup stayed quiet and whatever Maggie was doing didn't seem to be disturbing her. They heard the sounds of straps being tightened and plastic buckles snapping into place. Then, at last, she turned around to show them the pup.

The back half of the brown dog was fastened into a harness, its lame legs held aloft by a couple of loose belts. The harness itself was mostly shiny aluminium. Two bars ran along either side of the ribs, then curved downwards by the tail. At the end of each bar was a small rubber wheel. The pup looked back at the harness and wheels, then up at Ash.

Ash took a few steps back and then, patting her thighs, said, 'Come here, girl.'

The dog took a tentative step forward with her front paws and the wheels followed. Then she took another step, and another. Before they knew it, the little pup was running around the barn, barking excitedly. They all laughed to themselves, watching her go.

'You remember my old dog Snowy who got hit by a car when he was getting on in years?' Cousin Maggie explained through chuckles. 'He lost the use of his hind legs so I had to get him one of those doggy wheelchairs. I was hoping it would fit her and I was right!'

'Of course,' said Stace. 'That was when I was pretty young and Ash was only a baby. I'd totally forgotten about him!'

'We should give her a name,' Max suggested, slightly out of breath from laughing.

'Let Ash name her,' said Maggie. 'She found her.'

All eyes were on Ash. She patted her legs again and the pup came rushing over to her. Ash crouched to rub her back and thought about the perfect name. She wanted something that would sum up the dog and how they'd found her. Something with a bit of mystery.

'I have it!' she said. 'How about "Ice"?'

The rest of them considered it, slowly nodding their heads.

'I like it,' said Arthur. 'Ice.'

Ice looked up at Arthur, as if she knew it was her name, her tail wagging so much that it whacked against the aluminium bars.

Cousin Maggie stayed true to her word and wouldn't allow Arthur or Ash to leave the house for the next twenty-four hours. She had Ash and Max swap beds to keep the two ill friends confined together. (Stace wasn't too thrilled about having to share a room with her younger brother and even suggested that he should sleep on the living-room couch – a proposal Maggie had laughed down.) She fed them steaming bowls of chicken soup, with buttery crusty rolls on the side, followed by two juicy mandarin oranges with a scoop of real vanilla ice-cream each. She believed that the vitamin C in the oranges would help stave off the flu germs, while the ice-cream was just a well-earned treat.

From the moment they'd been rescued to the moment they got back to Maggie's, Arthur had felt fine. He guessed the adrenaline must have kept away any sick feeling because now, lying in a bed across from Ash, he felt terrible. And, clearly, so did she. Even though they were both bundled up in two blankets and a duvet each, with hot-water bottles warming their toes, the pair of them shivered involuntarily every so often. Arthur had a sore throat and Ash's voice had grown even hoarser in the past couple of hours. Aunt Maggie had carried Ice upstairs so they could all keep each other occupied. Ash would call Ice to her and the little dog would scamper around the room and occasionally even attempt to leap up onto Ash's bed. She never made it but at least her cracks at it kept Arthur and Ash giggling.

'Laughter is the best medicine!' Cousin Maggie declared when she was done administering some sweet cough syrup to them. 'And sleep is the second best. Which you two should be doing now.' With that, she picked up Ice, switched off the light and shut the door behind her. Before Arthur knew it, he had fallen into a heavy sleep and didn't dream once during the night.

The following day, he woke to find Ash kneeling on the floor and playing with Ice.

'How are you feeling?' he asked.

'Much better,' she answered, her voice still croaky. 'You?'

'Great, actually.' And it wasn't a lie either. There were still faint echoes of the pain in his legs, and his throat was still a little raw, but overall he felt really rested.

'See?' Cousin Maggie said when she saw how much they'd improved. 'I told you my chicken soup could work miracles!'

Although she still didn't want them leaving the warmth of the house in case their colds flared up again, there was still plenty to do and the day went by quickly. Stace and Max stayed indoors with them out of sympathy and they spent the day playing board games or being chased about by an excitable Ice. As promised, Cousin Maggie had put signs up around the town with Ice's picture, but so far no one had claimed her.

When Arthur woke up the following day, his heart sank. It was Friday, he realised, which meant that it was time to go home. Cousin Maggie made them breakfast and they all ate it noisily, clearly wanting to forget the fact that their brief holiday was coming to an end. Arthur really had enjoyed his time at Maggie's, despite nearly drowning and the ensuing stint in bed. As he chewed on some crunchy bacon, he looked across the table at Ash, who was feeding the end of a sausage to Ice. He wondered how she'd react if she had to leave the pup behind.

Mr and Mrs Barry arrived shortly after eleven in their large people-carrier. They gave their children tight hugs, particularly Ash. Mrs Barry surprised Arthur by embracing him too.

'What you two did was so reckless,' Mrs Barry said crossly, then in a gentler tone, 'but we're glad you're safe.'

They all went inside for a cup of tea before the return journey. Before Maggie could offer them all third helpings of her rhubarb crumble, Mr Barry announced, 'It's time we hit the road. Put your bags in the boot and we'll be on our way.'

'Dad?' Max piped up.

'Yeah?'

'Can we bring Ice with us?'

'What's Ice?' As if on cue, the little dog hobbled into view in front of Mr Barry.

'Oh no!' he said. 'No dogs.'

'Why not?' Stace demanded.

'For starters, you wouldn't walk it or clean up after it. And you know who'll end up doing it all? Muggins here!'

'Please, Dad!' begged Ash. 'She won't need much walking and I promise I'll feed her and brush her and do anything else that needs doing.'

'No and that's final. Get your bags.'

A few minutes later they were all squashed into the car, watching Cousin Maggie and Ice get smaller as they pulled away. There were tears in Ash's eyes as she looked back at them. Suddenly, Ice started running after the vehicle, yapping loudly. Mrs Barry, who had been watching in the rear-view mirror, turned to get a proper look at the dog. At this rate she would never catch up with them, but it was heart-breaking watching her try.

She laid a hand on her husband's arm as he steered towards the laneway.

'Francis,' she said imploringly.

He looked at her, catching the sympathy in her eyes.

'They won't look after her, Ann,' he said as reasonably as he could manage, his voice softening. 'You know that.'

By now, Arthur, Stace, Ash and Max were looking at the adults, silently praying for the answer they wanted to hear.

'If they don't,' Mrs Barry said, turning around to address her children face on, 'then we bring Ice back to Cousin Maggie. Sound fair?'

'That definitely sounds fair!' proclaimed Stace.

'You won't have to do a thing, Dad!' promised Ash.

'I'll walk her and bring her to the shops and play football with her and build her a kennel and wash her and do everything!' added Max finally.

Mr Barry slowly took his foot off the accelerator and the car ground to a halt.

'All right then,' he agreed reluctantly.

Ash whipped her seatbelt off, swung open the car door and ran to meet the puppy. She swept her up and the dog licked her face joyously.

'We can keep her!' Ash shouted back to Cousin Maggie, who was still standing by her house but now with a big smile gleaming across her face. 'We can keep Ice!'

CHAPTER EIGHT

In a time before history was written down, in Asgard, the realm of the gods, it is said that the great wolf Hati pursues the moon across the shifting night sky. If this is so, then the chase goes on now, as the sun has fallen behind the horizon for the day and the moon has taken its place high over the land.

Loki, the Father of Lies, stands on a hilltop staring up at the great celestial body. In Asgard, the moon shines larger and brighter and fuller than in any of the other worlds and he can see the pits and cracks and mountains on its face clearly. And, moments later, he watches something fall from the moon to Asgard. It soars across the sky – a falling rock with a tail of flame trailing behind it. He looks on as it plummets to the ground and feels the impact shudder through his legs, even from this distance.

The Trickster God smiles and spreads out his arms. The black cloak he is wearing falls in thick folds, then, with a flash of vivid emerald light, transforms into wings. He looks at his arms, now covered in expansive green feathers, and laughs. He flaps the colossal wings once, twice and with that is in the sky, flying over the mystical land.

Below him forests spread out as far as the eye can see. There are trees as tiny and fragile as a single hair on the back of his hand and trees as tall and monstrous and sturdy as Odin All-Father's great dining hall. There are trees of wood so dark and dense that the inhabitants of Asgard are always in danger of wandering too close and being absorbed into their endless blackness, and there are trees of timber so light that they are invisible to the eye and you would not be aware of them until you bumped into them. There are trees that grow so fast that you can hear them groaning, trees that walk and move and run, and trees that need centuries to take root. There are trees that aren't even made of wood: they are formed from iron and steel, marble and stone, flesh and bone. There are some trees that are even created from dreams and nightmares or hopes and fears – psychedelic, shifting things that most dread to look upon. This, then, is Asgard.

Twelve gods and twelve goddesses call the realm their home. At the head of their society is their ruler, Odin All-Father. Although he has but one eye, he can see all. Or almost all, Loki snickers to himself, batting his gigantic wings. He, the god of mischief, is a joke to the other gods, as demonstrated the previous night. In Odin's hall they had all laughed as a giantess had sewn Loki's mouth closed and he'd sworn it would be the last time they shamed him. As the sun rose on a new day, Loki had put his plan for revenge into action. He had created the Jormungand, the serpent that would destroy the world. Since then, the Jormungand had travelled to Midgard, the realm of Man, and the gods, roused into action, still have not found Loki. And now he will create his second child, the next stage in his brilliant scheme.

There is a clearing where the rock fell to earth, the trees burned away by the force of the collision and the earth scorched black all around. He extends his wings as wide as possible and soars gracefully into the centre of the clearing. As his feet alight on the ground once more, there is a flash of green light and his wings transform back into a pair of strong arms, the black cloak hanging from them.

Loki looks up at the moon. It is hanging directly above him, the white light falling into the clearing and illuminating his way. He walks towards the centre and can feel the heat scorching through his boar-leather soles. There is a small mound in the middle of the clearing, little more than an anthill. The point of impact. And there, on the top of the mound, is the thing that fell.

At first glance, it is just a white pebble. But Loki knows it is so much more. Even from here, standing a few feet away, he can feel great heat radiating from it. It is smoothly curved and white hot from breaking through the atmosphere. The Father of Lies yearns to touch it, to feel its power. He reaches forward and picks it up, gripping it tightly.

He smells the acrid stench of the flesh of his palm burning and singeing as he holds it. He keeps his hand like that for as long as he can, relishing the pain and savouring the power. Then he loosens his grip slightly between his index finger and thumb. He blows into the hollow he has created. Icy air escapes from his lungs and envelopes the moonstone. It cracks and hisses and whistles sharply as it cools. The burning sensation is gone now, but the pain remains.

He opens his hand. His palm is red raw; the skin has burned off it completely, exposing strips of blood and muscle. It is not pretty to look upon and the pain is inching further up his arm but he doesn't mind. His attention is focused on the small pebble.

Now that it has cooled down, it no longer appears white but is transparent, like a piece of glass. He takes it in his other hand – with a flash of green light, his burned hand repairs itself – and examines it more closely. The pebble isn't fully clear: pale swirls of green and pink dance in the glass and motes of moon-dust glitter throughout. It is a perfect circle, with a smooth convex curve on each side, and the moon itself is magnified behind it as Loki holds it up to the light.

'A piece of the moon,' he says to no one but himself. 'Did the Moon-wolf Hati bite you off?' Hmm. Hati's Bite. A suitable name.

He can't take his eyes off it. Such a small and pretty trinket and yet so powerful, so dangerous. The destruction it has caused in this clearing will be a drop in the ocean compared to what he will do with it. It is just what he needs.

A noise unexpectedly breaks through his train of thought. It is a whining sound, coming from the edge of the clearing, shrill and piercing like the cry of an animal in pain. Loki turns towards the noise and squints at the source through the darkness.

With the beast's black coat, Loki has trouble spotting it at first, but then he notices a shape. 'Oh,' he says with glee when he sees what it is. 'Fortune favours me tonight.'

It is a wolf, lying on its side under a half-fallen tree. Its head rolls around and it is whining, clearly hurt. Loki walks towards it to get a closer look. The fur on one side of its body has been burned away, presumably scorched by the impact of Hati's Bite. Bare skin and muscle are exposed underneath and he can see the animal's ribs shuddering up and down with each laboured breath.

Loki kneels by the wolf and slides his arms underneath it. At first the beast growls at him but then whimpers when Loki lifts it off the ground. Its head lolls to one side; it is too weak to lift it.

'Fortune favours you, too,' Loki tells the wolf as he carries it back into the centre of the clearing. 'I will make you better. Better and stronger and more powerful than you have ever been. You will walk on two feet and you will make me an army.' He crouches down, laying the beast on top of the small mound. Its back twists awkwardly over the bump. 'I will give you a piece of my power. For you are my second child, my Fenris Wolf.'

With that, he points Hati's Bite at the moon. Rays of moonlight fall through the glass, contracting into a single beam of white. Loki murmurs words constructed from the ancient and primordial language of runes and tilts the piece of moonstone, focusing the light beam over the wolf's face and into one fearful eye.

There is a sudden and blinding flash of light.

❋❋❋❋❋

'Argh!'

Arthur sat bolt upright in bed, drenched in sweat. He'd finally had it! The dream he'd been expecting and dreading ever since his pendant had glowed a few days ago – he'd finally had it. He felt a dull, throbbing pain in his right hand. He looked down at it, holding it palm-up. It looked fine, but the memory of soreness was still there. He recalled with great discomfort that Loki had burned his own right hand in the dream. Whatever was wrong with Arthur's hand, the pain was gradually fading, so he put it out of his mind.

A pale white light flowed in through the curtains of his bedroom. Some of the glass had been smashed while Arthur had been away. He assumed correctly that it was a result of the hammer breaking through, while Joe thought it had been some neighbours' kids and a misplaced football. Either way, the hole was now patched with a sheet of cardboard; Joe had promised to get it fixed on Monday. Arthur glanced at the phone on his bedside locker. It was still dead from the frozen lake. He'd tried the trick of holding it under a hair-dryer but to no avail. He got up, walked barefoot across a chilly floor to his desk and switched on his laptop. By the time it had finally booted up, it was 7.21. Far too early to be up on a Saturday morning. However, he knew that there was no chance of getting back to sleep again after that dream.

When they'd arrived home the day before, Joe had still been at work so Arthur had spent most of the evening in the Barry house, playing with Ice. Joe came knocking around seven and, after simultaneously commending Arthur for rescuing Ash and reprimanding him for putting his own life at risk, he took him to a local pizzeria for dinner.

Arthur sat down at his desk, his cold toes curling under the chair, and logged on to Skype. The instant-messenger service popped up on the screen, telling him that Ash was online. That didn't mean much as Ash usually left her laptop on overnight anyway, downloading the latest updates for all her favourite pieces of software. And Ash had a lot of favourite pieces of software.

However, it was worth a try, so he double-clicked

on her name. The tone of a phone played through the speakers. It rang six or seven times and Arthur was just about to hang up when–

'Morning,' Ash croaked and a dark and grainy image of her face filled the screen. 'It's very early, Arthur. What's up?'

'Sorry,' he said, tilting his own webcam so she could see him better. 'I know it's early but can I call over? I have something to tell you.'

'What is it?' She rubbed her eyes, still not awake enough to look concerned.

'I had one of the dreams.'

Those words managed to shake her awake and she looked at him on the screen with wide, worried eyes.

'You'd better come over, then.'

Ash was still in her peach-coloured pyjamas and dressing gown when Arthur arrived at her door a few minutes later. Ice was at her feet, wagging her tail merrily at him.

'Have you eaten yet?' she asked, leading him into the kitchen. The house was quiet; all the other Barrys were sensible enough to still be in their cosy beds. Even from downstairs, he could hear Granny Barry's ragged snores from the spare room.

'No, I wanted to tell you right away.'

She opened a cabinet over the sink and pulled out a box of cereal. 'Fancy some?' He nodded and she started collecting bowls, spoons and milk.

'Listen, Ash …' he started as she worked.

'No,' she said. 'Wait till we're finished eating.'

'Why?'

'Because the longer I put off hearing about the dream, the longer I can imagine he's not back.' She sat down and poured herself a heaped bowl of Cornflakes, splashing milk liberally over them. Arthur watched in silence as she started to eat, then sat down across from her and copied her.

For the next few minutes, they didn't speak. The only sound in the kitchen was the crunching of cereal and Ice's paws and wheels rolling on the tiled floor. The tension didn't break until Ash slurped the last of the milk from her bowl and put it aside.

'OK,' she said. 'Tell me.'

He told her. He told her about Loki's flight through Asgard, about the moonstone and the clearing, and lastly he told her about the Fenris Wolf. As he recounted the story, he paced the room, looking anywhere but at Ash. He studied the floor, the ceiling, the plates in the open dishwasher.

And most of all, he studied Ice. She sat in front of him, looking at him with her big black eyes and with her ears cocked as if listening to his tale. The more he watched her, the more he was filled with a sense of unease about the pup. The way she was looking at him seemed to be intense, intelligent, almost human.

When he was done, all Ash could manage was, 'Wow.'

'Yeah,' he said. 'But that's not the worst part of it.'

'What's the worst part?'

Before the pup had time to react, Arthur picked her up and dropped her out into the hallway, shutting the door between them. He urgently turned back to Ash, who had a confused look on her face.

'Why did you–' she started.

'Listen, Ash,' he leaned over the breakfast table, whispering frantically, 'just as I was telling the story, I realised something. Have you ever noticed how Ice looks just like a wolf cub?'

Ice was scratching the door, whining to get in.

'What?'

'Think about it. The long snout, the pointy ears. What dog looks like that? She looks just like a younger version of the wolf in my dream.'

'Arthur don't be ridic–'

'Look at how we found her! On the ice. How did she get out there by herself? She could barely crawl to you, let alone make it that far out.'

'It's like Cousin Maggie said: someone put her there to die.'

'No, don't you see? She was there deliberately waiting for us.'

The scratching had become increasingly fevered. Ash looked at Arthur, the accusation hanging in the air between them.

'You think ... you think that my puppy was trying to kill us?' She raised her eyebrows as she said it and he could see she was sceptical.

Arthur let out the breath he'd been holding and said, 'Look, I know it sounds crazy, but if you'd had my dream you'd be suspicious too.'

'So what do we do now?' Ash asked. 'How do we prove or disprove your theory?'

'I don't know,' he replied.

'Wait! I have an idea!' Ash tapped Arthur's chest. 'Loki can't touch the pendant without it hurting him,' she reminded him. 'Surely the same would apply to this child of his, this Fenris Wolf.'

Arthur thought it over before nodding. 'You could be

right.'

Ash got up, walked to the door and opened it. Ice practically fell into the room. Ash smiled for a second as the cute pup licked her ankles innocently then picked her up and carried her to Arthur.

He took the pendant from around his neck and dangled it over the little pup in Ash's arms. She gawked up at it, the bronze disc reflected in her dark eyes.

'OK,' he said. 'Here goes.' He lowered the pendant until it hung just above Ice's fur. He hesitated, bracing himself in case of the blast that had happened every time Loki had touched the pendant, then placed it against Ice's back.

Nothing happened.

The dog twisted in Ash's arms and snapped at the pendant as if she thought Arthur was teasing her with it, but he snatched it away before she could catch it.

'Well, that answers that,' said Ash with a relieved smile. She nuzzled her face into Ice's fur before setting her back down.

'I'm not sure it answers anything,' Arthur warned.

'What do you mean?' Ice looked from one friend to the other, wagging her tail excitedly.

'We don't really know if the pendant would have any

effect on the wolf. I had no chance to try it against the World Serpent,' Arthur said. 'We can't let ourselves be fooled again.'

'Be fooled? What do you mean? Look at her, Arthur. She's tiny and helpless – do you think she's faking the problem with her legs? How could she possibly hurt us?'

'Listen–'

'No! You listen to me.' She was suddenly furious, more so than Arthur had ever seen her, and he decided it would be prudent to stay quiet. 'You're obviously scared of Ice. I know she almost got us drowned, but it wasn't her fault. It was mine. Clearly that wasn't a real Loki dream you had; it was just an ordinary nightmare. A bad nightmare – like Max has been having.'

'Yeah … OK, maybe you're right,' Arthur admitted, putting the pendant back around his neck. An awkward silence ensued and then, 'Well, I suppose I should go home. You probably want to get a little more sleep.'

'Yeah, I'm still pretty tired, actually.'

They didn't say anything else to each other as Arthur let himself out. On the walk back to his house, he wondered about his dream. He wasn't at all convinced by Ash's idea that it was a simple nightmare. He was sure that it had been a vision and that Loki's second child was a wolf, so he had a bad feeling and really didn't know what to think about Ice. Despite the lack of reaction to the pendant, he couldn't shake the feeling that they shouldn't trust the little dog. He'd been tricked once before and it had almost cost him, Ash and Max their lives. Even if he couldn't convince Ash, he wasn't going to make the same mistake again.

CHAPTER NINE

Arthur walked to the bus stop by himself on Monday morning. He left early, hoping to avoid Ash, but she'd obviously had the same idea. When he got there he found her sitting by herself.

They hadn't spoken since Saturday morning when they'd had their disagreement. Arthur knew they should have been over it by now, but this was their first argument and it felt strange – uncomfortable, somehow. The rest of the weekend had passed slowly. He'd spent most of it playing an Xbox game that Joe had bought him for Christmas. His heart wasn't in it, though, and he barely noticed any time one of the computer-generated zombies attacked his avatar. As he stirred some soup for himself and Joe on Sunday afternoon, he spotted Ash through the kitchen window. She and Max were on the green chasing after Ice while the pup rolled after a football. Arthur could have gone out and said something, but he didn't know what to say. He certainly wasn't going to apologise, as he was still certain that his hunch about Ice was spot on, but he knew that Ash wouldn't want to hear about it again.

'Hey,' Arthur said as he got close to the bus stop.

Ash looked up. 'Oh, hi.'

'Going in early?'

'Something like that. Listen, Arthur–'

'No need to apologise.'

'Apologise?' she said, affronted, her voice rising. 'Why would I apologise?'

'Oh, so it's me who's in the wrong, is that it?' Arthur shouted, equally outraged.

Ash didn't reply, but the way she crossed her arms and stared at him said it all. Just then, a bus pulled up to the stop. They boarded in silence and sat at opposite ends to each other.

It was the first proper day back to normality after the Christmas break for thousands of workers and schoolchildren so the traffic moved frustratingly slowly. Whatever their reasons, it turned out it was a good thing they'd left early because otherwise they'd have been late for their first day back.

The morning bell rang as they walked across the car-park in front of Belmont School – Ash keeping twenty paces ahead of Arthur at all times, pointedly ignoring him. The building was modern and boxy, with one side completely constructed from glass. At the sound of the bell they started to run, and as they dashed inside they found that they weren't the only ones late and racing down the hallway. Other students and even some teachers were speed-walking towards their classrooms, including their own Miss Keegan.

'Hi, Miss,' Ash said when she caught up with her.

'Oh, good morning, Ashling. Arthur.' Her strawberry blonde curls cascaded out from under a pink, woollen beanie and she was wearing a matching cardigan with a yellow blouse underneath. She was younger than most of the other teachers in Belmont and certainly the most fashion conscious.

'I saw you two on the news last week,' she said as she walked with them. 'You were lucky Arthur was there, Ash.'

Ash's face flushed red as she muttered grudgingly, 'I know.'

From the stony silence that followed, Miss Keegan realised that all was not well between the two friends so she quickly changed the subject. 'We have a couple of new students today, so you're no longer the new kid, Arthur.'

Despite their argument, Ash and Arthur looked at each other, concerned. Could this mean Loki was back in his Will-disguise? Like the rest of the world, Miss Keegan had been hypnotised to forget that Will had ever existed, so he could easily have slipped back into class and only Arthur, Ash and Max would know that he was a threat.

Their fellow pupils were mostly sitting around on the desks when Ash, Arthur and the teacher reached the classroom. They were swapping lists of Christmas presents or sharing funny stories about things that had happened over the break. When they saw Miss Keegan, they all shuffled into their seats with much scraping of chair legs on the linoleum floor. Arthur took his seat next to Ash and quickly scanned the room. No sign of Will. In fact, there was no one new here at all that he could see.

'I trust you all had a nice break,' Miss Keegan was saying, taking off her coat and pulling some books out of her large handbag. 'I hope you're all so well rested that you can't wait to get back to work!'

There were some groans at this. Kevin and Colin – the ginger O'Toole twins – said in sync, 'Go easy on us, Miss!'

'Yeah, Miss,' Rob Tynan spoke up. 'We need to warm up first.'

The class made some general sounds of agreement as Miss Keegan chuckled to herself. Just then, there was a knock on the door. The teacher went over to answer it, holding a finger to her lips at the class. Arthur caught a glimpse of their principal before the teacher shut the door behind her. As the other pupils started murmuring and whispering to each other again, Arthur turned to Ash.

'Could you see the newbie?' he asked.

'Nope. Do you think it's him?'

'Will?'

She nodded.

'I hope not.'

The door opened again and the class fell back into hushed silence. Miss Keegan re-entered, ushering a boy and girl in front of her.

The boy was almost as tall as Miss Keegan but of a much broader build. He had small brown eyes through which he squinted at his new classmates, a large and crooked nose that looked like it had been broken at some stage and a strong, square jaw with hints of facial hair already sprouting along it. His black hair was shaved close to his head and he grimaced at them with an expression that said *I'm bigger than you, so don't test me*. He had a backpack slung over one of his powerful shoulders and his brown school uniform was a couple of sizes too small for him, with the sleeves stopping well short of his wrists. Arthur doubted that they even made the Belmont uniform in his size.

The girl, on the other hand, could easily be summed up as petite. Standing at just over four feet tall, her slim frame was a twig compared to the trunk that was the gargantuan boy behind her. Her straight black hair was pulled back from her face by a light-blue hairband and hung in a bob just above her neckline. Her deep brown eyes popped out from her sallow skin; they were watchful, studying each face in the class. When they landed on Arthur they stopped and he couldn't help but look away, discomfited. It felt as if the eyes were looking into his soul. Unlike the boy's, her uniform fit her perfectly. However, the coat she wore over the uniform was far too large for her and bunched at the elbows. It was an adult-sized trench coat and it trailed along the ground by her feet, only serving to add to the illusion of her littleness. Instead of a backpack, she held a cracked leather attaché case in her right hand. She smiled a toothy grin at them all, clearly pleased and excited to be there.

'Class,' said Miss Keegan, 'this is Ellie and Xander Lavender. They'll be joining us for the rest of the term.'

'Ex,' said the boy Xander. His voice was a deep baritone rumble, certainly more grown-up sounding than anyone else in the class.

'I'm sorry, Xander, what was that?' Miss Keegan asked.

'I prefer to be called Ex, Miss Keegan.'

'Oh, I'm sorry.' She turned back to her pupils. 'Ellie and Ex Lavender.'

The boy nodded his head slightly while the girl waved.

'Maybe you'd like to tell the class a little about yourselves?' Miss Keegan suggested. 'Ex?'

'No, thank you.'

'I'll do it!' Ellie said eagerly. She put her case carefully on Miss Keegan's overflowing desk and took a step towards the class. 'As Miss Keegan said, I'm Ellie Lavender and this is my brother, Ex. He's thirteen, nearly fourteen. And I'm eleven, just gone. Usually, we're home schooled although I've been in five real schools in the past. But our parents are archaeologists, you see, so they're pretty intelligent. And they've gone on a dig in Greece for a few months, so here we are! Speaking of which,' she turned to Caroline Cusick in the front row, 'I see that you have just come back from Greece.'

'How did you–' started Caroline.

'Thank you, Ellie.' Miss Keegan cut her off mid-sentence. 'If you'd like to take a seat, we'll begin the class.'

Two vacant chairs sat right in front of Arthur and Ash, which the Lavender siblings went straight for. Ex sat right down while Ellie busily took off her massive coat. She hung it on the back of her seat and put her hand out to Arthur.

'Hi,' she said. 'I'm Ellie. What's your name?'

'Ellie,' Miss Keegan said, turning away from the blackboard she'd been writing on. 'Maybe you could make time for introductions during break? We have work to get on with.'

'Of course, Miss Keegan. Sorry, Miss Keegan.' Ellie sat down and faced the teacher studiously.

Arthur looked at Ash. She swirled her index finger in little circles at her temple and crossed her eyes, indicating that Ellie was nuts. She was right, Arthur reflected. Whoever this pair were, they definitely weren't like Will. Despite that, he still felt wary of them. He suspected that any new classmates would take a long time to earn his trust nowadays.

When the bell for break rang, the fifth- and sixth-class pupils trooped out to the all-weather pitch at the back of the school. The pitch had been the last piece of construction work to be completed when the new school was being built and it was a much appreciated addition for the majority of the pupils.

Rob Tynan, who liked to consider himself the best sportsman in the school, tossed a rugby ball from one hand to the other.

'How about some rugby?' he asked loudly. The ball fell between his arms and bounced unevenly away. He stretched to catch it, then nonchalantly rubbed his hand through his hair as if nothing had happened. 'Rugby, yeah?'

'Can the girls play too?' Tara Egan asked, taking a step forward and grabbing the ball from him. Rob wasn't a fan of letting the girls join in and often suggested rougher sports for lunch break to put them off.

Rob gave her a pitying look. 'Really? Ha!'

With that, Tara threw the ball. It soared far and wide across the pitch and Megan Gallagher caught it mid-air. She held it above her head triumphantly.

'Yeah,' Tara said, as the other girls giggled, 'really.'

'OK,' Rob agreed reluctantly. 'But I bags captain!'

'Bags!' Tara said quickly before anyone else could claim the second captaincy.

They picked teams. Almost the entire class agreed to play, so the pitch was quite cramped. Rob picked first and went for the new boy, Ex Lavender. They didn't know what he was like on the pitch so it was a gamble, but judging by the new boy's powerful physique, Rob guessed the gamble would pay off. Tara's first choice was Megan, followed by Arthur. While Tara's team was quite evenly mixed, Rob didn't want to pick any girls. He eventually had to take one – Ash, the last one standing. Just once, Ash thought, just once I want to be picked first. Ciara O'Connor and Caroline Cusick were both too precious about their hair and nails to join in, so they sat on the sidelines with a couple of like-minded fifth classers and the new girl, Ellie.

Although Arthur had been Tara's second choice, he thought that her faith in him was misplaced. He loved basketball, and had even won medals for his efforts back in Kerry, but rugby was one sport he had never excelled at. His uncle in Kerry, who was a huge rugby fan, boasted that the sport was more ingrained in his blood than any other, including Gaelic. (This, of course, was considered blasphemy by the GAA supporters in their town, but it always made Arthur laugh to hear his uncle wind them up on purpose.) Coming from Munster, Arthur naturally enjoyed watching rugby. But playing it was out of the question. He had a light, slim frame – perfect for basketball, not for rugby.

This game, however, was getting off to a flying start and Rob's team had already scored one try, partly thanks to a vital pass from Ash. Arthur's team now had the ball. Niall Fitzgerald passed it to Mark Curtis, who passed it to Brian Savage who passed it to Robyn Power who passed it to–

'Arthur!' she shouted as the ball bounced feebly off his chest and onto the ground. Arthur had drifted away, not really paying attention. He looked down at the ball by his feet, rocking over and back.

'Pick it up!' someone shouted at him.

He did as they said, grabbing the ball and clutching it tight to his chest, then he ran in the direction of Rob's goal line. His heart was thumping as his legs pounded off the rubbery all-weather surface. Since it was still freezing, they were all wearing coats, hats and scarves; a drop of sweat rolled into his eye, stinging it. But he ignored the discomfort and kept going. He hadn't far to run now: he could see the line coming up before him and no one was in the way, just footsteps thundering after him.

Suddenly, something yanked him backwards. Whoever it was had grabbed the back of his coat, stopping him in his tracks and pulling him in the opposite direction through the air. He heard the hood of his coat, caught in the grip of his attacker, rip as easily as tearing toilet paper. The person let him go and he fell with a heavy thud onto his back. The ball flew out of his arms and straight into those of Ex Lavender, who was looming over him. That's who had been pulling him backwards! Without even giving Arthur a second look, Ex kicked the ball back down the field to cheers from Rob's team.

Arthur stood up, his back stiff and sore. He arched backwards and heard a loud crack, which actually helped relieve some of the pain.

'You all right?' asked Ash, who was standing nearby.

'I will be. I'll just sit out the rest of the game.' He hobbled off the pitch and sat on one of the bleachers, making sure he wasn't anywhere near Ciara and the other girls. He didn't feel like listening to them prattle on about eyeliner and shades of nail polish, especially when he was already in pain. The game went on without him, everybody too engrossed to notice his absence and, as he grew bored of watching, Arthur's thoughts once again drifted off.

'Sorry about my brother.' Slightly startled, Arthur looked up to find the source of the voice. Ellie Lavender had left the girls and was standing over him. Her too-big trench coat danced in the breeze.

'It's OK,' he said. 'Not your fault.'

Without asking if she could join him, she sat down.

'Arthur, right?' she said. 'I'm Ellie. Nice to meet you.' They shook hands.

'Sorry again about Ex,' she continued. 'I got the brains in the family and he got the brawn. I like to think I got the best deal.'

'He's pretty strong,' Arthur agreed.

'He doesn't know his own strength.'

'He's older than the rest of us. What's he doing in sixth class?' Arthur instantly regretted such a straightforward question, but when he looked at Ellie she didn't seem to mind. She seemed pretty straightforward herself, he supposed.

'Like I said, I got the brains and he got the brawn. He's always struggled at schoolwork. Any time we're in a school, teachers like to keep him a year behind.'

'And they put you a year ahead?' Arthur asked.

'Sometimes two years!' Ellie said proudly. 'Home schooling is better for Ex. He doesn't feel as out of place there.'

'Neither do you, I bet.'

'I can talk to anyone. About anything.'

'Really?' He nodded to Ciara, Caroline and the other girls, who were staring at her out of the sides of their eyes and whispering frantically. 'Even them?'

'I don't think they like me very much ...'

'How did you guess about Caroline's holiday in Greece?'

'Oh, that was easy. I spotted the tan lines on her face as soon as I came into the class.'

'What tan lines?' Arthur looked over at the girl in question.

'See how her face is tanned but there are whitish patches around her eyes?' Arthur did notice them now that she'd pointed them out. Ellie continued, 'That told me that she was recently somewhere hot and sunny – she needed to wear sunglasses. And then I noticed the airport tag that was still stuck on her backpack. The letters on it were ATH – the code for Athens. I just put two and two together.'

'Wow!' exclaimed Arthur, genuinely impressed. 'You got all that so quickly?'

'It's a game I like to play, although sometimes I think it scares people. I shouldn't have said it in class. Those girls don't really like me now.'

'I'm sure they'll come around.'

'Maybe.' She looked at the game and watched as her brother scored yet another try to great applause. 'Like I said, I'm not afraid to talk to anyone but … well … I'm not very good at making friends. People don't seem to get me.'

Before Arthur could comment, she turned back to him. 'So, Arthur, tell me about your adventure.'

He was taken aback and rendered momentarily speechless. 'Uh, adventure?'

'You did nearly drown a few days ago, right? You and Ash? Ciara and Caroline were talking about it and I may have eavesdropped.'

'Oh!' He breathed a sigh of relief. 'Yeah. Quite the adventure, all right.'

Just then, the school-bell rang, announcing the end of break-time.

'So?' Ellie urged. 'Tell me what happened.'

'That's the bell, though,' he said. 'We need to go back to class.'

'Oh, yeah.' She seemed disappointed. 'It always takes me a while to get used to following the school-bell routine.'

Ellie had got the hang of the school-bells by the time the last one of the day rang, and she rushed from the classroom as eagerly as the rest of her classmates. Before they went, the teacher reminded them that the annual parent–teacher meeting would take place in a couple of weeks' time and gave them all flyers to take home. Arthur and Ash walked silently together to their bus stop just outside the school, the air between them still not clear. They stood in silence, neither quite knowing what to say to the other.

'Oh, hi guys!' Ellie said, catching up with them. Ex was standing behind her; he just nodded at them and grunted.

'Hi, Ellie,' Arthur said. 'Have you met Ash yet?'

The two girls shook hands.

'This is Ex,' Ellie said, reaching up to lay her tiny hand on her huge brother's shoulder. 'Say "hello" Ex.'

'Hello Ex,' said the older Lavender sibling as Arthur and Ash's bus pulled up.

'Ooh!' said Ellie, as Arthur and Ash started to board. 'The number 11 bus! Eleven's a good number. It's lucky.'

'Really?' Arthur asked, stepping onto the bus.

'Yup! Well, goodbye, Arthur! Goodbye, Ash! See you tomorr–!'

The bus door whooshed shut, cutting off the end of the word.

'What a pair of weirdos,' Ash said, walking up to the second deck of the bus and finding a seat near the back. Arthur sat next to her.

'I like them,' he said.

'Even Ex? After what he did?'

'He was only playing the game. Maybe he doesn't realise his own strength. I kind of feel sorry for him.' He took this as his opportunity to make up with Ash. 'Actually, speaking of which …'

'Yeah?'

'I just want to say I'm sorry for arguing with you.'

'I'm sorry too,' she said.

'I still think you should be careful around Ice, though.'

'And I still think you're wrong.'

'I guess we'll just have to agree to disagree then,' said Arthur.

Ash studied him for a moment then nodded. 'Friends again?'

'Friends!' agreed Arthur.

CHAPTER TEN

The bright spell of weather had passed but the cold snap remained on the day Podge McGarry found the jar. The sky was overcast – yellow clouds threatening snow – as he made his way across the Usher's Quay Metro site. The ground was hard and would have been slippery with ice if not for the uneven scattering of pebbles and rubble giving extra traction to his boots. He pushed a wheelbarrow over the bumpy ground. The heavy jackhammer in it bounced severely on every pothole.

Podge was in his mid-forties. The top of his head was completely bald, but he made up for it with a bushy grey moustache. A pot belly – the result of too many greasy breakfast rolls – hung precariously over his belt. He was wearing a padded bomber jacket, cargo work pants, a pair of steel-toed boots and a worn beanie embroidered with the Citi-Trak logo. He was also sporting a bright-yellow high-visibility jacket, as was compulsory on the worksite. He walked with a slight limp – the result of a teenage car accident.

There weren't many people about on the main site today. Most of the excavators were down in the tunnel, operating the huge drill or building support systems. The engineers – the bossmen, as Podge liked to call them – were holed up inside the warm Citi-Trak on-site offices. These were essentially a pair of long and low prefab buildings full of computers, plans, paperwork and, most importantly, electric heaters, tea and biscuits. Lucky sods, Podge thought bitterly, heaving the wheelbarrow through a particularly troublesome pothole.

He didn't mind working on his own, though. In fact, he enjoyed his own company far more than anyone else's. He could drift off into his own thoughts, nothing to bother him except the droning sound of the jackhammer. His job today was a simple one. The icy weather had caused havoc with the water system all over the country of late. Water froze solid in the pipes, bursting them and creating leaks that wasted thousands of gallons of water. Old pipes lay under the site and Podge's job was to find them so that the on-site plumbers could replace them. If one of the old clay pipes burst while excavation was ongoing, there's no telling what damage it could do.

He turned a corner to the first spot he had to dig. A young engineer, whose name he thought was Ruairí, was spray-painting a large red X on the ground. As always, he was unshaven, with tousled, unkempt hair. But, for a change, he didn't have that other young engineer – Deirdre, Podge thought – with him. Since the pair had started going out a few months ago, they'd been inseparable.

'Hi, Podge!' Ruairí said pleasantly, putting the cap back on the paint can.

'Hullo,' grunted Podge, barely looking up. He put the wheelbarrow down and lifted the jackhammer out. It was so heavy he could only manage to shuffle it over to the spot the engineer had marked.

'This should be where the first pipe is,' Ruairí explained, indicating the X. 'Need a hand with anything?'

'No, it's grand.'

'OK. I'll let you get on with it so.' He walked off in the direction of the heated office. Lucky sod, Podge thought to himself again.

He put a hard hat on over his beanie, followed by plastic goggles and a pair of ear defenders that clung tightly to the side of his head, turning all outside sound into a distant echo. He positioned the chisel of the jackhammer right on the centre of the X, then switched on the pneumatics.

The internal hammer pounded up and down rapidly. He could feel each vibration juddering up his arms and even into his teeth as the chisel broke through the top crust of earth. He was so used to the machinery that he was able to drift away, humming a tune softly in his head, yet still instinctively know when he was coming close to the target. But he was shocked out of his thoughts when, suddenly, the chisel ground to a halt underneath him. The machinery screeched and spluttered. He could feel heat rising from it and saw a small trail of white smoke seeping through one of its vent holes. Before he did any real damage, he shut the jackhammer off. It wheezed to a stop and he laid it on the ground next to the shallow hole he'd made.

He knelt down and examined the hollow. It was only a few inches deep. He brushed aside the remnants of dust and earth and found the source of the problem. He'd hit rock.

Podge knocked his knuckle on it. He didn't know one type of rock from another, but this one seemed harder than most; it didn't give off the hollow ring that limestone did. The jackhammer could probably break through it, but only given time and probably a couple of replacement chisel pieces. Both of which he didn't have. His best option would be to work around it then lift it out to reveal the pipe.

Unsure how big the piece of rock might be, he decided to start fairly close to the original spot and move further away by stages as necessary. He lifted the jackhammer back up and placed the chisel two feet away from his first attempt. He straightened his hard hat then switched on the machine once more.

This time he concentrated on what he was doing, keeping a close eye on the chisel hammering into the ground. When it passed lower than his previous effort, he breathed a sigh of relief. But this was short-lived as he felt a sharp crack through the vibrations in his hands. Suddenly, a lumpy cream-coloured substance started to ooze up out of the second hole. He immediately turned the jackhammer off and laid it aside.

Although the substance quickly stopped seeping out, it gave off a strong, sour stench. Gagging, Podge pulled his jacket collar up over his nose and mouth to try and filter out the smell and bent down for a closer look. The gunk wasn't the only thing that had come out of the hole, he now saw. A small piece of red pottery was lying on its surface. He reached out and picked it up, hoping that it wasn't a shard of the water pipe and that he hadn't done more damage to it than the ice had.

For a moment he almost panicked as he saw that it was a rounded chip of earthenware, similar to an old pipe. But then he realised that this was no pipe. This was different. A pattern of swirls and interweaving loops was carved into the shard. Whatever this was, Podge realised, it was clearly very, very old.

Deirdre had left the noise of the tunnel and was heading towards the engineers' office when she spotted the excavator looking intently at something in his hands. She was tall and slim, and her hips wiggled when she walked. Her hair was, as usual, tied into a neat bun under her hard hat and her thick, round glasses magnified her brown eyes to almost twice their size.

She diverted from her course and strode over to Podge.

'What've you got there?' she asked. Suddenly, the sour stench slammed her in the face. 'Pee-ew! And what's that awful smell?'

'It's that stuff.' He pointed at the creamy slime oozing out of the hole he'd made. 'Do you reckon it's sewage?'

'I doubt it. I've seen sewage down in the tunnel and it doesn't look – or smell – like that!'

'Found this too.' He handed her the slice of pottery. 'I think it's pretty old.'

She studied it for a beat, tracing her fingertip over the carved swirls. 'I reckon you're right,' she said.

Within minutes Deirdre had gathered up Ruairí and Joe Quinn from the office. They were all standing around Podge's find, holding their noses. The grumpy excavator stood to one side smoking a cigarette – if only to block out the stench.

'What is it?' Ruairí said, his voice sounding unusually nasal as he pinched his nose.

'Haven't a clue,' answered Deirdre.

'I think I know what it is,' Joe said, turning the shard of earthenware in his free hand.

'What?' Ruairí asked, looking up at his boss.

'It's butter.' Joe turned away from the hole and paced quickly back towards the office.

'Butter?' Deirdre repeated, as the pair of them trailed after him.

'Yup, butter.' He didn't seem too pleased with the

discovery. 'In college, one of my lecturers told me that he was working on an excavation in Cork years ago. Work had to stop when they found a jar of butter left under the ground by the Celts. He even showed us photos of the stuff and it's just like this. Shortly after that it was made law that all big digs like this had to have archaeologists survey them in advance of work starting.'

'Which means that …?' Ruairí prompted, unsure of the situation.

'We're going to have to call in the experts.'

Joe made the call to the University College Dublin archaeology department personally. The lady who took the call promised that they would send someone over to have a look within the hour and, true to her word, an archaeology professor along with a couple of volunteer students arrived forty minutes later. Soon the students were on their knees, chipping away at the surrounding earth with tiny chisels and hammers.

The day wore on. Joe and the engineers stayed in the office, waiting to hear from the small team what had been found and sipping mugs of instant coffee.

'Shouldn't we call Luke Moran?' Deirdre spoke up at one stage. Joe was shocked he hadn't thought of it himself. Luke Moran, the CEO of Citi-Trak, should have been the first person he'd called.

He dialled Moran's number on his phone, only for the secretary who answered to tell him that Moran was out of the office, making an appearance on a cookery programme. It was a well-known fact that Luke Moran enjoyed self-publicity as much as he enjoyed making money or getting angry and shouting at his staff. Joe left a message with the harassed secretary, saying that they'd found something on the site and had had to call in some archaeologists.

Eventually, there was a knock on the prefab door. Joe rushed to answer it. Dr Martin, the archaeology professor, stepped in. He brushed his dusty hands on his trousers to clean them and leaned against the prefab wall.

'It's Viking,' he said, clearly excited from the pitch of his voice. 'We can't be sure of the date yet but I'd approximate some time between AD 1000 and 1100. My students are just collecting some specimens of the butter. Possibly the best example we've ever discovered in Dublin. And it's–'

'But what will this mean for the tunnel excavation?' Joe interrupted him.

'Oh, you'll have to put it on hold,' the head archae-ologist said, as if it was the most obvious answer in the world.

'But it's only one jar!'

The professor rolled his eyes as if he'd heard this objection before. 'So far there's only one jar, but we'll have to do a complete new survey and some trial trenches to see if there's anything else.'

'How long will that take?'

'It's difficult to tell exactly. It could be that there actually is only one find or it could mean that we're standing over a whole Viking settlement. Could be a month; could be twelve. This is a big site. Either way, we'll have to shut down excavation for a while.'

Joe, Deirdre and Ruairí sighed in united despair.

'I'm sorry,' Dr Martin went on, sensing their dejection. 'I realise this is probably quite a blow to your schedule. I'll just see if my students are finished and we'll be on our way. I'll be in touch shortly.'

As he left, they heard the *fwump-fwump* of an approaching helicopter. Joe ran to the door and looked skywards at it. The Citi-Trak logo was painted on both sides. It hovered there for a moment before lowering itself carefully to a clear area in front of the prefabs where the ground was more even than elsewhere. The blades cut through the air, blowing up huge clouds of dust and debris. Luke Moran and his ever-present personal assistant, Piers, came running through the clouds.

For such a broad and fat man, Moran had a long stride and even the tall, lanky Piers struggled to keep up. Moran saw Joe, Deirdre and Ruairí standing in the doorway.

'What's all this about archaeologists?' he shouted over the roar of the helicopter. Always straight to the point, thought Joe. Unlike Moran, he wasn't keen on yelling across the site so he waited until his boss reached them.

'Well?' Moran asked again as they led him into the office.

Joe took a deep breath, preparing himself. Moran wouldn't like what he had to tell him, he realised. It's just like pulling off a plaster, Joe thought to himself: best to get it over and done with fast. So, as quickly and succinctly as he could, Joe filled Moran in on all that had happened.

'We're going to have to suspend work for a while,' Joe finished. As he was speaking, he hadn't been able to look Moran in the eye and found himself staring at a piece of lint attached to the man's jacket shoulder instead. Now that he *did* look at Moran directly, he saw that he'd turned an unhealthy deep shade of red.

'You let archaeologists onto *my* site?' He spoke slowly, enunciating each word clearly with rage.

'Of course,' said Joe. 'We had to. It's the law.'

'Sod the law! They had their time to survey the site before we started and found nothing.'

'Well, they've found something now!' Joe was aghast. 'We had to let them survey. There could be something of great historical importance here.'

'Oh, shut up, you idiot.'

Now Joe saw red. 'I show you respect, Mr Moran, and you should do the same for me.'

'Oh, really?' Moran spat back in a mocking tone. 'And what are you going to do if I don't respect you? Quit?'

'Yes, actually, I am.'

Arthur and Ash stopped for a hot chocolate on their way home from school. It was exactly what they needed after the first few days back, and the warm sweetness felt perfect running down their throats on this icy evening. By the time they got back to their estate, Stace had also just arrived home.

'Hey, Arthur!' she shouted from across the road where

a friend had dropped her off. 'Wait up!'

Arthur looked at Ash in confusion. '"Wait up"? What does Stace want with me?' he asked. Ash shrugged her shoulders, just as bewildered.

'What's up, Stace?' Arthur said when she reached them.

'I was just wondering,' she started, a little out of breath from her sprint across the street, 'if your hot cousin is coming around any time soon?'

'Who?' questioned Ash.

'Eirik,' Arthur told her with a wink.

'Oh!'

'So when's he visiting you next?' Stace asked again eagerly.

'Uh … probably not for a while. He doesn't visit that often. Sorry.'

'Arthur, you have to get him around! Invite him to the cinema or something.'

'And you'd just happen to be there, right Stace?' Ash said, sniggering. 'Wearing your best outfit and make-up too!'

They were outside Arthur's house and, before Stace could send a retort Ash's way, he promised that he'd try his best to invite Eirik over.

'Although, he's kind of a loner so I can't guarantee anything,' Arthur said, going in through his front door.

Joe was sitting in the kitchen, going over some paperwork in silence. Rather than disturb him, Arthur headed for the stairs until–

'Arthur.'

'Yes, Dad?'

'Come here and sit down for a minute. I have something to tell you.'

Arthur took the seat opposite his father, slightly anxious – it was unlike his dad to be this formal and he was worried that he was in trouble for something he couldn't remember doing.

'What's up, Dad?'

Joe took off his reading glasses and set them down on the paperwork. He looked his son straight in the eye for a beat before speaking.

'The Metro excavation has been suspended.'

'Why?'

'We found some Viking artefacts on the site so all work has to stop.'

'Oh.' Arthur looked down, half-wondering what artefacts had been discovered. 'What does that mean for us?'

'Work on the tunnel might not start up again for

another year. It's all up in the air at the minute. So I've quit my job. We're moving back to Kerry.' He said the last bit with a huge smile.

'What! When?' It was a blow he hadn't been expecting. It had been something he'd wished and prayed for when they'd first moved to Dublin, but now that his wish had come true, he found that he wasn't even slightly pleased.

'I had to give them four weeks' notice. There's a lot of paperwork to finish before I leave. So we go home in a month.' Joe stopped when he realised that he wasn't getting the excited reaction that he'd expected. 'Arthur? I thought this was what you wanted. Aren't you happy?'

'Yeah,' Arthur lied and forced a weak smile onto his face. But he wasn't happy. He wasn't happy at all.

CHAPTER ELEVEN

A week passed and Arthur still couldn't bring himself to break the bad news to Ash. It was something he just didn't want to think about. Despite this, it was on his mind constantly. Even when he did manage to concentrate on schoolwork or something on TV, the thought of leaving was still there. A niggling, negative thought in his subconscious. He felt like a drone during those days. He'd get up, go to school, do his work half-heartedly and return home with Ash in near-silence. Eventually she noticed the change in his mood and asked what was up.

'Nothing,' he'd answered monotonously, still hoping to avoid the issue with her. 'I'm just tired, that's all.'

The new girl, Ellie Lavender, also tried engaging him in conversation during the lunch-breaks, asking about his family, where he was from, what he liked to do at the weekends. But to no avail. Arthur just replied with one-word answers.

It was Friday lunchtime when Ash gave him some news that brightened his humour. The students were on their way back to class when her phone beeped shrilly. She and Arthur had each bought new phones with Christmas gift vouchers after their old ones had been destroyed in the frozen lake (even Ash wasn't able to fix them). Arthur went for a small touchscreen that fitted neatly in the palm of his hand, while Ash chose a state-of-the-art smartphone which she spent hours happily playing with. She flicked the screen to read the incoming text, then squealed in delight.

'What's up?' Arthur inquired.

'It's a text from my mom. Cousin Maggie is coming to visit!'

'When?'

'Tomorrow! She's showing some paintings to a gallery on Dawson Street. She said she'll meet us there around one and take us out for the day!'

'That's great!' Arthur was so pleased at the thought of a much-needed distraction that he didn't notice Ellie and Ex walking slowly in front of them. Or the small and knowing look that Ellie shot at her brother.

Although it was only mid-January, a thaw had set in on the Saturday morning and they took the bus into town. It was still cold and their breath puffed out in clouds of condensation, but the day didn't have that biting frostiness that they'd been used to for weeks now. Arthur, Ash and Max all disembarked from the bus outside St Stephen's Green. Stace couldn't come as her mock Leaving Certificate exams were rapidly approaching and she wanted to use the spare time to study.

The pavements weren't icy and slick any more, but rather uneven with residue from the salt and grit that had been scattered on them during the treacherous weeks. Dublin city centre was busy once more – the opposite of the Saturday Arthur and Ash had visited the Vikings. The improving weather had obviously encouraged the shoppers too.

They crossed the road at the traffic lights and walked down Dawson Street. Most of the Christmas lights, trees and decorations had been taken down and packed away until next November. But all the shops that lined the street had bold, red SALE signs placed prominently in their windows. Shoppers piled in and out of stores, carrying bags stuffed with bargains and spending the last of their Christmas savings and gift tokens.

They reached the art gallery Cousin Maggie had mentioned about halfway down the street and next to a large bookshop. The shop-front of the gallery was old, with intricately carved wooden pillars and mouldings that were thick with layers of paint. Polished bronze letters stood out on the sign, spelling the words CHEVALIER GALLERIES. A lone painting hung in the single window. It was a landscape, depicting a windswept and harsh field in Connemara. The oil paint had been applied densely and globs of colours popped out here and there on the canvas. It was selling for €23,000.

'Twenty-three hundred!' exclaimed Max in shock.

'That's twenty-three thousand, Max,' Arthur said.

'Twenty-three *thousand*! For that? I prefer Cousin Maggie's ones. They're not as depressing.'

As if on cue, Cousin Maggie appeared inside the shop, stepping out of a back room with a couple of gallery employees. She smiled and waved through the glass, then turned back to a stern-looking man in a three-piece suit. Arthur assumed that he was the gallery owner. They talked for a moment. Then Maggie shook his hand and walked out to the street.

Straight away, she hugged the three of them at once.

'How are you all?' she asked, finally letting them go.

'We're good, Cousin Maggie,' Ash answered for them. 'How are you?'

'I'm great, Ash!' She pointed over her shoulder into the gallery. 'The owner, Mr Branigan, is a famous artist himself, but he's agreed to show my paintings to some interested buyers later today, so I couldn't be better!'

'That's amazing news,' Arthur said. 'Well done!'

'Fingers crossed it goes well. Now,' she clapped her gloved hands, 'who's up for some celebratory milk shakes. I saw a place down the street that looked nice.'

Without waiting for an answer, she turned and strode briskly away. Max ran after her. Arthur and Ash started to follow but stopped when–

'Arthur! Ash!'

They turned in the direction of the voice calling to them. Ellie and Ex were running across the street to them, dodging the dense traffic. Arthur almost didn't recognise them out of their brown school uniforms. Ex was wearing clothes that fitted for a change, although Ellie was still in her too-large trench coat.

'Hi, guys!' said Ellie when they reached them. 'We were just passing. I thought I saw you and I said to Ex, "Hey, isn't that Arthur and Ash?" and he was like, "I dunno," and I was like, "I'm pretty sure it is," and then I called your name and, lo and behold, it is you!' She took a short breath. 'So what are you up to?' Through it all, Ex stood silently behind her, studying his feet.

'Just meeting up with Cousin Maggie,' Ash said, indicating Maggie, who was striding up the street.

'Oh, she's your cousin?'

'No,' Arthur said with a wry, knowing smile. 'But it's a long story.'

'Oh. OK. Well ...' Ellie looked from Arthur to Ash and back again, waiting. 'Well ...' she said again.

'Hurry up, you two!' Cousin Maggie called, already halfway towards the milk shake bar. Then she noticed Ellie and Ex. 'Bring your two friends along if you like!'

Ellie turned back to Arthur and Ash. 'Well, we wouldn't want to intrude.'

Ash was about to say, 'Then don't,' before Arthur cut her off.

'You wouldn't be intruding at all.'

With that, Ellie skipped off in the direction of Cousin Maggie and Max. Ex plodded along behind her. Arthur and Ash trailed after them in silence, Ash glaring at Arthur in quiet irritation the whole way to the milk shake bar.

'Ow!' cried Ellie, rubbing her temple furiously. 'Brain freeze!'

'Don't drink it so quickly,' Cousin Maggie advised, sipping at her own shake more slowly.

The milk shake bar was designed like an American diner from the 1950s, with black and white chequerboard tiles, a chrome countertop running the length of the kitchen area and comfortable booths with seats covered in bright red vinyl. Rock 'n' roll music boomed from a jukebox in the corner and the waiters wore costumes from the period.

They were all squeezed into one of the booths, with Max opting for a tall swivel stool at the end of the table. He swung in small arcs on the seat as he drank his milk shake.

'So, how do you all know each other?' Maggie asked.

'We go to school together,' Ellie piped up before anyone else could answer. 'We just started there – Ex and I. That's Xander, my brother.' Ex nodded his head at Cousin Maggie as he was name-checked.

'Do you like it there?'

'It's all right. It's a bit lonely, though. We don't really know anyone yet.' She bit the end of her straw and sipped, looking sideways at Arthur. He didn't know what had prompted the look, but thought he could read some sadness in her eyes. Suddenly her expression changed and she beamed up at Maggie. 'But the farm must be quite lonely sometimes too, right? Although I guess it's good for painting.'

'It can b–'

'Hold on!' Ash cut Cousin Maggie off. 'How did you know she's an artist who lives on a farm?'

'Oh …' Ellie blushed. 'It's that silly habit I have. Sorry.'

'How did you know?' Ash pushed once more.

'Well, I knew she was an artist because I saw the spots of paint under the fingernails. Oil paint is notoriously difficult to clean off. I knew she lived in the country because I noticed the smudges of dirt around the hems of her trousers. We've had dry weather for a few weeks now in Dublin, so the dirt must have come from the countryside. When I saw the long white animal hair stuck to the back of Cousin Maggie's coat, I realised that she must live with or near animals. So I put it all together.' She blushed once more, looking up at Maggie. 'Sorry. It's just a weird thing I do.'

'It's kind of creepy,' Ash murmured to no one in particular.

'I think it's fascinating!' Maggie enthused. 'So very

clever. And to answer your question, the farm can be lonely at times. But that makes days like today even better.' She looked around at the rest of them, then back to Ellie. 'You know, I'm bringing this lot somewhere fun after this and you're more than welcome to join us.'

Ex looked at Ellie, as if he was waiting for her to decide.

'Sounds good,' she said eventually. 'Where are we going?'

'Oh,' said Cousin Maggie with a mischievous wink, 'somewhere very special. Back in time!'

Cousin Maggie led them up the adjacent Kildare Street, walking too briskly as usual.

'Hustle, hustle!' she said. 'You'll love this place.'

They passed Leinster House – a grey and overwhelming building that Arthur knew was the seat of the Irish government – then went towards a smaller entrance on the right. They climbed a few short steps up to the main entryway: a couple of heavy wooden doors held open by strong chains. Beyond, they found themselves in a round entrance hall. The entire floor was covered in an intricate and beautiful mosaic showing the twelve signs of the zodiac. Arthur quickly spotted his own sign of Aquarius: a Greek figure pouring water from a jar. Around the edges of the hall were souvenir stands selling trinkets and jewellery, posters and books. And overhead was a domed ceiling with a glass centre, allowing natural light to fill the hall.

'Welcome,' Cousin Maggie said, stretching her arms wide, 'to the National Museum.'

'Wow! It's amazing!' Arthur said.

'You think this is impressive? We're just in the souvenir shop now!' She turned on her heel and marched off once more. 'Follow me.'

They emerged into an even greater hall. The entrance had been a sight to behold, but this room took Arthur's breath away. The ceiling was higher in here, with glass panels running along its length. The floor below him was covered in a series of mosaic patterns running the length of the hall and huge, timeworn portraits hung on the walls themselves. There were exhibits everywhere he looked – bowls and chalices from the Bronze Age gleaming in glass enclosures, mannequins wearing the remains of costumes and jewellery from the Iron Age, jars and pottery and early examples of writing all out for display. And this was only on the ground floor. He could see a balcony running the entire way around the hall, with people examining other exhibits on the second storey.

'Let's explore,' suggested Cousin Maggie.

Max didn't need any prompting and ran off to look at a selection of Iron Age weapons. They were housed in a glass cabinet, with a little thermometer inside keeping track of the temperature in case it got too hot or too cold – the wrong temperature would damage the fragile artefacts.

'Look at that one!' he cried, pointing to a rusty Celtic dagger, complete with a shining bronze hilt inlaid with gold filigree and bright-blue detailing. The colours in some of the Celtic jewellery really surprised Arthur. He couldn't imagine how the ancient craftsmen could have created such lively and vivid shades of green, red and blue.

They found a room filled with Celtic high crosses. These stone monuments towered above them, with images of saints or demons carved into their surfaces. Some of the images were still as intricate as when they'd first been carved, while others hadn't stood the test of time as well and had eroded to faint shadows of their former glories. Another room housed the famous Ardagh Chalice, a silver cup decorated with Celtic knots and spirals and insets of coloured enamel. It wasn't as large as Arthur had thought it would be from pictures in history books, but it was no less impressive. He remembered seeing the world-renowned *Mona Lisa* in the Louvre in Paris a couple of years ago on holiday and expecting it to take up half the wall, but he'd been surprised to find that it was barely larger than a standard comic book.

They wandered upstairs where it was much quieter, and into the Egyptian Room. There was sand under the glass floor with pink neon lighting to give it a mystical feel and there was a sarcophagus in the centre of the room. The great coffin had an Egyptian prince painted on the lid, his arms crossed and his eyes wide open.

'Do you think there's a mummy in there?' asked Max.

'Probably,' Cousin Maggie said. 'Let's hope it doesn't get you, Maxie!'

They continued out of the Egyptian Room. Arthur was about to follow them until he noticed a sign on the wall, with an arrow pointing in the opposite direction, which said Viking Room. He looked at the others: they were intently studying a medieval gown so he didn't disturb them. He walked towards the Viking Room.

'Can I come?'

He turned back to find Ellie behind him.

'Sure,' he said and went on.

'Arthur, can I ask you something?' she said as they walked along the balcony overlooking the main exhibit hall.

'Go ahead.'

'Ash doesn't like me, does she?'

Arthur stopped and looked at her. She seemed so small and fragile right then that he couldn't help but feel sorry for her. 'Uh … she just doesn't know you yet.'

'No, it's not that. She doesn't trust me. I can tell.'

'Don't be daft, Ellie. Of course she d–'

'Do you trust me?'

'Ellie, I barely know you.'

'But do you trust me?'

He considered for a second. Despite all the weird tricks and showing off, despite the jokey, playful confidence she seemed to exude, Arthur could see her underlying insecurity. She just really wanted to be liked, to have a friend.

'Yeah,' he said eventually. 'I guess I do. You're my friend, after all.'

'Great!' she said, a smile breaking out on her face once more as she strode towards the Viking Room.

The room was long, with exhibits arranged along either side. Thanks to low-wattage ceiling lighting and dark red walls, the room was very atmospheric.

A Viking longboat stood against one wall. The timber was black and smooth, worn by time but preserved in a peat bog, according to the little sign next to it. They walked past cabinets with leather helmets, boots and tunics, with longswords and bows and arrowheads, all rusted and falling apart. One glass case was full of Viking pendants. They were all much smaller and flimsier-looking than Arthur's. Some were shaped like the hammer, others showed the symbol of the Jormungand to ward off evil spirits, while some even featured Loki's face with the intelligent eyes and sneaky grin.

'Arthur,' Ellie started, gazing at the exhibits, 'friends confide in each other, right?'

'Huh?' he said, looking up from the pendant collection.

'I was saying that friends confide in each other. Tell each other secrets. You know?'

'Yeah,' he said. 'Yeah. But, listen, Ellie, can you give me a minute here? I want to have a look around by myself if that's all right.'

She looked confused and disappointed but, without saying anything else, turned and left. Arthur actually did want to be left alone, but he also didn't want to have to field any more questions about secrets and honesty.

He continued on through the Viking Room by himself, taking in the different coins and weapons as he passed. There was nobody else in this gallery and the only sounds were his own footsteps on the parquet floor and the soft ticking of the heaters in the ceiling.

He reached the end of the long hallway and turned a corner into a smaller alcove, where a selection of aged shields and bows hung in tall glass cabinets. As he examined them, comparing them to the ones his own Vikings had, he gradually became aware of footsteps entering the gallery. The steps were light, treading softly and slowly on the floor, and he assumed Ellie must have come back despite what he had said. Yet when he peered around the cabinet to check, the sound stopped and there was no sign of anyone.

Arthur turned back to the bows, leaning in closer to see some intricate carving on a grip. After a moment, the footsteps broke the silence once more.

'Ellie,' he said, exasperated, stepping out of the alcove. 'Is that y–'

A Japanese tourist, complete with a 'Kiss Me, I'm Irish' sweater, a bright-yellow plastic poncho, a green cap emblazoned with shamrocks and a Nikon camera hanging from his neck, was standing in the middle of the gallery, staring right back at Arthur. He smiled pleasantly, then shot off a photograph of the bemused boy. The flash was blinding, sending little blue and red dots spiralling in Arthur's vision. The tourist nodded once then turned back to the nearest display.

Arthur rubbed his eyes and went back to his alcove. But as he did, he became distracted by a strange feeling. He could feel a warmth starting to emanate from a point on his chest. At first he hoped that it might be a blast of heat from a nearby air conditioner. But as it grew hotter, he knew it wasn't that. He put his hand against his sweater and felt his pendant underneath. Without even looking, he knew it was glowing. It usually only did this when he was in danger; his stomach clenched with fear.

'No ...' he whispered to himself just as a third sound broke the peace of the gallery. It was a hollow, rolling sound and it was getting louder. Louder and closer. Whatever it was, whatever was rolling across the wooden floor, bumping on some of the indentations in the parquet, was making its way towards Arthur.

Before he could peer out of his alcove again, the approaching menace arrived. The basketball bounced off the wall at the end of the gallery before coming to a complete stop. Cautiously, as if it actually was a ticking bomb, Arthur picked the ball up. There was nothing out of the ordinary about it, except that it was a basketball in the National Museum. But he knew what it meant. And it wasn't good.

Slowly, Arthur turned on the spot. He could feel the heat rising in his face, the sweat on the palms of his hands.

There was no sign of the tourist. In his place was a boy of Arthur's age, wearing a basketball vest, shorts and fresh-out-of-the-box sneakers. The boy had platinum-blond hair, icy blue eyes and a long, stately nose that Arthur was more than familiar with.

'Hey, Artie,' Will said. 'Fancy a game?'

For a split second there was silence in the room and all Arthur could hear was his own panicked breathing. Then, suddenly, there was a loud bang and the scream of the museum's security alarm pierced the room.

CHAPTER TWELVE

Max was leaning against the balcony, shuffling his feet anxiously, as Cousin Maggie, Ash and Ex closely studied the stitching on a medieval dress. He'd enjoyed their first few minutes in the museum, but then the sight of all the old costumes and weapons on display brought back terrifying memories to him: the Vikings, the World Serpent and, of course, Loki.

He wondered where Arthur and that other girl had gotten to. No matter how frightened or wary he'd felt over the past months, having Arthur or his sister nearby always put him at ease. He knew he was safe around them. But now Arthur was suddenly missing.

'Where's Arthur?' he asked out loud, his voice reverberating around the quiet museum.

He looked over the balcony into the main exhibition

hall. There were lots of people down there, tourists and families milling around and gazing with fascination at the artefacts. Cousin Maggie and Ash joined him at the rail and peered over. No sign of Arthur or Ellie anywhere.

'Oh, I'm sure they've just gone exploring,' Maggie said, then turned back to the medieval mannequins. 'Something wrong, Ex?' The boy's eyes were wide, staring straight over their heads at the ceiling. Cousin Maggie, Ash and Max followed his gaze.

Through the glass they could just about make out some shadowy figures moving about. People in black were walking along the roof, stepping over the rafters and supports that held the glass in place, but taking care not to stand on the glass itself. It was difficult to say how many there were, but there were enough to disrupt the faint January light that had been coming through.

'Who on earth is that?' Cousin Maggie muttered, her eyes fixed on the ceiling, but no one answered her as they all stared upwards. The people around them noticed their staring and looked up. Soon everyone on the balcony and the floor below was watching the glass and exclaiming to each other.

A shiver ran up Max's spine and he had a strong feeling that whatever was going on wasn't good. No, he thought. No, not again. Arthur. Where was Arthur? Max had just made up his mind to go in search of him when one of the figures on the roof placed something the size and shape of a tennis ball on the centre of a pane of glass. Everyone watched as each figure placed their own dark ball on each of the panes.

'What do you think those are?' Ash managed to ask, the dread in her voice clear to her companions.

'Get down,' Ex said.

'What?'

'I said get down!' With that, he shoved them to the floor. 'Cover your heads!' This time nobody questioned him and they all did as he ordered, covering themselves with their coats. Ex did likewise, ducking down next to them and wrapping his thick, muscular arms over his head.

And just in time too, as a series of small explosions burst through the ceiling. They heard the sound of glass smashing, disintegrating to smithereens, followed by the security alarms blaring. They could feel shards of glass showering down onto their hunched backs, almost like rain. Cousin Maggie whimpered next to Max, and the shrieks and terrified screams of other visitors filled the air. As the noise subsided, Ash, desperate to see what was happening, took a chance and raised her head, peering over the edge of the balcony.

Slivers of glass coated the lower floor, twinkling where the remaining light reflected off them. It would have been a beautiful sight if not for the sounds that accompanied it: the screeching alarm, the screams and clattering as people ran for the exits, some of them bleeding from cuts caused by the falling shards. She looked up at the ceiling. The glass was totally gone now, blown out by whatever explosives the figures had used. And she could see the dark figures more clearly now. They were all dressed from neck to toe in fitted black Lycra overalls with black gloves on their hands. Motorcycle helmets covered their heads, perfect dome shapes that shone like ebony. As she watched, they each pulled a metallic cord from their belts and attached them to the rafters with a carabiner clip. The other end was still attached to them and, before she knew it, they were dropping into the museum, the cord extending from their belts as they abseiled to the ground with a whoosh. And, Ash saw with alarm, they each had a crossbow strapped to their backs. The figures dropped past the balcony, descending to the floor below.

The others joined Ash at the edge of the balcony now, peeking over carefully. Cousin Maggie gasped as the figures in black – both male and female from their shapes – unhooked the cords from their belts and aimed their crossbows at the people cowering below who hadn't managed to make it out. The attackers didn't shout any commands at the frightened people, probably because they wouldn't be heard through their thick helmets, Ash assumed. Nevertheless, the people understood what they wanted them to do and all moved together in one group to the centre of the hall, shaking with terror. More of the figures came in through the door from the anteroom, leading other terrified visitors and museum workers from the souvenir shop. They shut the huge wooden doors with a bang that echoed throughout the hall.

One of the figures grabbed a security guard by the collar of his jacket. His hat fell off as the black figure shoved him through a side door marked Staff Only. Seconds later, the alarm stopped. The sound continued to ring in their ears for a second, but then all they could hear were the whimpers of the people held captive.

Ash looked around for a way out. At the corner, past the row of medieval mannequins, she spotted an emergency exit. She tapped the others, put her finger to her lips then pointed at the door. They all nodded in agreement, apart from Max. He was shaking, his eyes squeezed shut, and whimpering, 'No, no, not again' over and over. Ash squeezed his shoulder lightly to get his attention. He looked at her, tears glistening in his eyes, then nodded. With that, they all carefully shuffled across the upper balcony, keeping their heads low in case anyone on the ground floor spotted them.

Ash could feel her heart beating a mile a minute and hear the blood pumping in her ears as she approached the door. Nearly there, she thought. If we get out, we can get help. She put her hand on the aluminium bar and pushed hard. It swung open but, rather than freedom, she found herself facing the pointy end of a crossbow bolt.

Will smiled. 'I thought I saw you coming in here,' he said. 'Who was that girl I passed a few minutes ago, Arthur? Did you find my replacement so soon?'

A burst of green vapour enveloped him. When it dissipated, he had transformed into Loki. He was wearing a long black coat with black suit legs peering out from underneath and highly polished shoes. The ball that Arthur had been holding disappeared in a puff of smoke. The alarm shut off and the last ring echoed around the exhibits.

'What are you doing here, Loki?'

'Oh, Arthur,' he said menacingly, taking a step forward. 'I can't tell you that. It would spoil the surprise.' Suddenly, he shot his right hand out against the nearest display unit. His fist crashed through the glass. When Loki withdrew it, clutching a longsword tightly, blood was seeping from cuts on his knuckles and shards of glass stuck out of his skin. He looked at his hand, as if surprised to see blood on it. There was a flash of green light. When it cleared, Arthur saw that the hand was completely healed.

Loki turned back to Arthur. The sword was badly rusted but, by the looks of it, it could still do some damage if wielded correctly. He swung it over his head in a fluid demonstration of strength and skill, all the while grinning.

'I never was much of a swordsman,' he said, examining the blade. 'But that doesn't mean I don't enjoy using one. Back in Asgard, before Odin banished me, I would amuse myself by skinning cats. I'd disguise myself as a mouse, trick them into chasing me, then lead them right into my trap.' As he spoke, he sauntered towards Arthur, swinging the sword lazily by his side. 'Then I'd take them back to my hall and hold them down. I'd start by slicing from here ...' he pointed the tip of the blade towards Arthur's throat and traced a line down to his waist, 'to here. Then I'd start to peel away the skin ... at this point, the cat would be in unimaginable pain and making a terrible racket, but I'd just keep going ... it was fascinating the way the blade slid so easily into the flesh ... it would be so tender, so fragile ... I'd try to take my time, go verrrry carefully ...' Watching Loki, Arthur could see the madness in his eyes. 'But then I'd make a total mess of it! I always did – I was just too impatient. So I'd just start chopping ...' he swung the sword down, 'and chopping ...' he swung the blade again frenziedly, 'and chopping. Until the cat was completely unrecognisable. Just a piece of meat.'

Arthur shivered – he couldn't help it – but he hoped Loki hadn't noticed his apprehension.

'Now,' Loki went on, 'I've never tried to skin a boy before. But I'm sure the principle is the same.'

Arthur pulled the pendant from his shirt and let it fall on his chest. Loki recoiled a little at the sight of it.

'If you try to touch me, I'll use this,' Arthur said. 'And we both know how much it can hurt you.'

Loki lowered the sword by his side once more and looked down at the floor. He shuffled his feet, turning slowly away from Arthur.

'You're right,' he admitted eventually, still staring at the ground. 'But you've forgotten one thing, Arthur.'

'Oh, yeah? What's that?'

Loki swivelled sharply around on one foot and faced Arthur again, grinning. 'I'm a god.'

With that, every sword and axe on display crashed through their glass cabinets. They hung in the air momentarily then turned their blades gradually towards Arthur.

Arthur had no time to think, as every weapon in the room flew straight for his forehead, and only a split second to react. He threw himself to the side just in time, feeling a gentle movement in the air next to his ear as a blade flew past, narrowly missing him. He landed on his hip with a painful crash and cried out in agony. He watched as most of the weapons thunked into the wood-panelled wall behind where he'd been standing. The ones that didn't just shattered on impact.

He turned back to see that one of the large glass cabinets just above his head, which was filled with Viking coins and medals, was rocking crazily back and forth. It teetered before the front two legs finally snapped and the cabinet fell slowly forward.

Arthur rolled sideways as fast as he could. The cabinet

crashed to the ground. Glass smashed and precious Viking artefacts clattered out. Arthur sat up groggily and pushed himself back against a wall for support, at the same time looking round frantically, trying to locate the god. But as he did so, a Viking shield hanging on the wall above him, which had been set swaying dangerously by the vibrations caused by the impact of the cabinet, fell from its fixing and hit him on the crown of the head, sending him tumbling into unconsciousness.

Ellie turned when she heard the crash of the display unit from the Viking Room behind her. She briefly considered going back to investigate but didn't want to risk getting caught.

When she'd left the room a few minutes previously, she'd been on her way back to her brother. Just in time, she spotted the figures on the roof and ducked back inside the entrance to the gallery. And now, just moments later, the museum was in total chaos. The glass ceiling had been blown out and some raiders dressed all in black had abseiled in. A young couple on her side of the balcony crouched behind a large map of excavation sites in Ireland, just out of sight of one of the raiders standing sentry on the balcony. He held his crossbow across his chest, poised and ready. She followed the couple's lead and hunkered down behind another exhibit, peering carefully around the edge of the cabinet to watch what was going on.

A few of the raiders had herded all the frightened people on the ground floor into the centre, crossbows armed and aimed at them. The rest were looting the place. They smashed the glass cabinets open with the blunt ends of their crossbows and filled black sacks with the more valuable contents. They gleefully ran from exhibit to exhibit, pilfering everything in sight, grabbing chalices, jewellery, illustrated manuscripts, weaponry and more.

While the raiders busied themselves, Ellie pulled her mobile phone out of her coat pocket and looked at the screen. No Service, it read in bold black text.

A lot of help you are, she thought bitterly, dropping the phone back in her pocket. More than likely someone had heard the alarm outside and the Gardaí had been notified already. But Ellie didn't want to take that chance, and the alarm had been shut off so quickly she was sure the raiders probably would have been able to spin the

Gardaí a yarn about a malfunction. She needed to get word to the outside world as quickly as possible. And if she could somehow scare off the raiders, all the better.

Then she spotted the perfect solution. The only problem being that it was at the far end of the upper balcony, past the hiding couple and the sentry …

The raider at the emergency exit stepped towards Ash, keeping his crossbow aimed directly at the space between her eyes. Ash, Max, Cousin Maggie and Ex all took a step back. The raider nodded his helmeted head towards the corner. The four of them understood instantly and crouched down on the ground where he'd indicated, their backs against the wall. He gestured with the crossbow and they understood again, putting their hands up.

'Why are you doing this?' Cousin Maggie asked.

There was no response from the raider. All they could see was their reflections in the polarised helmet glass – a distorted view of them all sitting in the corner, terrified.

'Let the children go,' pleaded Maggie. 'Just let them out the emergency exit.'

Still no answer.

'Please!' Maggie said, growing desperate now.

The raider simply kept his crossbow aimed at them. From the ground floor, they heard the smashing of glass as the others broke into the cases.

Max leaned closer to his sister and, in a trembling voice, whispered, 'Ash, do you think it's something to do with–'

The raider grunted behind his helmet and thrust the crossbow pointedly at Max.

'Yes, Max,' Ash said, looking defiantly at the raider, 'I do.'

Ellie inched on her hands and knees along the wall towards the young, cowering couple. The wall was to her immediate left, a row of glass-enclosed exhibits to her right and, just beyond that, the balcony rail. The sentry was standing at the rail so the exhibits were between him and Ellie as she scuttled along.

The couple saw her coming and she could see the fear in their eyes as they very subtly shook their heads at her, afraid that any large movement would attract the sentry's attention. Ellie understood their fear. They didn't want her making noise and getting them caught. But she had to reach the end of this row of exhibits. It was her only chance of alerting the Gardaí and saving everyone. So she kept on crawling.

When she reached the couple, the man grabbed her arm.

'Stop moving,' he whispered, 'or you'll get us killed!'

She shook his hand off. 'Let me pass,' she hissed back angrily. There wasn't much space between the main wall and exhibits and the couple were in her way.

The woman shook her head. 'Hold on to her, Seán,' she said to her boyfriend.

Ellie craned her neck and peered through the display unit to her right. The sentry was just beyond it, overseeing the entire hall, with his back to her. He still hadn't noticed them, but if she was forced to step over the couple he just might. Still, those helmets probably made it pretty difficult to hear, she reasoned. She turned back to the couple furiously.

'If you don't let me through, I'll scream,' she threatened.

'You wouldn't!' the man whispered, hoping to call her bluff.

'Oh, wouldn't I?' With that, she took as deep a breath as her lungs could manage. But before she could let the scream out, the woman clamped her hand over her mouth.

'OK, OK!' she conceded. 'Please, just be quiet!' The couple pushed themselves against the wall, making just enough space for Ellie to squeeze through. She looked towards her destination. Not far now.

She continued to crawl as quickly and silently as she could. She finally reached the end of the row of exhibits. Here the balcony turned off to the right, where it ran along the entire length of the main hall. She glanced down the length of the balcony and gasped in shock. In the opposite corner, huddled on the ground under a raider's crossbow, were Ex and the others. Her brother was staring up at the raider with resentment while the others were too afraid to look away. She'd have to help them. But first she had to complete phase one of her plan.

A little red box was fixed to the wall across from her. It had a piece of glass in it that said BREAK IN CASE OF EMERGENCY. A fire alarm. If she set it off, it was sure to get the attention of the Gardaí. And, if they were lucky, it might spook the raiders enough to send them running. The only problem was that she'd have to step out of her hiding place to set it off.

She looked back the way she had come. The sentry was standing stock-still, keeping an eye on the main hall. The couple were watching her intently, their eyes pleading with her not to do anything stupid. She'd have to be quick about it, she knew. There was no other way. She took her phone out of her pocket then slipped her shoes off. They had a tendency to make a lot of noise on tiled floors and she didn't want to risk it. Finally, she counted in her head to ten.

She stood, taking care not to make a sound, and tip-toed from her hiding place. As she crept towards the fire alarm, she glanced over her shoulder. The sentry behind her was still watching the goings-on down below. Each step seemed to take forever, but eventually she reached the alarm. With one last glance at the sentry, she positioned the end of her phone on the small glass panel and pushed hard. The glass cracked abruptly and an alarm rang through the museum for the second time in a few minutes.

As soon as the second alarm started, a number of things happened very quickly. The sentry behind Ellie turned and immediately pointed his bow at her. The cowering couple threw themselves to the floor, hands over their heads. The sentry guarding Ash and the others turned to see what was happening. Meanwhile, Ex looked up to see his little sister standing by a broken fire-alarm panel, a mobile phone in her hand and a sentry with his crossbow advancing on her. Ellie was motionless with fear. Ex looked up at the man guarding them. The raider's attention was also – momentarily – focused on Ellie. Taking his chance, Ex sprang into action and threw himself at the man, hitting him with his full body weight in the chest. The raider fell backwards with Ex on top of him, knocking his head against the parapet, while his crossbow flew out of his hand and skittered across the floor and over the edge of the balcony. Before the stunned raider could recover, Ex was on his feet and racing towards Ellie. As his feet pounded the wooden floor, he barely slowed to pick up a folding metal chair that a security guard would usually sit on.

'Get down!' Ex shouted to Ellie, sprinting as fast as his legs could carry him – which was, much to Ash's surprise as she watched from their corner, quite fast indeed.

The sentry had heard the commotion with Ex and turned towards him. He aimed the crossbow and let a bolt loose. Ex threw up the chair like a shield just as quickly and the bolt bounced off it with a clang. By now, all of Ex's attention was focused on getting to Ellie.

'Get down!' he shouted again. This time she listened, snapping out of her trance, and slid back behind the relative safety of the glass cabinets.

The sentry kept Ex in his sight as he dashed along the balcony, cranking another bolt into the crossbow. Judging that he wouldn't be able to break through Ex's makeshift armour, he aimed a few feet above the boy and loosed his arrow. The glass in a painting smashed overhead and rained down on top of Ex, but the boy kept on going.

He turned the corner, his feet pounding as he passed Ellie and the couple crouched behind the exhibits. The sentry was busily cranking another bolt when Ex lunged forward with the metal chair, whacking the raider straight on the side of the head. The raider's head snapped to the side and he toppled to the ground, unconscious.

'Come on!' Ex urged the three hiding behind the display units. The four of them ran back across the balcony towards Cousin Maggie, Ash, Max and the other raider, who was still lying stunned on the floor.

By now they could hear footsteps clattering up the stairs: more raiders with more crossbows. Ash, Maggie and Max were all standing by the doorway as the first new raider rounded the corner.

'Go, go, go!' Ellie shouted, urgently waving everyone out.

They all raced through the door and slammed it behind them before anyone could release another bolt. In front of them was a flight of stairs that led to the lower floor and they started down.

'Wait!' Ash cried after the first couple of steps. 'Arthur! We have to go back and find Arthur!'

'No time!' Ex yelled. 'Just go!'

Ash tried to force her way back up the stairs but with everyone pushing in the opposite direction it was impossible.

'Arthur!' she screamed at the top of her lungs back up the stairwell as she was swept along by the others. '*Arthur!*'

Loki was in a gallery adjacent to the Viking Room when the fire alarm went off.

That wasn't part of the plan, he thought to himself, going to see what was happening. He walked through the wreckage of Viking artefacts and looked out at the commotion on the balcony. He saw the large boy run across and save the little girl. And he saw Ash and Max.

'I should have known,' he muttered to himself. 'The gang's all here, interfering in my plans as usual.'

He went back through the room, kicking aside glass and rubble and priceless artefacts nonchalantly. He looked down at the still-unconscious Arthur, the pendant glowing brightly on his chest, still protecting the boy.

'That's my cue to leave, Arthur,' he said, even though he knew the boy couldn't hear him. 'I'm sure I'll see you soon. And when I do, you'll breathe your last breath.'

He turned and walked back out of the room. On the balcony Ash and Max and the others were gone and one sentry was helping another to his feet.

'Time to go!' Loki shouted, his voice spreading further than should have been possible. All over the museum, the raiders tied the ends of their black sacks and prepared to leave.

※※※※※

Arthur's eyes fluttered open. There was a ringing in his ears. No – not in his ears. There was a ringing everywhere. An alarm was going off. Time for school, he thought, but then realised he was lying somewhere uncomfortable and wasn't at home in bed.

He sat up, confused. Then he saw the Viking shield on the floor next to him and it all came flooding back.

'Loki!' he exclaimed to himself. He looked around and spotted the Trickster God on the balcony overlooking the main hall. He was wearing a long green coat now, like something a soldier would wear. As he watched, the god turned and strode down the main staircase.

Arthur pushed himself to his feet with all the strength he could muster. As he stood upright, his head spun and he stumbled backwards. He paused for a second, regaining his balance, his hand braced against the wall beside him. When he felt better, he walked carefully through the carnage Loki had left in the Viking Room. Glass and debris covered every surface.

The balcony area was empty and Arthur, as he looked down on to the room below, could see innocent bystanders evacuating the building through the main entrance below. He spotted Loki escaping in the other direction, through a Staff Only door, his green coat billowing behind him. Arthur ran down the stairs and headed for the door. As he passed through it, he noticed that the security keypad on the wall had been disabled by some kind of blast – a hand-shaped black mark was clear on its surface.

Loki was already halfway down the corridor when Arthur came through the door, striding along behind countless figures in black carrying sacks. There were filing cabinets on both sides of the corridor.

Loki and his gang of raiders turned a corner and Arthur sped up to keep up with them. He wasn't quite sure what he was planning to do, but he wanted to see what Loki's next move was going to be. He heard a door slam and rounded the corner to find himself suddenly face to face with the Father of Lies.

The corridor went on further but there was a door here, fitted with fire-safety glass. Loki was standing just beyond it, grinning and waving at Arthur as the raiders ran away behind him. Arthur tried to pull and push the door open but to no avail. It was tightly locked.

Still grinning, Loki mouthed, 'See you soon,' and with a last wave he turned and followed his raiders. At the far end of the corridor was another door. One of them pulled it open and daylight streamed in. They stepped outside, bright sunlight swallowing them. Loki went last. And just like that, he was gone.

CHAPTER THIRTEEN

Arthur walked back down the corridor, shuffling his feet and feeling sorry for himself. Now that the adrenaline of the chase had worn off, his hip and head were both throbbing. He came back into the main exhibition hall and surveyed the damage. Most of the glass display units had been smashed and ransacked, while some had even been kicked over. There was no one left in the museum but him; all the raiders had escaped with Loki, and the hostages had run to freedom through the front doors, which were now ajar. He limped towards the main entrance slowly. Halfway through the hall, he came to a bronze chalice on the ground. Maybe it had been thrown aside or maybe it had fallen out of one of the raiders' sacks. Either way, he didn't like the thought of it just lying there on its side. He picked it up and gazed at the Celtic patterns and green enamel inlay. Reflected in the bronze he could see his face. He had a small cut on his forehead and was surprised to see a trickle of blood running down his cheek.

He stepped to one of the cabinets that was still standing. A few glass shards hung precariously in the frame. The shelves in the unit were totally bare. He placed the chalice on the centre shelf and stood back to admire it. It looked very lonely there all by itself.

By now his legs felt like jelly and he decided that it would be better for him to sit on the ground, careful to avoid any particularly sharp chunks of glass, before he fell over. He was still looking at the chalice when a Garda squad stormed through the front doors. He was too weary to look up at their faces but could hear the hustle as they burst through the anteroom and then into the main hall. One of them cut off the fire alarm. They were wearing riot gear – bullet-proof vests and helmets – and carrying Perspex shields. Most of them crowded around him, some with guns trained on him.

They shouted commands: orders to stand up, to name himself, to go with them. He ignored them all, still dazed and in his own little world. Eventually, one voice drowned out the others.

'Stop!' it shouted. 'Let me through!'

The Gardaí parted to let the man through. He held one hand out to Arthur.

'Hello, Arthur,' he said. 'Remember me?'

When Ash and the others had escaped through the emergency exit, they came out into what had become a bright January day, the sunlight almost blinding them. They emerged at the side of the building and had to walk through a narrow alley to reach the front and the other relieved hostages.

The Gardaí had arrived at this stage, as had countless members of the press. Photographers stood behind crash barriers, aiming their cameras, zooming in with telephoto lenses and straining to get a good picture of any of the distraught hostages. News reporters shouted questions to the Gardaí but got no answers in return. While a squad of Gardaí stormed the now-evacuated museum, a few others lined up the hostages to gather names and statements.

Cousin Maggie was thoroughly shaken by the ordeal and Max, who had recovered quickly once they'd escaped, was busy comforting her, rubbing her back and telling her repeatedly that it was all right, that they were safe. The young couple that Ex had saved ran straight to the nearest TV camera, recounting their tale in great detail. Ash kept her eyes fixed on the main entrance, hoping to see Arthur come out safely. The Lavender siblings, meanwhile, stayed very quiet. Ex appeared to be in his own world again, as silent as he was before. Ellie, however, seemed to be deep in thought.

'Ash,' Ellie spoke up after a while, 'can I ask you something?'

'What is it?' Ash was standing with her arms wrapped around herself, tension written on her face.

'Do you have any idea who those people could have been?' Ellie finished.

Ash did indeed have an idea, but it was a theory she didn't want to voice. Loki had to be involved. It would be too much of a coincidence for him not to be.

'No,' she lied. 'Not a clue.' Her expression told a different story, but before Ellie could question her further, Max exclaimed, 'There's Arthur!' and pointed at the door. Ash followed the direction of his finger and gave a sigh of relief. Arthur was being led out of the museum by a man in a lilac shirt and tie. The man had shaved red hair and was tall with an athletic build. She vaguely recognised him but couldn't think from where.

'Arthur!' she called out, waving to him. He spotted her and headed towards the group. The man in lilac followed.

Before Arthur could say a word, Ash embraced him tightly.

'Was it Loki?' she whispered into his ear.

'Yup,' he whispered back, then let her go and looked at the others. 'Before anyone asks, I'm fine.'

'He's probably a bit dazed,' the man said behind him. 'He got knocked out, apparently.' He pointed at Ash. 'You're Ashling, right? Ash?'

'Uh … yeah …' she answered hesitantly.

'This is the Garda who helped when Dad was attacked,' Arthur explained and it all came flooding back to her. When Loki had beaten Joe last October, this Garda had notified Arthur. He'd stayed on watch at the ward and even drove Arthur to and from the hospital.

'Garda Morrissey, isn't it?' Ash said.

'Actually, it's Detective Morrissey now,' the man said proudly. 'Or, rather, Trainee Detective Morrissey. Are your parents here?'

'No. We came with Cousin Maggie, my grandaunt.'

The detective wasn't phased by the odd naming of the

aunt and turned to her. 'I have some questions for Arthur here, Ma'am. Is that all right with you?'

Maggie, who was still dazed by the whole experience, just nodded her head.

'Thank you. Shouldn't be long.' He put his hand on Arthur's shoulder and led him away.

Detective Morrissey brought Arthur into the back of a Garda van. The interior of the vehicle was decked out with computers and TV screens and machines that went blip. Surveillance equipment, Arthur realised, having seen similar kits on every cop movie he'd ever watched. One Garda was sitting at a panel reviewing the security-camera tapes of outside the museum. There was a small round desk in the centre of the van, which Detective Morrissey sat at. He indicated the chair opposite him and Arthur took it.

'So here's what we know, Arthur,' Morrissey said. 'At 2.21 exactly, the security cameras inside the museum suffered a malfunction. All of them shut off at once. At 2.22 exactly, a gang of raiders all dressed in black, numbering between twenty and thirty and armed with crossbows, blew out the glass roof, setting off the alarm, and abseiled into the building. After shutting off the alarm, they proceeded to loot the place. At 2.36, the fire alarm rang. A minute later, the hostages escaped through the front door. That's all we know so far. Maybe you can fill in some blanks since you were in there the longest?'

'I told you,' he said. 'I blacked out, woke up, stumbled downstairs and saw all the mess. And then ...' Arthur hesitated. He liked Morrissey. The Garda had stayed in contact with them for a few weeks after Joe had regained consciousness and had retained an interest in their case. Arthur felt sorry for him because the case was never likely to be solved; or rather, because he could never tell him the truth of the matter. And now he was faced with the same dilemma. He didn't like not telling Morrissey the whole truth. But he also knew that no one in their right mind would believe his story about a Viking god breaking in to a museum to steal all those artefacts. In fact Arthur himself couldn't understand why Loki would do such a thing. Besides, if by any chance Morrissey did believe his story, then Arthur would only be getting him involved in a situation that could get him hurt or worse.

'Go on,' Detective Morrissey prompted as Arthur paused, eager with anticipation, leaning forward in his chair.

'Well,' Arthur continued, 'when I saw the mess, I heard a noise behind me. I turned to see someone running through a Staff Only door. I didn't know what was happening, so I followed.' Arthur could feel the eyes of the other Garda on him now, too. 'When I went through I saw a gang of people – all dressed in black and carrying sacks – running down the corridor through the fire door. It locked behind them so I couldn't get through. But I saw them go out the back.'

'You shouldn't have followed them, Arthur – you could have been hurt. These guys clearly meant business. But since you did, can you show us where this all happened?'

'Yeah,' Arthur said to Detective Morrissey, looking him straight in the eye. 'I can.'

As they walked down the corridor, Arthur was in front, followed by Morrissey, a couple of senior detectives and a handful of Gardaí.

'They came down here,' Arthur said as they went. 'They were running pretty fast so I couldn't catch up with them.'

'It's a good thing you didn't,' Detective Morrissey said. 'These people were dangerous.'

They came to the locked door halfway down the passageway.

'This is as far as I got,' Arthur said, then pointed

through the glass to the shut door that led to the outside. 'They went out through that door there.'

Detective Morrissey tried the inner fire door but it was still securely locked.

'Can somebody open this for us?' he shouted back to the people following him. One of the museum security guards stepped forward, jangling a hefty set of keys. He put the right key into the lock and turned it with a click. They all pushed through, hurrying to the last door along the corridor of filing cabinets. Detective Morrissey ran in front, leaving Arthur trailing behind.

The trainee detective reached the door before anyone else. He swung it open. As before, sunlight streamed into the dim hallway.

'What the–?' Arthur heard Morrissey utter, followed by excited chatter as everyone else saw what was awaiting them outside.

Arthur squeezed through the crowd to get a look for himself. There was a small yard with a few skips and recycling bins lined up against one wall. Cigarette butts littered the ground by the door; staff obviously used the area for smoking breaks. But what had caught all the Gardaí's attention was the sight of black costumes scattered on the ground: black Lycra overalls, surgical gloves and shiny onyx helmets. He recognised them instantly as the raiders' uniforms.

Detective Morrissey knelt down and gingerly picked up one of the helmets, studying his distorted reflection in it.

'So either they were wearing these over their clothes, or we're looking for some naked raiders,' he said miserably.

'It wasn't quite the day I expected,' Cousin Maggie said as she pulled her brown Volvo into their estate. She looked around at Arthur, Ash and Max, studying their faces for any signs of stress. They all seemed, remarkably, to be taking it in their stride – much better than she was.

After Detective Morrissey discovered the black uniforms, half of the Gardaí started to go through the museum with a fine-tooth comb looking for evidence, while the rest interviewed the waiting hostages. Most of the witnesses said the same thing: the raiders burst in through the skylights, herded them together and took what they wanted. No one had much new to offer until they interviewed those who'd been stranded on the second floor. Detective Morrissey listened with rapt attention to the story of the two sentries and how Ex had used a folding chair to shield himself from the crossbow bolt. He was also pleased with Ellie's detailed descriptions of the raiders, their positions in the museum and their weapons. In fact, Morrissey was surprised by how detailed the descriptions had been. She made 'guess-timations' (as she called them) about the raiders' heights and weights. She even made note of what hand they used for firing their weapons. She'd counted thirty-two raiders in total, not including the man in the Viking Room who had attacked Arthur. As he led them back towards Cousin Maggie, Morrissey complimented her amazing recollection of events. She blushed, murmuring something about being good at noticing things.

'Hmm ...' Morrissey mused to himself when Ex had left the Garda van after recounting his story in as few words as possible.

'What is it?' asked the Garda working at the bank of computer monitors.

'Either that boy is exceptionally fast,' he said, 'or exceptionally lucky.'

'How do you mean?'

'I don't think I'd have the reflexes to deflect a crossbow bolt with a chair. Would you?'

The interviews continued for a couple more hours. No one was permitted to leave the enclosure around the museum until they were all done, in case any hostage needed to be questioned again. The Gardaí supplied tea, coffee and sandwiches while the statements were being recorded.

When they were allowed to leave, they all climbed into the Maggie-mobile and she drove them back to Ranelagh. Ellie and Ex made their own way home, hopping on the first bus that passed.

'Would you like to come in for tea, Cousin Maggie?' Ash asked as her grandaunt idled the car next to the Barry house. 'Or something to eat?'

'No thanks, pet,' she said. 'What I need now is my own bed.' Arthur, Ash and Max all climbed out of the car and gave her a wave as she drove off.

'I know how she feels,' Ash said, watching her go. 'I don't want to have to start telling the whole story again to Mom and Dad.'

'Maybe we shouldn't tell them now?' Max suggested, somewhat hopefully. 'Could we wait until the morning at least?'

'Good idea. Cousin Maggie will probably call then to see how we're doing. What about you, Arthur? Are you going to tell Joe?'

There was no response. She turned to find him staring at the green.

'What is it, Arthur?'

'There's someone out there,' he said, 'standing behind that tree.'

She squinted her eyes to get a better look. It was dusk and starting to get dark now. The street lamps blinked on as she looked, buzzing with electricity. Arthur was right. There was a figure there, half-hidden by the trunk of the tree and watching them. Without warning, Arthur strode across the road and onto the green.

Ash was about to call him back, but Max went after him, jogging to keep up, so she did likewise. As they got closer, the figure became clearer and sharper in the twilight gloom. From the build, it was clearly a man, wearing a few layers of bulky clothing by the looks of it. His hair was messy, yellow curls falling over his forehead and around the nape of his neck. His face was unnaturally sallow due to the thick make-up he was wearing.

'Hi, Eirik,' Arthur said cheerfully to the Viking, breathing a sigh of relief.

Eirik stepped out from behind the tree and met them halfway. He had a longsword strapped to his back; the pommel peeped out above the collar of his coat. He wore a grim expression as he nodded and grunted back.

'So I'm guessing you sensed we were in danger again,' Arthur proposed. 'You couldn't get your costume ready in time to help us in the museum but you got there anyway and then followed the pull of the pendant here?' Eirik nodded, looking ashamed.

'It's OK, Eirik,' Max said. 'We're safe now.' He looked around him in the darkness. 'I think.'

'He's right,' Arthur said. 'We're safe now. So you can go back to the others.'

The Viking shook his head furiously.

'Eirik, go back to the others!' Arthur said again, with more force this time.

Once more, the soldier shook his head.

'Why not?'

'Because,' guessed Ash, 'he wants to be close by the next time something happens, to protect us. To guard us.'

This time, Eirik nodded and smiled.

'But where are you going to stay?' Arthur asked the Viking. Eirik indicated the small clump of trees behind him at the edge of the green. 'You're sure?' The soldier nodded in response.

'OK,' Arthur conceded. 'You can guard us then. But just be sure that no one sees you. Especially–'

He was about to say Stace's name but, almost as if she'd sensed it, she stepped out onto the porch and called out. 'Ash! Max! Come in – your dinner's rea–!' When she saw who was standing with them on the green, the words caught in her throat. She wasn't wearing a jacket, so as she jogged across the grass towards them, shivering, she wrapped her arms around her torso for extra insulation.

'Hi!' she said when she reached them. 'Hi, Eirik!'

'Let's go inside, Stace,' Ash said, taking her sister's arm and trying to lead her back to the house. She wouldn't budge, however.

'Ash, stop being so rude!' she said, then turned back to the Viking. 'So, Eirik, are you staying with Arthur?'

Eirik nodded before he noticed Arthur shaking his head frantically behind Stace's back.

'Oh, you are!' she said, as Max joined in with Ash's attempts to drag her away. 'Maybe we'll bump into each other some time …'

'I'm sure you will, Stace!' Arthur said, taking Eirik's arm and leading him away. 'But Eirik was just leaving now. He has friends to meet in town.'

'Friends?' she said. 'Maybe I can be a friend?'

'Of course you can,' said Ash. 'But not tonight. Dinner's ready, remember?'

'Oh, yeah. Dinner.'

Arthur led Eirik around a corner onto the main road and out of sight of Stace, while Ash dragged her sister towards their house. Arthur waited till he heard them go into the house and close the door. Then he gestured to Eirik to stay and walked back around to the green.

'All safe now,' he called to Eirik. 'But keep out of sight, just in case. Stay in the shadows.'

As Arthur turned to go he noticed a gemstone in the pommel of the hilt of Eirik's sword glinting in the amber streetlight. He paused for a moment, then said, 'Eirik, I think we – Ash, Max and me – maybe we should learn to defend ourselves after all. What do you think?'

Eirik looked at Arthur for a beat, as if surprised by the question. Then he nodded enthusiastically. With that, Arthur turned and headed home, leaving the Viking standing in the shadows.

CHAPTER FOURTEEN

The following morning was bright and chilly as Arthur strolled across the estate to the Barry house. There was a crispness to the air that told him an early spring was on the way. When he reached the house, he realised that the family people-carrier wasn't in the drive. Hoping it didn't mean that Ash wasn't in, he rang the doorbell. Almost instantly, he saw a shadow pass over the eyepiece and then a moment later he heard several locks clicking open within.

'Arthur, it's you,' Max said, peering through the crack between the door and the jamb. His eyes were bloodshot, with dark circles underneath them.

'More nightmares, Max?'

The boy shook his head, stepping back to let Arthur in. 'I didn't sleep at all in case Loki …' He trailed off.

'You looking for Ash? She's in the living-room.'

Arthur stepped past him and Max shut the door urgently, once more fastening each lock. He sat down on the floor, clutching a hurl tightly to his chest. With one last look at the boy, Arthur went into the living-room. Ash was stretched on her belly across the sofa, twiddling a minute screwdriver at the inner circuit boards of what looked like her new mobile phone. Ice was sitting up on the rug, staring at the television – it was almost as if she was watching the cookery programme that was on. She looked at Arthur when he entered the room, then turned back to the television without greeting him, clearly remembering what had happened the last time he was in the house.

'Something wrong with your phone?' Arthur asked, collapsing into the nearest armchair.

'Nooo,' Ash replied, concentrating on the screw she was tightening. 'Just adding a few extra features.'

'Such as?'

Ash clamped the cover back on the phone. She threw something across the room to Arthur, which he just managed to catch. It was a plastic sphere about the size of a ping-pong ball and when he turned it in his hand he discovered a lens staring up at him in the front.

'A webcam?' he asked, looking back at her with raised eyebrows.

She walked over and turned the phone towards him. A live video stream filled the three-inch screen – a close-up of his own chin! He looked down at the webcam in his hand and back at the phone. The stream was coming directly from the camera he was holding.

'Wireless connectivity between that camera and my phone,' she explained. 'A makeshift security camera!'

'Great idea,' he said, admiring the camera once again, with one eye on the video of himself on the phone.

'It was simple enough. I had the camera lying around, but I added a few extra features to it: GPS, a two-year battery and so on. I still have to get the recording function working but I'm sure I'll manage it.'

'Cool.'

'I figured it might come in handy. What with … well, you know.' She didn't feel like saying his name out loud. If she did, it made it real in her mind. Loki was back. She nodded to shut the living-room door. 'Max has been guarding the front door for hours, ever since our parents and Stace left for the day. He won't move, no matter how much I ask. So what's up with you? Did you tell your dad about yesterday?'

'Well, luckily he was out late last night so I didn't have to face the Inquisition. I told him this morning before I came over here.'

'And?'

'Same as always. He warned me not to get myself into dangerous situations any more.'

'Our parents were the same when we told them at breakfast,' Ash said. 'But it's not like it was our fault this time so they kept the nagging to a minimum. So what are the plans for today?'

Arthur was about to answer when he noticed that Ice's attention had strayed from the television and she was watching him with her big black eyes.

'Um … Ash, can we …' He nodded at the staring pup. Ash instantly understood what he meant and rolled her eyes.

'Really?' she said, mildly irritated.

'Yes, really. Please, Ash.'

'OK.' She sighed, then got to her feet, took Ice by the collar Stace had bought her and dragged her out of the room. She shut the door but Arthur just knew the pup was still waiting outside.

'You still don't trust her?' Ash asked, exasperated, sitting back down.

'No,' said Arthur in a hushed tone. 'I don't.'

'Why are you whispering?'

'Because.'

'OK.' Ash rolled her eyes again but fell into a whisper to appease him. This wasn't the time to be falling out. 'What's your plan for today?'

'We should go to the Vikings. And learn to defend ourselves.'

'You mean with weapons?'

He considered for a beat before answering, 'With whatever it takes.'

'But didn't you say—'

'I know,' he said, louder than he meant to. 'Weapons are dangerous, blah, blah, blah. But not as dangerous as Loki. Not as dangerous as all those raiders shooting arrows at us. We need to be prepared in case they come back. You, me and,' he glanced at the door meaningfully, 'Max.'

'Actually, I agree with you.' She stood up determinedly. 'My parents and Stace are bringing my granny back to her place so they'll be gone for the day and won't miss us. I'll try to convince Max to leave the door.'

Max didn't take much convincing. He would have happily gone anywhere with Ash and Arthur on that day, but the idea of learning to defend himself made him even more delighted to go. When the three of them were ready, they mounted their bicycles. It was still freezing, but not cold enough for them to choose the bus over the freedom of the bikes.

On the way out of the estate, they stopped by the clump of trees on the green. Eirik was sitting on the ground with his back against a tree trunk when they walked up. He leaped to his feet and stood to attention immediately. Arthur told him to relax and then explained where they were going. Eirik nodded sagely as he listened; he clearly thought it was a great idea. They hopped onto their bikes once more and the Viking waved them off.

Meanwhile, back in the Barry house, Ice was frantically scratching her paws at the front door and yelping to be let out. Her claws dug into the wood of the door, making deep indentations. A rage built inside her at being trapped indoors by herself.

Seconds later, Eirik was stretching his back with a loud creak. He rubbed his belly and looked at the sun through the trees. It was early in the day and his charges wouldn't be home for hours yet, so he could relax because he knew they'd be safe with the others. Back in Scandinavia, when he'd been alive, Eirik had loved to go hunting. He would happily chase down a boar for days through the wild forests of his homeland, never tiring. The hunt gave him strength, gave him an unrivalled energy, adrenaline coursing through his body. He was contemplating going hunting again – even just for a small bird or a rabbit maybe – simply to feel that thrill. As he was wondering if he could find a suitably barren piece of land to hunt in Dublin, something caught his eye on the green.

A little dog was racing across the grass. Only her front legs worked; a set of wheels acted in place of the crippled hindquarters. That was the girl Ash's pup, he knew. The one they had rescued from the frozen lake. He half-wondered if he should catch the dog and return it to the house, but then he remembered that Arthur had warned him not to be seen. So he remained in the shadows, watching it go.

Bjorn grunted happily when Arthur told him what they wanted. After the boy had rejected the suggestion previously, the Viking had been concerned that it was a mistake. He was pleased to hear that the boy had had second thoughts on the subject.

He clapped his leathery hands and snorted a loud

command. Three soldiers emerged from the watching mob, each holding a weapon. The one on the left had long scraggly wisps of hair falling from a mostly bare head. He had no beard on his narrow jaw and no teeth left in his dry gums. In one hand, he held a shield: a perfect circle of hard wood with an iron ring around the edge and a matching bump in the centre. Rays of black and yellow were painted on the wood, spreading out from the middle. In his other hand, he held a wooden longsword. Arthur recognised it as one of the Viking Experience props. It was in pretty good nick and with a hilt shaped like a tree, the branches forming the cross guard. The Viking's name, Arthur remembered, was Gunnar.

Next to him was Knut. He also had uncut and greasy hair, as well as a bushy beard. He was shorter than Gunnar but with broader shoulders and muscled arms that hadn't withered much during death. He squinted his eyes continuously, which gave him a fierce appearance. Arthur knew, however, that he could be as gentle as a kitten and loved to play-fight with Max when they visited. Knut was carrying a bow and arrow.

Last in line was the Viking known as Magnus. He was the shortest of any of the surviving men, barely breaking the five-foot mark. But he was also stout, with great thick legs and arms and a barrel of a chest. He was totally bald with a thick handlebar moustache sitting on his upper lip and a unibrow over his eyes. As with the other two, he carried a shield. In his spare hand he held a war-hammer. It was smaller than Arthur's and the iron head had rusted brown over time.

Just then, Arthur's phone vibrated in his pocket. He looked at the screen: an unknown number. Feeling all the eyes around on him, he pressed the little red phone icon, cancelling the incoming call.

Gunnar pointed at Ash and stalked away. With a quick glance at Max and Arthur, she followed him. Knut led Max to the far side of the Viking Experience, while Magnus lumbered away with Arthur. Training had begun.

The day flew past and before they knew it, it was time to go home. The sun was low along the horizon, casting their shadows far inside the Viking Experience. No one else will ever do anything like we did today, Arthur thought as he met up with Ash and Max to leave, although he still hadn't decided whether that was actually a good thing or not.

The three Vikings had begun by instructing their wards about the correct use of their shields. The shields were made from thick timber and iron and felt like they weighed a tonne, so first they were taught how to carry them – the proper way to hold them to minimise the stress on their arms while maximising their effectiveness. The Vikings drilled into them time and time again the importance of protecting their faces, throats and chests. Lunchtime arrived and, before Max could moan that he was getting tired, the soldiers moved on to the second part of the training.

They'd covered the basics of defence, now it was time to start on offence.

Gunnar had taken one of the unused mannequins out of storage and set up a practice area for Ash. He demonstrated how to assault an enemy first. He ran at the mannequin, swinging and hacking his sword through the air and roaring a harsh battle cry. In one swift movement, he chopped the mannequin's plastic head off. It bounced onto the ground with a hollow thud. Gunnar looked down at it and chuckled a throaty laugh, then nodded to Ash, who was holding the wooden sword.

'I don't want to chop off anyone's head,' she told him. 'I just want to learn to defend myself if they have a sword.'

Gunnar gave her a look that clearly suggested he was surprised that anyone wouldn't want to know how to decapitate a foe, but slowly nodded. He ducked into one of the nearby huts then came out with a broom. He brought the broomstick down on his knee and it cracked in two. He discarded the shorter end that had the mop head and twirled the longer pole in his hand, appraising it. He grinned, seeming happy with his own wooden sword, then sliced it through the air at Ash's head.

She barely had time to react and failed to raise her sword in defence, but Gunnar stopped his assault just shy of her face. She looked up at him, slightly shaken. The Viking was smiling. He tapped her longsword with his own.

'Oh!' Ash murmured, getting the picture. She swung back with hers, sending the Viking's stick clattering to the ground. He looked at it in shock, then back at her with a satisfied grin and a nod.

In another part of the Viking Experience enclosure, Max was learning the basics of archery. Knut had also raided the props room and arranged a variety of fake plastic fruit on the window ledge of one of the huts. He led Max away from the ledge, as far as he could in the confined space. Max looked back at the fruit. It seemed so distant now; he'd be surprised if Knut could hit any of the pieces.

The Viking dropped to one knee and lined up a shot, squinting even more than usual. He held the arrow steady, keeping the bow string as taut as possible, and then loosed it. Max heard a whistle as the arrow sliced through the air. Before it had even found its target, Knut was lining up the next shot. He fired again and immediately aimed and loosed arrow three. He left the bow on the ground and the two of them walked back to the ledge. Max was shocked to see that Knut had made all three shots: an arrow speared through each piece of plastic fruit. The Viking pulled the arrows out and handed them to Max.

Back at the opposite end of the archery range, Max picked up the bow. It was light but clearly very strong and came up over his hip. He put an arrow in the little nocking point and pulled back the bowstring. He strained to wrench the string back far enough and Knut even motioned to him a couple of times to pull it more. By the time the Viking was smiling, Max's arms were quivering. He heard the wood groan as he held it and part of him hoped it wouldn't snap. He shut one eye and focused on the first piece of fruit – an apple. It was so far away he could barely see it. He was about to loose the arrow when Knut held up his hand to stop him. The Viking put one hand on Max's shoulders and another on his lower back and straightened his posture, pushing his chest out. He grunted at the boy, satisfied now. Max looked back at the apple then let the arrow go. It flew through the air – nowhere near as straight or steady as Knut's – but it still managed to reach the far end of the range. He saw it sail just over the apple and into the plywood wall behind. Even though he hadn't hit the target, he was immensely pleased with himself. Knut patted him on the back proudly, then gestured for him to continue.

Arthur wasn't having as pleasant a time with Magnus. This Viking had always struck Arthur as grumpy, cantankerous and sullen, but he really had no idea how bad-tempered he was until he started training with him. Magnus hadn't put in as much preparation as the other two Vikings. He began by simply heaving his hammer down a narrow laneway. It tumbled through the cold air and smacked into one of the metal emergency-exit doors that were peppered around the exterior wall. The force of the blow gave off the sound of a church bell, which rang throughout the Viking Experience. Magnus picked up the hammer and wobbled back to Arthur, pushing it into his waiting arms.

Even though this war-hammer was smaller than Arthur's own one at home, it was much heavier. Or, at least, it felt much heavier. He was able to pick his own up one-handed but had to use both hands to lift this monstrosity.

'It's too heavy,' Arthur complained.

'Grnk,' Magnus grunted ambivalently and stood with his arms crossed, waiting.

'Fine!' Arthur said. He swung both his arms backwards between his legs, then let the momentum carry the hammer forward again. As it reached the peak of the arc he let go. It landed with a hefty clang a few feet away.

'See?' said Arthur, looking at Magnus. 'It's too heavy.'

The Viking just grunted and pointed to the hammer on the ground.

'Again? You want me to do it again?'

Magnus nodded impatiently, so Arthur took a second try. This time was no better. Arthur looked at the Viking but he only pointed to the hammer once more.

'But it's not going to work this wa—'

Magnus rolled his eyes up to heaven and grunted a high-pitched and whiny imitation of Arthur. When he was done, he nodded to the hammer once more. Arthur picked it up and tried again, his biceps feeling the strain already. The day continued like this. Arthur would try to reach the door and fail, and Magnus would have him do it again. There was only a marginal improvement after a few hours. On top of that, Arthur's phone rang a couple of times throughout the day – always with the unknown number. Even though he always cancelled the call, Magnus sighed loudly each time. Arthur was understandably delighted when it was time to go home.

※※※※※

The sun was just setting when they got back to the Barry household; Stace and her parents were already home. Arthur, Ash and Max were about to run upstairs to discuss their training in private when Mr Barry called Ash into the living-room. He and his wife were sitting on the couch and Arthur could guess from the redness in his neck that he was annoyed about something.

'Where have you lot been?' he asked furiously.

'We just went to the cinema,' Ash lied.

'And you left the front door wide open!' Mr Barry accused.

'No, we didn't,' she cried. 'I definitely locked it on the way out!'

'Well, it was wide open when we got home,' said Mrs Barry. 'How do you explain that?'

'I don't know but I definitely locked it, didn't I?' She turned to Arthur and Max and they both instantly backed up her story. Arthur distinctly remembered Ash making sure the door was tightly shut.

'And what about the scratches on the door?' Mr Barry went on. 'If it's that dog of yours, we're getting rid of her!'

'Scratches?' Ash repeated, running into the hallway. She knelt down and studied the deep grooves etched into the wood of the door. They definitely looked like claw marks. Before anyone could say anything else, she ran through the house, going from room to room and calling her pup's name. Ice was nowhere to be seen.

'Arthur,' she said, out of breath, when she was finished her search, 'Ice is gone.'

Flashlight beams broke through the darkness of the estate as calls of 'Ice!' shattered the silence. They walked the length and breadth of the estate, shining their torches under cars, behind wheelie bins and down the narrow alleys that ran between every second house. Even Mr and Mrs Barry were going from door to door, asking the neighbours if anyone had seen the dog. While Stace and Max concentrated on the far end of the estate, Arthur took his chance to search the green.

Eirik was concealed in the depths of the trees when Arthur got there, keeping a close eye on the proceedings in the estate. He wore a pained, worried expression.

Arthur felt his phone vibrating in his pocket. A quick glance told him it was the unknown number again. He still didn't have time to talk to anyone so he cancelled the call once more. He looked up at Eirik.

'Have you seen Ash's dog, Eirik?'

The Viking nodded in response and pointed at the green, drawing the line with his finger where he saw Ice run earlier in the day.

'She followed us?' Arthur asked. Eirik nodded. Why would she follow us, Arthur wondered as he headed off in the direction Eirik had indicated. He snuck through the brush rather than going around it as he usually would. Whatever Ice was up to, he aimed to find out for himself, without Ash's input.

He emerged right at the edge of the road that ran behind the estate. Two lanes of traffic flew at breakneck speeds in both directions. Car headlights blinded him and trucks rattled loudly, shaking the very ground beneath his feet, but there was no sign of the pup.

Arthur was about to turn back when he heard the bark.

It was a high-pitched yap – not unlike Ice's own cry – and it was so faint that Arthur wasn't sure if he had heard anything. A second bark confirmed that the sound had been real. It was distant and broken, the sound bouncing to him from across the busy road. There was a third bark, this time accompanied by a persistent and shrieking yelp. Whatever animal had made the sound was clearly in some pain or discomfort.

He squinted across the road. There was a matching estate and clump of trees on the opposite side. Although he couldn't get a clear view through the hurtling traffic, he could just make out some of the low bushes moving over there. It could have been caused by the wind or by the gusts from the cars, but the shuddering of the shrubs seemed too urgent to be either.

The nearest set of traffic lights – and pedestrian crossing – was a few hundred yards from where he'd seen the bushes move. However, in the other direction was a footbridge over the road itself, which Arthur headed straight for, taking extra care on the narrow pavement along his side of the road.

Both sides of the footbridge had a set of steps and a long, winding wheelchair ramp. At the top of the stairs on each side were tall poles with a pair of iron suspension cables holding the bridge itself aloft. The walkway spanned the entire four lanes of the road. Arthur took the steps, bounding up them two at a time. As he passed over the walkway, he felt the slightest vibration of the traffic below his feet. He came to a stop midway and peered over the edge. It was a strange sensation, being up so high over the busy road. Despite the fumes and noise, it felt oddly peaceful to look down at the disappearing lights. After a moment, he continued on across the bridge.

A figure was slowly moving up the ramp he was approaching. He squinted in the amber glow of the streetlights and the person came into focus. It was an old woman, frail and hunched over, with a headscarf fluttering in the slight breeze. She was heaving a shopping bag on wheels up the last few feet of the ramp. From the way the bag bulged at the sides, it was clearly very heavy. Arthur ran forward to help her with it.

'Oh, thank you, dearie!' she said, her voice crackling with exhaustion as Arthur took hold of the trolley. She wore green eye-shadow and bright-pink lipstick – both applied liberally. Her teeth were yellowed – no doubt the result of a lifetime of smoking. And she reeked of flowery perfume. 'Me legs aren't what they used to be.'

'No problem at all,' said Arthur cheerily as he set the cart down on the walkway. 'Would you like a hand down the far side with it?'

'You're very good. But I should manage that side by myself. Thank you again, dearie.' The woman gripped the handle and went on her way.

Arthur continued down the ramp – half running, half skipping – and then towards where he'd spotted the rustling bushes.

'Ice?' he called as he walked. 'Ice, are you there?'

There was no discernible sound over the traffic now. No barking or yelping. Just his own footsteps and the speeding cars.

'Ice?' He ducked into the shrubbery in a gap between two dense briar patches. As soon as he was inside the clump of trees, the noise of the traffic lowered to a distant groan. The trees were denser here which meant that it was darker than on his side of the road and he had to use his phone flashlight to see anything.

'Ice? Come here, girl.'

No answer, no sound.

Arthur moved deeper through the trees and bushes.

All he found was the remains of a campfire and beer cans that some teenagers had probably been responsible for. After a few minutes, he gave up and trudged back towards the footbridge.

He went back up the ramp more slowly than before, lost in his thoughts. Where was Ice? Why had she followed them? Or, rather, had she been following them?

Arthur shuffled his feet dejectedly across the walkway, gazing down at the hurtling lights. He thought of all the people in all those cars and wondered where they were going, where they were coming from, who they were with. Regardless of the answers, he was quite certain that they didn't have to deal with the same kind of problems that he did.

He was midway across the bridge when his foot kicked off something. He bent down and picked it up.

An iron nut.

It was painted black but with a fine layer of rust around one of the threads. He looked at the metal floor of the walkway around him and spotted the matching bolt. It was around six inches long, also painted black and also with a crust of rust along some of the threads. Odd, he thought, turning the two of them over in his hands. Where did they–

He looked behind him. There, where the ramp met the walkway – the railing of the ramp should have been attached to that of the bridge but there was a gap. It was slight but it was definitely there. He'd missed it because he'd been looking at the traffic.

He turned back in the direction of home. The old woman with the shopping bag was standing at the far ramp. There was a wrench by her feet, a bolt-cutter in her hand and a grin on her face. She turned her fist over, dropping a handful of nuts and bolts. They thumped heavily onto the walkway. When Arthur pulled his shocked gaze away from them, the woman was lost in a cloud of green light. It faded away, revealing Loki in her place.

Arthur was rigid with fear as Loki swung the bolt-cutter up over his head. He vaguely recognised it as the same one that Will had used all those months ago at the Metro site. With one screeching shriek, like nails on slate, the god snapped one of the suspension cables.

The walkway lurched underneath Arthur's feet, shaking him from his stupor. Without waiting to watch Loki cut through the second cable, he turned and sprinted in the opposite direction.

Every second counted, yet every footstep felt like an eternity.

All the muscles in his body were straining to get him off the bridge, to safety.

Above Loki's laughter, Arthur heard the second cable snap behind him and felt the bridge lurch downwards.

He gave one last push, his legs cramping, and–

He landed with a thud on the ramp, crashing onto his hands and knees. He turned, just in time to see the far end of the walkway ploughing into the road below. The squeal of brakes reverberated around him as the traffic tried to avoid hitting the bridge. One car screeched to a stop just in time to avoid being squashed underneath it. The cables above Arthur's head groaned and creaked but stayed attached to the bridge. He heard the crunch of metal below him as someone failed to react in time. He really hoped no one was seriously hurt.

When he looked back across the chasm that had been the bridge, Loki was gone.

Chapter Fifteen

In the confusion that followed the accident, Arthur snuck across the road, where all traffic was now at a standstill, and ran back to his estate. His legs were still shaking and he had a few small scratches on the palms of his hands but, other than that, he was unhurt. He didn't feel like having to talk to the Gardaí for a second time that week.

Joe's car was in the drive when he got back. Ash was standing talking to him with Ice in her arms.

'Look, Arthur!' Ash exclaimed gleefully. 'Your dad found Ice!'

'I saw her sitting by the side of the road into town when I was coming home,' Joe told Arthur. 'I recognised her wheels so I stopped and picked her up.' He held up a cardboard box heaving with files. 'Anyway, I'll just drop these inside.' Joe turned and left them alone.

'Isn't it great!' Ash hugged Ice closer to her.

When Arthur didn't answer she raised one quizzical eyebrow at him.

'Something wrong?'

He quickly filled her in on what had happened, keeping his voice low so that no one would hear that he had been at the accident that would soon be all over the news.

When he was done, Ash set Ice down on the ground and took Arthur in a tight hug, then gave him a once over for any injuries.

'I'm fine Ash, I'm fine. It's just …' He shot a look at Ice.

'What?'

'I thought I heard Ice. That's why I crossed the bridge to start with.'

'And?'

'It was all a trap, Ash!' he cried impatiently. 'And Ice was the bait.'

Ash protectively picked up the pup again. 'So you think Loki took Ice?'

'No. I think Ice was in on it.'

She sighed heavily and rolled her eyes. 'You've had a shock, Arthur. You're not thinking straight.'

'I'm fine, Ash. I know what I heard. And–'

'Don't be daft, Arthur! We're not getting into this again. Even if you did hear a dog it was probably Loki imitating Ice.'

'How would Loki have known Ice was missing? In fact, how would he even know you have her?'

'He's a god, Arthur, who knows what he knows? I wish you would just give up on this idiotic theory of yours. Besides, if she was across the road a minute ago, how could your dad have found her on the road into town?'

'I don't know but–'

'Stop,' Ash said curtly and turned, starting back towards her own house. Then, unwilling to part on such a sour note, she called back, 'I'm glad you're OK. I'll see you tomorrow before school. Thank your dad for me again.'

'Yeah,' Arthur said. 'See you.' As Ash walked away, Arthur could have sworn he saw the pup looking back at him with what could only be described as a smug look on her face. If only Ash would listen to me, he thought, watching his friend until she went inside her house and closed the door.

As soon as Arthur was back in his bedroom, his phone started vibrating again. Finally able to answer the unknown number, he pressed the green phone key.

'Hello?' he said, a little too sharply.

'Hi,' said a girl's voice on the other end. 'Arthur? It's Ellie. Ellie Lavender. From school.'

'Hi, Ellie. How did you get my number?'

'It's a long story involving Ciara, Megan, Robyn, Brian and Caroline,' she answered. 'Listen, I was hoping I'd catch you to talk about what happened yesterday.'

After his long day of trying to please the grouchy Magnus, and then his encounter with Loki, Arthur really wasn't in the mood for discussing the museum.

'Sorry, Ellie,' he said. 'I'm just too tired to talk about that now.'

'But can I just ask you–'

'Goodnight, Ellie.' And with that he hung up and collapsed onto his bed.

In a time before history was written down, in Asgard, the realm of the gods, there is a lake called Amsvartnir. It stretches as wide as the eye can see and is unfathomably deep and the water is ever-shifting shades of blue and green and yellow. The lake is always still, as if the wind itself is terrified of disturbing its strange and wondrous beauty. In the centre of Lake Amsvartnir is an island called Lyngvi. It is insignificant, rocky and dusty; no life can flourish here. And it is this island that the gods are heading for on this day.

There are usually twelve gods and twelve goddesses in Asgard. But with Loki imprisoned and Thor still engaged in battle with the Jormungand, it is down to those who remain to travel to Lyngvi.

Odin walks in front. He is known as the Battle God, as the One-Eyed, as the All-Father, and he is the leader of Asgard. He wears a dark cape that trails on the ground and a wide-brimmed leather hat that casts an eternal shadow over his face. His left eye is watchful and intelligent, shifting quickly back and forth in its socket. His right eye is gone. He traded it years ago for knowledge. A tan eye-patch covers the empty socket. The satchel across his chest looks empty.

They walk across the lake, their feet travelling on a stone causeway hidden just below the water's surface. These hexagonal-shaped boulders start at the shore and end at the island and are wide enough for all the gods and a single carriage to pass along. The carriage is being pulled by a boar, following Odin closely. It snorts and grunts with every step, struggling to haul the cart across the lake. Though there is only one passenger in the carriage, it weighs more now than at any other time the boar has pulled it. The boar, with its great tusks and strong legs, is terrified of the sole beast in the buggy.

The Fenris Wolf sleeps soundly in the wagon, lying on his back, his tongue lolling out of his slack mouth. If he was to stand on his hindquarters, he would be as tall and as broad as Thor himself. But now, thankfully, he is unconscious. The only way the gods had of transporting him was by casting a series of spells to capture him and send him to sleep. In the short few days of his life, under Loki's command, he has slaughtered men, women and children. A small round piece of glass hangs on a string around his great neck, but even now none of the gods is brave enough to try to take it off for fear of the jaws snapping down on their wrists. They know the spells will only work on such a powerful being for a short time.

They reach the island and all clamber onto it. There is barely enough space for them all.

'Fenris Wolf,' Odin says, keeping his one eye fixed on the beast, 'awaken and face your fate.'

The wolf's eyes shoot open. In one swift bound, he leaps off the carriage and lands on the stony ground, watching the gods warily. The boar, happy to be relieved of his burden, turns as quickly as he can and proceeds to pull the – now much lighter – carriage back to the mainland.

Fenrir backs up against a tall and craggy boulder sticking out of the ground. He snarls at the gods, baring razor-sharp, bloodstained teeth. His black fur bristles across his back.

'Quiet, Fenris Wolf,' Odin snaps. 'You are here to pay for your crimes.'

The wolf stops growling and suddenly breaks into a booming laugh.

'My crimes?' the wolf cries in a deep, rumbling voice. All the gods but Odin recoil in horror at the terrifying sound. 'You think you can make me pay?'

Odin waits while the wolf laughs derisively. As his mirth trails off, the All-Father reaches into the seemingly empty satchel. Even though the leather bag appears no larger than a purse, he thrusts his arm in up to his elbow and fishes about for something. As he does so, he keeps his one eye fixed on the wolf and the wolf stares back with ferocity.

Eventually Odin withdraws his arm. In his hand is an immense chain with thick and powerful-looking links. He holds it before him so all can see.

'This chain is called Laeding,' he announces loudly. 'We, the gods of Asgard, forged it from the strongest iron in all the nine worlds. No man nor beast has the strength to break these links.' He lowers it and takes a tentative step towards the wolf. 'Even you can't escape this chain, Fenris Wolf.'

The wolf looks at the chain with wide eyes, then abruptly howls with laughter.

'You think you can trap me with that, old man?' he sneers. 'All right. You can try. And to make it easier for you I won't even move from this rock so that you can bind me to it.'

The lesser gods look from one to the other, nervous of the animal's mocking words. Odin accepts the challenge, calls forward the three strongest gods present and hands them Laeding. They set about binding the wolf to the crag in the middle of the island. They coil the chain around his belly, twice around each leg and thrice around the rock before sealing the two loose links with magic. And all the while, the Fenris Wolf remains calm, letting them entangle him.

When they are done, they step away to look at their handiwork proudly. There is no way the Fenris Wolf can escape these bindings.

The wolf looks back up at them. He places his paws steadily on the ground, as far away from each other as he can manage. Then he opens his powerful jaws and inhales. As he fills his lungs, he tenses every muscle in his body. The iron groans under the strain momentarily and then, without warning, the links of the chain fly apart. Pieces of shrapnel spin through the air as the iron snaps into tiny pieces. Laeding is destroyed and the Fenris Wolf is free and laughing.

'So it goes,' Odin says sadly to himself.

As the wolf roars in triumph, the All-Father reaches into his satchel once more. This time his arm plunges deeper, until he is up to his shoulder in the bag. His hand comes out with a second chain. The links on this are even thicker, constructed of a black metal that shimmers weirdly in the faint light of the day.

'If Laeding couldn't hold you, Fenris Wolf,' he says, showing the wolf the new chain, 'this will. It is called Dromi and was forged by the Giants from the strongest metal found in the deepest volcano in all the nine worlds. None can escape its binding.'

'Ha!' guffaws the wolf. 'None but I! Wrap that chain around and see me escape.'

Odin hands the chain called Dromi to the three strongest gods and, as before, they bind the wolf to the rocky ridge. This time they coil the chain around his belly three times, each leg six times and the boulder nine times. Then, just to be fully sure, they tie his legs together like a hog and strap his jaws tightly. Finally, they seal the loose links by casting some rune magic and step back to watch what happens.

The wolf's eyes watch them from behind his black manacles. There is a mischievousness in them, Odin notices. The wolf rolls onto his back, with his hog-tied legs in the air. Then he straightens his arched back and, with an enormous crack, the chain Dromi disintegrates. Fragments of the shimmering metal fill the air and once again the Fenris Wolf is free.

As the wolf rejoices, Odin reaches into his satchel. Even up to his shoulder, he can't seem to find what he's looking for, so he has to duck his head straight into the bag. Finally, up to his chest in the leather satchel, he finds what he wants and re-emerges. In his hand is a long and slender ribbon that flows around his ankles in the slightest breeze. It is silky smooth and golden; it glimmers incandescently in his grip. The Fenris Wolf, who has stopped laughing long enough to see what Odin has in store for him this time, starts sniggering again when he sees the flimsy-looking ribbon.

'Do not laugh, Fenris Wolf,' the All-Father warns. 'This is Gleipnir, a gift from the Dwarves. It has been forged from the sound a cat makes as it moves, the beard of a woman, the breath of a fish, the roots of a mountain, the sinews of a bear and the spit of a bird.'

'A bird's spittle?' the wolf taunts. 'A woman's beard? I've never heard such folly! These things don't exist.'

But they do exist, Odin thinks to himself. Just because we cannot see them doesn't mean they don't. And the magic they possess is great.

'Do you accept the challenge then?' Odin asks. 'May we bind you with Gleipnir?'

'Of course! Wrap that ribbon around me a hundred times – no, a thousand! I'll still escape!'

The three gods step forward to take Gleipnir from the All-Father, but Odin shakes his head.

'I will secure the wolf this time,' he says.

He wraps the ribbon around the stone precipice once and binds it with runes. Then he kneels by the wolf and ties the loose end around one of his legs in a similar magical knot. The wolf watches him closely, wondering to himself at the stupidity of the god.

'Goodbye, Fenris Wolf,' Odin says, standing and walking to the edge of the island.

'Wait!' cries the wolf. 'You haven't seen me escape yet.'

'And nor will I,' Odin says, swivelling to face his foe. 'You will never escape Gleipnir.' He turns once more and crosses the causeway back to the shore. The other gods follow him in silence. None of them so much as looks back at the wolf on the island.

The wolf watches them go. He waits until they are back on the mainland before looking down at the ribbon around his leg. The fools, he thinks. Leaving me here all alone to escape. Wolf-father Loki will be so proud of me. I will enact his plan just as he instructed.

He pulls his bound leg sharply away from the rock, expecting the ribbon to snap instantly. It doesn't. He tries again but gets the same result. He attempts it a third time, jerking his leg even harder. But this time, the ribbon snaps backwards in response and the wolf bounces off the ground, as it pulls him towards the rock.

Now he sets his jaws to Gleipnir, ripping at the delicate silk with his serrated fangs and grinding the ribbon together between two rows of teeth. He spits it out, expecting it to have snapped. But Gleipnir is still whole and completely undamaged by his onslaught.

He pulls and grunts and bites and claws at the ribbon and all to no avail. The gods have tricked him, he realises, whimpering. He is well and truly trapped. Odin was right; there is no escape from Gleipnir.

He throws back his head in anger and lets a deafening howl burst from his lungs. He bays at the setting sun and wails at the rising moon, knowing full well that he is imprisoned for all eternity.

CHAPTER SIXTEEN

Krzzz! Krzzz! Krzzz!

Arthur groggily opened his eyes. His phone was vibrating harshly on his bedside cabinet. He grabbed it and tapped the screen irritably to read the incoming text message. It was from Ash: 'Im outside. Where U?' He looked at the time on the corner of the display. It blinked to 08.47. Usually he left his house at half-past eight. He was late!

He threw the covers back and barely had time to register the cold before throwing off his pyjamas and pulling on his school clothes. Luckily the brown uniform had been draped over his radiator so it warmed him up. He legged it into the bathroom and studied himself in the mirror. His eyes were pink, with yellowish chunks of gunge at the corners, as if he hadn't slept. A clump of hair stood to attention at the crown of his head. He threw some water on his face, then on his hair, patting it down while brushing his teeth. As he gargled, he recalled the dream he'd had: the gods capturing the great Fenris Wolf. There was no doubt now that the first dream of the wolf had been real. Ash would have to believe him whether she liked it or not.

He raced downstairs, grabbing his school bag on the way, and swung open the front door. Ash was waiting there, leaning against the railing and tapping her foot impatiently.

'Sorry!' he apologised. 'I slept in.' He went to shut the door behind him.

'Wait!' Ash stopped him, putting her foot in the door jamb. She pulled something out of her coat pocket and offered it to him. It was another webcam, the same size and shape as Ash's only with a label stuck across the top with his name. 'I made you one, too,' she went on. 'Just put it in your window so we can see if Loki or any of his raiders come around.'

He grabbed the camera, bounded back upstairs, left it on his windowsill and sprinted down again. He was out of breath as he locked the door.

'Listen, Ash,' he said through pants as they ran towards the bus stop. 'I've something to tell you …'

※※※※※

As soon as the bus pulled up outside Belmont School, Ash got off and marched towards their classroom before Arthur could catch up. After he'd described his dream in detail to her and emphasised again his theory about her dog, the atmosphere in the upper deck of the bus had turned icy.

'So Loki's second child is definitely a wolf,' she'd said. 'I believe that much. What I don't believe is that you still think that my little puppy is that very wolf!'

'But–'

'Look, we know Loki has a gang of raiders. We know that whatever he wants was in the museum. And where was Ice through all of that? At home.'

'Ash don't be so–'

Without another word, Ash had changed seats. Arthur stared at the back of her head for the rest of the journey to school. If she won't listen, he thought, I'll have to act. I'll do something. But what?

The morning bell had already rung when they'd reached the school and Arthur walked across the car-park by himself, watching his friend trudge ahead of him.

'Hi, Arthur!' a voice called from behind him. Without even turning around, he knew it was Ellie.

'Hi, Ellie,' he said, still facing forward. 'You're late.'

'So are you,' she said as she caught up with him. Ex was trailing alongside her, kicking pebbles out of his path as usual. Ellie noticed Ash storm through the main entrance of the school ahead of them. 'Did you and Ash have a falling out?' she asked.

'You could say that.'

'What about?'

'Long story.' He liked Ellie but he really wasn't up for her constant stream of queries this morning, so he picked up the pace to a jog. 'Come on. Or Miss Keegan will give us detention.'

'Oh, look who's turned up!' said the teacher as the three of them piled in the door sheepishly, only moments after Ash had arrived in. 'Did *everyone* sleep in this morning?'

'Sorry, Miss,' Arthur said, taking his seat next to Ash. He could feel her stiffening beside him as he sat down.

'Apology accepted, Arthur,' Miss Keegan went on. 'I was just reminding the class that our annual parent–teacher meeting will take place this evening from six. Just be sure to remind your parents it's on in case they've forgotten.'

'Miss!' Ellie said, raising her arm. 'Our parents are on a dig in Greece.'

'Yes, I'm aware of that, Ellie. You can invite your guardian.'

'But that's my grandfather, Miss. He's nearly blind and he can't drive any more.'

'Just let him know anyway, Ellie,' Miss Keegan said, exasperated.

The remainder of the day didn't go as quickly as Arthur would have liked. In fact, occasionally it felt as if time had not only ground to a halt, but was flowing backwards. He was sure he spotted the minute hand on the clock over the blackboard tick backwards at one stage. Ash avoided him all day, sending glares his way during lunch as she sat with Ciara O'Connor. He ate lunch with Ellie, Ex and Rob Tynan, who wouldn't shut up about motor-racing the whole time. Ordinarily this would have driven him crazy (no pun intended), but now he was pleased that Rob's incessant yapping managed to drown out Ellie's questions. Eventually the bell rang to announce the end of the day and the class scrambled out of the building as if their very lives depended on it.

He watched from afar as Ash and a few other pupils walked to the bus stop. He couldn't bear to ride in the same bus as Ash after the uncomfortable journey that morning, but the next one would be over an hour. There was nothing else for it, he realised. He'd have to walk the forty minutes home by himself.

As he set off – passing the bus stop on the way and hoping that Ash wouldn't notice him – he heard some small footsteps clatter along the street behind him. They were followed closely by a set of heavier, thumping footsteps.

'Where are you going?' Ellie asked, coming up alongside him.

'Walking home.'

'We'll walk with you,' she said, indicating Ex lumbering behind them.

'Won't it be out of your way?'

'Doesn't matter.'

He laughed to himself. Whatever else you could say about Ellie, he thought, she was certainly very persistent.

'OK,' he said, bowing to the inevitable. 'I'd be happy to have the company.'

As they went on, Ellie started to swing her arms vigorously by her sides. Arthur looked at her for a minute before curiosity got the better of him.

'Why are you doing that?'

'To stay warm,' she told him, keeping her arms swinging.

'Well, why don't you wear a warmer coat?' She had the adult-sized trench coat on as usual and, though it was far too baggy for her, it didn't look like it held in much heat.

'Because this is my mom's,' she answered reasonably. 'She leaves it for me any time they go away without us. So I don't miss them as much. It still smells like her.' She put a loose bunched-up sleeve to her nose and inhaled her mother's scent.

'Do they go away much?'

'A couple of times a year. Usually they bring us. But not this time.'

'So your granddad is taking care of you guys?'

'Yup!'

'Don't you have to be home on time?'

'Oh, he won't mind. He's old now and he mostly just sleeps in a chair by the fire.' She stopped swinging her arms and put her hands in the over-sized pockets. 'So what do your parents do?'

'My dad works on the Metro. Well, worked on the Metro.'

'Worked?' This seemed to pique her interest.

'He quit his job. Which means we'll be moving back to Kerry in a couple of weeks.'

'Wow,' she uttered, staring down at the pavement. 'That sucks.' After a moment's silence she brightened up again. 'I've travelled all over the world with Mom and Dad. I've seen the sunrise in New Zealand, polar bears in the Arctic, the slums of Mumbai. But I've never been to Kerry. Is it nice?'

'It's all right, yeah.' For the past couple of weeks, he had dreaded the thought of moving back there. But now that he had fallen out with his best friend, Kerry was looking better all the time.

'We should visit you when you move back,' Ellie said. 'Me and Ex and Ash.'

'Yeah,' he said, noncommittally.

'What happened in the museum, Arthur?' she asked suddenly.

'Uh …' He faltered, thinking of Loki's grinning face as it was on that day. 'I can't really remember. I blacked out.'

Ellie stopped in her tracks. Arthur looked back at her. They stood like that for a moment as Ex kept on kicking pebbles.

'That's not true. You showed the Gardaí something,' she said, finally breaking the silence. 'What did you see?'

'Just forget about it, Ellie,' he said. 'I saw the raiders leaving, that's all.'

'I thought we were friends.'

'We are.'

'You said you trusted me.'

'I do, Ellie. But, well, you just need to trust *me* on this one.' He walked on, wondering if Ellie could understand everything he knew, if she'd be as trusting and as carefree with that knowledge. Knowing about Loki and all he had done had made Arthur so paranoid and suspicious that he couldn't even trust an injured puppy. He resolved there and then to put the argument with Ash behind him, to give Ice another chance and to apologise to his best friend.

Ellie joined him by his side. 'Sorry,' she said. 'No more questions.'

For the rest of the walk home they chatted about school and the other pupils and their favourite things. Anything but the museum. Before long, they reached the estate.

'Could I use your bathroom?' Ellie asked as he turned towards his house. 'It's just that it's a longer walk to ours. I'll be really quick.'

'Of course you can.' The three of them walked to his door. Arthur opened it and let Ellie in first.

'Up the stairs,' he instructed her. 'First door on the left.'

She thanked him and loped up to the bathroom. Arthur was about to follow her inside when Ex spoke. It was the first time he'd opened his mouth the whole way home, so he took Arthur by surprise.

'So this is where you live,' he said. It was more a statement than a question, but Arthur still felt he should reply.

'Sure is,' he said, starting to go inside again.

'And Ash lives here too?' Ex asked before Arthur could get out of the cold. Arthur took a step back and pointed out the Barry house.

'She lives just there,' Arthur said, then moved to go in again.

'Nice,' admired Ex. He nodded at the green. 'Do you have many kick-arounds there?'

Halfway through the door, Arthur sighed and turned back to Ex.

'Sometimes,' he answered. 'But not as often as Max would like.'

'Hmm,' mused Ex.

'All done!' Ellie cried, springing down the steps and out the door. She stopped in front of Arthur and looked him straight in the eyes.

'If there's ever anything you want to talk about, you have my phone number,' she said. 'I'm very understanding.'

Then abruptly, with a brisk wave to him, she skipped merrily out of the estate. Ex trailed after her, silent once more. Arthur finally went into his own house and collapsed in front of the television, exhausted.

·········

As soon as Ash got home, she went up to her room. Ice jumped up at her thighs when she got in the door so she carried the pup up with her.

She dropped her backpack, lay on her bed and lifted the pup onto it too. Ice walked in a tight little circle before finding a comfortable spot to lie down. Ash put her hand on the pup's curled back, stroking the silky fur.

'What a long day,' she said to Ice, knowing she couldn't understand the words. 'And all because of you.'

She took her phone out of her pocket to check her emails and texts. None of either. Then she switched on the application that was linked to the webcams. She accessed her camera first. The image that filled the screen was the view out her bedroom window. She could see the whole estate here. It was nearly four o'clock and quite quiet. The old lady across the street was out walking her dog, trying to act casual as it pooed on the pavement. All was still on the green, although she knew that Eirik was hidden in the trees, guarding them. She noticed two figures standing outside Arthur's house. One was Arthur, obviously, but there was someone else next to him. She squinted her eyes at the low-resolution image and was able to make out Ex. She wondered what he was doing there, then switched her view to Camera Two.

The second webcam was the one she'd given Arthur only that morning. She expected to see outside his window so she could get a closer look at Ex but, to her surprise, the phone display was filled with a shot looking into Arthur's bedroom. Obviously he hadn't placed the camera in the correct position in his rush to leave that morning. Sunlight didn't fill the room at this time of the day so it was quite dark and ill-suited to a low-resolution camera. Nevertheless, she could make out the open door and hallway beyond, the piles of clothes heaped at the end of the unmade bed, the closed laptop on the desk. And Ellie. The girl was wandering around the bedroom, picking up books and pictures, examining them closely. Ash watched in shock as Ellie opened the laptop, found that it wasn't on and shut the lid again. Then she got to her knees and crawled along the ground, out of shot. For a few moments nothing happened, then there was a series of bright flashes. As each flash flared, the vision in the webcam blurred. When they were done, Ellie stood back up and left the bedroom. Ash watched as she popped into the bathroom opposite Arthur's room and flushed the toilet. Finally, she bounded down the stairs and out of sight.

Ash leaped off her bed and ran to the window. She waited until she saw Ellie and Ex walking away from the estate, then ran down the stairs and towards Arthur's house.

CHAPTER SEVENTEEN

Eirik stood at the edge of the tree cover to get a better look at Ash as she raced across the street and knocked on Arthur's door. After a minute, Arthur opened it. The Viking was still standing there, waiting to see what would happen next, when Stace arrived home.

'Oh, hi Eirik!' she chirped happily, stopping on her shortcut across the green. 'How are you?' Stace had had a trying and difficult day. It had been the start of her mock examinations, which meant sitting Irish and Biology papers – neither of which was a favourite subject of hers. The last forty minutes of the day had been set aside for study time but, following the disastrous couple of exams, she certainly didn't feel like sticking her head into another textbook. She left school early and strolled home slowly with her iPod blaring in her ears. She actually felt energised after the time to herself and, on seeing Eirik, felt even better.

The Viking grunted in response, then decided to creep around the shrubbery and out of the estate instead of back into it. He definitely didn't want to give away his hiding place to Stace.

'Wait,' Stace said. 'Where are you off to?'

Eirik stopped and looked at her, struggling to come up with an excuse or even a way to communicate with her.

'Let's go for a coffee,' she suggested, ignoring his befuddled expression. 'I could do with a coffee right now. It's been a stressful day.' She linked her arm through his and started leading him away from the green towards the main road. Eirik looked around desperately, hoping Arthur would notice and come to his rescue, but his luck was out. 'We'll just go to that nice little place around the corner.'

And that was how Eirik went on his first ever date.

※※※※※

'You can't be serious, Ash!' Arthur reproached her when she told him what she'd seen.

Before the doorbell had rung, he'd been sitting on the

267

couch. He'd switched on the TV but couldn't concentrate on it. He just kept thinking about the last thing Ellie had said before she'd left. That she was very understanding, that he could tell her anything. But would she understand, he wondered. He considered the implications of telling her what was going on. If she knew, it would be a whole other person involved, a whole other person at risk from Loki's insanity – in fact two other people, as Ellie and Ex seemed to be inseparable. On the other hand, Arthur was moving home soon and it might be good for Ash to have someone in Dublin to confide in.

The doorbell had rung then and as soon as Arthur opened the door Ash brushed in past him like a twisting tornado and ran up to his bedroom. By the time he reached his room, he found her waving around the little webcam she'd given him. She told him all that she'd witnessed – Ellie snooping around, checking his laptop, causing the strange flashes and finally pretending to use the bathroom.

Arthur just stared at her agog during the whole on-slaught, then said finally, 'You can't be serious, Ash!'

'Deadly serious.'

He took a breath and sat on the edge of his bed. He didn't know what to think. He just hadn't a clue.

Eventually he looked up at her.

'Did you record it?'

'No,' she answered, looking away, frustrated. 'I haven't fixed the recording function yet.'

He stood back up and paced the room. 'I think you're being a bit paranoid,' he said.

'What?'

'Look at it from my perspective, Ash,' he continued. 'Earlier today I don't trust your dog; then this evening you're suspicious of my new friend.'

'Your new friend?'

'Yeah, actually, my new friend. I'm allowed more than one, aren't I?'

Ash put the webcam in her pocket and sat down on the swivel chair by the desk. 'I didn't know you were that close.'

'She's a nice girl,' he said. 'You should get to know her instead of making accusations—'

'They're not just accusations! It's true! She was in here.'

'So what if she was in here?' he shouted back, suddenly angry. 'So she's nosy? She's curious. Big deal.'

'What about the flashes?' she said. 'Five or six bright-white flashes. It was like she was taking photos. Maybe of the hammer?'

'Or maybe your webcam malfunctioned.'

'It did no—'

'You said yourself the flashes blurred the picture. Have you considered for a second the possibility that something was wrong with the camera?'

Ash looked out the window, feeling too angry with Arthur to even look at him right then. When she turned back, he was sitting on the edge of the bed again.

'Look,' he said, his voice even and reasonable, 'with this whole Loki thing, we've all been really paranoid and jumpy lately. We keep waiting for Loki to show up and it's putting us all on edge. Take Max, for example, guarding the door the other day. It's understandable, really. But we can't both be right.'

'Maybe we're both wrong,' Ash muttered. She got up and sat on the bed next to him. She offered her hand. He wrapped his fingers through hers and held it there on the mattress between them.

'Ellie's nice,' he said. 'Granted, Ex is a bit weird.' They both chuckled, thinking of him kicking at pebbles. 'But Ellie's nice. Give her a chance.'

'I'll try,' she promised.

'Anyway …' he went on. 'I was thinking of filling her in on Loki.'

At that, Ash let go of his hand and stood back up. 'What!' she shouted. 'Why would you do that?'

Now Arthur stood up and faced her head on. 'So that you'll have someone to talk to when I–' He stopped mid-sentence, realising that he'd said too much.

'When you what?' Ash asked.

'When I move back to Kerry,' he murmured, sitting back down on the bed. 'In two weeks.' He stared at the carpet, unable to look his friend in the eye. 'Dad quit his job, so there's nothing to keep us here now.'

'Two weeks,' she repeated slowly.

'Yeah.'

'Nothing to keep you here. OK.'

'Ash, I didn't mean it like that. I'm …' He looked at her. Her eyes were glistening with tears. 'Sorry.'

'It's fine,' she lied, turning away from him. 'I'd better go home.' She walked out the door and then ran down the stairs. He heard the front door open and shut, followed by Ash's footsteps as she ran home across the estate.

He lay back on the bed. I messed that up big time, he thought with regret.

The café had low lighting, a blessing that Eirik was thankful for. Despite that, he kept what he thought of as his best side facing the girl, leaning back all the while into some shadows. Stace ordered them a large latte and a brownie each. When she put them on the table in front of Eirik, he looked at them bewildered. He picked up the brownie and sniffed at it. Then he licked the hard chocolate crust on top and smacked his lips, savouring the strange flavour. Next, he took the mug of coffee and blew at the foamed milk on top, sending it toppling over the lip of the cup.

'Is it too hot?' Stace asked, then took a sip of her own. 'No, just right.'

He shrugged his shoulders and dived in head first. (Well, he dived in head first metaphorically. If he'd dived in head first literally, he would have made quite a mess of the date.) He took a tentative sip, seemed to enjoy it and then glugged back more. The whole mug of coffee was drained in one go. He slammed it down on the table proudly.

Stace laughed. When he saw that she was studying his face, he once more leaned back into the shadows.

'Acne scars, huh?'

The Viking raised an eyebrow in confusion.

'Acne scars,' Stace repeated herself, twirling a finger

272

about her own face. 'You don't need to feel self-conscious, you know. I had really bad acne a couple of years ago but some tea-tree oil really helped clear it up. There was this one girl in my class who …' She noticed his bemused expression. 'Sorry. I tend to ramble sometimes. If I'm nervous or with someone I … never mind … I just always end up saying the wrong thing. And I shouldn't have brought up the … uh …' She bit her tongue, eager to change the subject. 'So where do you come from?'

'Grrr,' Eirik muttered, leaning his head to one side as he tried to come up with an answer.

'Oh!' Stace seemed to understand. 'You move around a lot!'

Eirik nodded frantically.

'You must travel quite a bit with your job.'

The Viking gestured in the affirmative.

'I bet it's fun working with horses.'

'Mmm,' Eirik agreed.

'I enjoy talking to you, Eirik,' Stace announced suddenly. 'Most guys are all "me me me". But you're a listener. That's good. I like that.'

And behind the thick layers of make-up, Eirik managed to blush.

Ash was lying face down on her bed, tears soaking into her pillow, when Ice started barking downstairs. She had gone straight to her room when she got back to her house, feeling very sorry for herself. How would she manage without Arthur? She always knew he was only staying for a year, but had never imagined him leaving so soon. She liked him more than any other friend she'd ever had. And now he would only be around for two more weeks.

'Ice!' Ash called down, rolling onto her back. 'Stop the barking!'

But the dog didn't stop. In fact, the yapping just got worse. She could hear her snarling now as well. With a sigh, she trundled off her bed and went to investigate. As she descended the stairway, she could tell from the way the sound reverberated that the barking was coming from the living-room.

'Ice, please stop,' she said again. 'I'm getting a headache.'

She pushed the living-room door open. Five of Loki's black raiders were waiting for her inside, decked out in their Lycra uniforms and matching reflective helmets. Ice was standing in the centre of the carpeted floor, barking up at them. Before Ash had any time to react, a sixth raider crept up behind her and shoved a black cotton sack over her head.

Ash kicked her feet and punched her fists. She tried to scream out in the complete darkness of the bag, but one of the raiders wrapped his strong arms around her and clamped a hand over her mouth before she got a chance.

Meanwhile, Arthur was in his living-room, back watching TV. He was still annoyed with himself for upsetting Ash, but the television helped to take his mind off it. It was some Australian soap opera and, even though he couldn't follow the storyline, it was nice to soak up other people's problems for a change. He was getting hungry so was glad when he heard a noise from the kitchen.

'Dad?' he called out. He hadn't heard Joe come in but, since the TV volume was up so loud, he could easily have missed him. He looked at the time. It was just turning 6.30. 'Dad?' he called again, getting up and moving in the direction of the kitchen. 'Did you forget about the parent–teacher meeting?' There was no response. 'Dad?'

Arthur swung open the kitchen door. The light was on but no one was inside. Must have been my imagination, he thought, turning back towards the living-room. He heard something swish through the air and then felt the collision as it knocked into the back of his skull before his legs gave out from under him. He was unconscious before he hit the ground.

CHAPTER EIGHTEEN

In a time before history was written down, in Asgard, the realm of the gods, a storm is brewing. Wind and sleet are lashing the harsh yet beautiful terrain. The gale is too much for the trees and they bow to the gusts, their great trunks creaking in the strain to remain rooted while branches are left bare by the squall. But one tree alone stands upright. Its branches are ripe with fruit and berries and bright-green leaves. Its trunk stands bold and fierce, straight as an arrow with no twist or gnarl blighting its perfect appearance. This tree is known as Yggdrasill.

The tree rises high above the land, balancing on the edge of a tall precipice over a waterfall. Its roots sink deep into the ground, reaching each of the worlds: those of the gods, of man and of the dead. The water that flows by it and over the edge of the cliff falls into a deep pool on the forest floor below. This pool is the Well of Urd. It is said to be bottomless and to contain all the knowledge that is, was and will be. And it is now, as winds howl across Asgard, that the Fenris Wolf emerges from the woodland next to the well …

He is no longer wolf-shaped but stands on two feet as a man. An hour ago, he managed to escape the binds that the gods had left him in. He could not have managed it on his own, however. The girl had helped. He looks down at her in his arms as he emerges from the forest and into moonlight. Her hair is strewn over her face. She is unconscious. Not dead, just in an impossibly deep sleep. It happened just after she freed him and he doesn't understand why, but he could not leave her there. He changed his form to a man so that he could carry her to safety. With his Wolf-father Loki bound somewhere and his brother the World Serpent about to fall, this girl, his sister, is all he has left. He needs to save her now as she has saved him. The Fenris Wolf knows that the gods will track him. Once they discover that he has left the island, they will rage and rant and follow him to the edge of the world. He must find somewhere to hide. But all he knows is Asgard. And Odin rules here.

He slouches past the Well of Urd, not realising what

it is, when he hears voices call his name. He looks back over his shoulder, certain that the gods have found him. So soon, he thinks with dismay. But there is no one there.

'Fenris Wolf, look at us,' the voices say again.

'Who …?' He swivels slowly towards the well, the source of the sound.

Three figures appear in the waterfall. He can tell from their long hair and hourglass forms that they are female, wearing sleek silk dresses that cling to their frames. They come to a stop just at the point where the water foams into the well. Any detail in their faces is obscured behind the rushing water. They stand so still that, for a moment, the Fenris Wolf wonders if his eyes are playing tricks on him. Perhaps there were statues there all along and the sense that they'd moved had been a mirage caused by the flowing water. But when one of them speaks again, he knows that they are real.

'Greetings, Fenrir,' the three voices speak as one.

'What manner of creatures are you?' He does not have much knowledge of gods but has never seen any god like these.

'We are not gods,' they tell him, as if reading his mind. 'We are the Norns. We can read the waters of this well and can tell you of your present, of your future and of your fate.'

'Tell me then!' he cries frantically. 'Tell me all!'

The Norn on the left looks into the well first. She stares at the deep swirling waters then looks back at Fenrir.

'I am Verdandi,' she explains. 'And I can read the present. You have escaped from Odin's binds with the help of the sister in your arms. He has just discovered your disappearance and even now is in his great hall, calling the other gods together to find you.'

Fenrir takes a step back at this.

'I must go,' he says. 'Tell me all I need to know quickly. How can I hide, Verdandi?'

'My sister may have more to tell you about that, Fenrir,' says Verdandi, as the Norn on the right-hand side now looks into the well. She studies the black waters even closer before looking up.

'I am Skuld,' she tells him, 'and it is I who can read the future. The Well of Urd tells me that you should escape to Midgard, the land of man. The gods will not reach you there.'

'But how, oh great Skuld?'

'Over the next ridge is the bridge Bifrost. It will take you to a place called Dubh Linn. You will find safety there for a thousand years.'

'A thousand years? Tell me more.'

'Only I can tell you of your fate, Fenrir,' says the Norn in the centre. 'I am Urd. And this well is mine and mine alone.'

'Tell me then!' He is growing impatient now as Urd looks into the frothing well. Eventually, after what seems like an eternity, she looks back at him and speaks.

'I am the oldest Norn. And I have seen your fate. No man, nor god, nor beast should know all of his fate, but I will tell you what I can.'

'Hurry then!'

'Your fate is also hers.' A ghostly, dripping arm points out from the waterfall at his sister. 'She will be locked in sleep until he returns.'

'Who?' Fenrir asks. 'Who returns?'

'Your Wolf-father, Loki.'

Fenrir becomes excited at this. It means he will be reunited with his father one day. And his sister will awaken from her slumber.

'So we will continue what we began,' he says excitedly. 'I will make him an army as promised and we will conquer all the worlds.'

'No creature should know their fate,' the Norn Urd mutters.

'Wait!' He stops and looks at the woman in the water.

'Why do you help me?'

'No creature should know their fate,' she says cryptically again before receding into the stone wall. The others follow and are gone from his sight in seconds.

He does as they said and climbs over the nearest ridge. It would be a struggle for a normal man, especially carrying the girl. But Fenrir is no ordinary man and manages it easily.

A glimmering rainbow awaits him over the ridge, the shades of colour shifting continuously. He has heard of it. Bifrost – the bridge between the worlds. Taking one last look over his shoulder, he races towards the bridge, towards Dubh Linn and towards Loki.

Arthur opened his eyes to a blinding light glaring into his face. He shut them straight away once more, wincing at the throbbing pain at the back of his head. With his eyelids tightly shut, he collected his thoughts. The last thing he remembered was the argument with Ash and how he'd felt after telling her he was going back to Kerry. He could still see her disappointed face in his mind, the way she'd blushed as her eyes started to glisten with tears.

After that he'd … what? Television! He'd watched some TV. And then he'd heard a sound, some noise from the kitchen. He recalled investigating it and then … pain. Blackness. Nothing. And now that he was awake again, the back of his head throbbed dully. It had probably come up in a lump. He went to touch the tender area but found that he couldn't move his arms. He was sitting in a hard wooden chair and his hands were restrained behind his back. Even his ankles were clamped somehow to the legs of the chair.

Just stay calm, he told himself. Wherever you are, whatever's going on, just stay calm and you'll get out of it.

He tried again to open his eyes and, even though he managed it this time, he still had to squint against the brilliant glare in front of him. He could make out the source now: it was a high-wattage desk lamp on a bare wooden table, positioned to face him. He could even feel the heat radiating from the bulb. He gazed around him. Apart from the lamp, the room he was in was in total darkness. It seemed to be a large room – with a parquet floor, he noticed when he looked down. His ankles, he realised, were bound to the chair with plastic cable ties: easy to get on, impossible to get off without something to cut through them.

'Hello?' he called, his voice echoing off the walls of the empty room. 'Let me out!'

As his voice faded he struggled in the chair, hoping to loosen the bonds, but to no avail.

Suddenly, a door opened at the far end of the room. He couldn't make out much through the glare of the light, apart from some shadows entering. They walked across the room towards him. He judged from the footsteps creaking on the old floor that there were two of them.

'Who's there?' he asked as the footsteps approached. 'Who is it?'

'How are you feeling, Arthur?' The person leading the way tilted the light so he could finally see.

'*Ellie?*'

She nodded to him grimly, laying her hands on the tabletop. She was wearing jeans, a cardigan and the ever-present trench coat. Ex stepped up behind her and pulled a chair out for her to sit on. She sat and crossed her legs, keeping her eyes on Arthur the whole time.

'How's your head?' she asked.

'It could be better,' he said, easily ignoring the pain in light of this new revelation. Ash had been right about Ellie. He should have listened to her.

'I apologise for that,' she said. 'As I told you the day I

284

met you, Ex doesn't know his own strength.'

Her brother grunted an apology from somewhere in the darkness.

'First you knock me out, then you kidnap me! What on earth do you think you're doing?' demanded Arthur.

'I have some important questions for you, and you wouldn't answer them when I tried talking to you normally.'

'That doesn't give you the right to go around kidnapping people. Now let me go!' Arthur fumed.

'Not until you tell us the truth, Arthur.'

'The truth? About what?'

She leaned forward, her face serious, and said, 'Everything.'

'About everything? You mean the museum?'

'That,' she said, relaxing back in her chair again, 'and about what happened last October.'

October, Arthur wondered. What does she mean? Ellie can't possibly know about the World Serpent. Loki wiped the memories of that day from everyone in the world. Everyone except him, Ash and Max, of course.

'I don't know what you mean,' he bluffed.

'Sure you do,' she said. 'There are no records anywhere in the world for 22 October last year. I want to know why and I think you know something about it. I'm also quite curious about the Viking war-hammer in your bedroom.'

So she *had* been snooping in his room.

'Who are you, Ellie?' asked Arthur suspiciously. 'Really?'

'Really, I think you should tell her what she wants to know!' Ex blurted, taking a step forward, his hands balled into fists.

'It's all right, Ex,' Ellie said in a soothing tone. 'He has every right to ask.' She turned back to Arthur and said, 'I'll tell you if you answer me first.'

'How do I know I can trust you?' How do I know she's not working with Loki, he thought to himself, pretending to be my friend so she can report back to the god on what I'm doing.

'You don't know. Except that you said we were friends and friends are supposed to trust each other, Arthur.' Her lips turned up in a wry smile. 'You said so yourself.'

'Friends don't usually kidnap each other, though, Ellie.'

'Hmm,' she said, seeming to contemplate his point. 'That's true.' She looked over her shoulder to her brother. 'Ex, will you do the honours?'

With that, Ex whipped a switchblade out of his

pocket. It swished open and gleamed in the bright light. Then he advanced on Arthur menacingly.

'Don't!' Arthur cried, struggling in the chair and trying desperately to snap the cable ties. 'Stay away!' But Ex just kept coming. He put a strong hand on Arthur's shoulder to steady him. Arthur's heart was pounding in his chest and he could feel the blood rushing through his veins. Then suddenly he felt his hands falling free. He raised them to his face: the wrists were bruised from the tight cable ties but not badly. Ex went around to the front of Arthur's chair and slid the knife into each of the other ties securing his captive. He cut them off and they fell to the ground by Arthur's feet.

'This was our last resort,' Ellie said when Ex went to stand by her side once more. 'But I'm not going to force it out of you, so you're free to go. If you wish, that is. But I suspect that you're as curious about us as we are about you.'

Arthur weighed up his options. Was she lying? Was he actually free to go? And if not, could he outrun Ex if he needed to? Even if he could, would he find his way home to safety? How did Ellie know that something had happened in October and that he was connected to it? She was right about one thing. He *was* extremely curious about her. He looked at her for a moment, mulling over his options. If she worked for Loki, she probably knew the story anyway so it couldn't hurt to tell her. If not, perhaps she and Ex could help him in some way. Ellie was certainly smart and resourceful, and he could do with all the help against Loki he could get.

'I'll tell you,' he said. 'The whole truth.'

She nodded her thanks and shot a look at her brother. Ex reached down and took Arthur's right wrist in his strong grip.

'Hey!' Arthur tugged back, but to no avail.

'Don't worry, Arthur,' Ellie reassured him. 'My brother won't hurt you. But he can feel your pulse and if it speeds up he'll know you're lying.' Ex's grip loosened until it felt comfortable. 'We just want to be sure we can believe you. Please begin.'

Arthur took one last look at Ex's hand on his arm, then started talking.

Eirik had some latte foam on his chin. Stace reached across the table and wiped it off with a napkin. Just then her phone rang – which was lucky for her as the conversation had dried up a few minutes previously and she didn't know how to keep it going – and lucky for him as she'd accidentally wiped off some of his make-up. Stace answered the vibrating phone to Max's voice.

'*What?*' she yelled, causing heads to turn curiously in the coffee shop. 'Have you called Mom and Dad? And have you tried Ash?'

As she talked, Eirik spotted the make-up on the discarded napkin. Before Stace could react, he grabbed the evidence and ran out the door. He'd have to return to the Viking Experience to top up, he realised. Stace was too engrossed in the phone call to even care that he was gone so suddenly.

'Call the Gardaí, Max. I'll be there in a few minutes.'

He'd never told anyone the story of what had happened before. Ash and Max were the only people in the world who knew it and they'd lived through it with him. It felt strangely exhilarating to recount the whole tale from start to finish, as if a great weight was being lifted from his shoulders as he spoke. He told Ellie and Ex about Will and described that first trip underground where he found the pendant. He even showed it to them and they both touched it with no ill effects. He spoke at length about that fateful day, of how Loki had tricked them and how the World Serpent had been freed, then eventually destroyed with the help of the Viking army. He told them how Loki erased everyone's memory with mass hypnotism. The one thing he held back was the whereabouts of the Viking army now. That was one thing Loki couldn't know and until he was absolutely sure of Ellie and Ex, Arthur felt it was important to keep that to himself. Finally he filled them in on what had been happening since: the museum, his dreams, the lake, the hammer and his suspicions of Ice.

Ellie never took her eyes from his as he spoke, trans-fixed by the whole crazy story. And Ex never released his wrist. When he was done, Ellie exhaled loudly, staring into the distance.

'Ex?' she said to her brother.

'Above average but a steady pulse throughout,' said the boy, dropping Arthur's hand and stepping away finally. 'He was nervous telling the story but it was the truth.'

'I thought as much. His body language told me he wasn't lying too. Now, Arthur, I just need to get my head around a few things–'

'Hang on. It's your turn,' he interrupted.

'Of course,' she said, then stood up and started pacing the room. 'I'm the world's youngest paranormal detective.'

'The world's youngest what?'

'Paranormal detective. Our parents are both paranormal investigators too.'

'You said they were archaeologists.'

'Well, archaeology often comes into it. They travel the world digging for supernatural artefacts, studying their true powers. We travelled with them for a few years, looking for the lost city of Atlantis, examining the Bermuda Triangle and so on. It turns out I have a knack for investigating. I have a high aptitude for deciphering clues and a photographic memory – all vital attributes.'

'So your parents just allowed you to investigate me?' Arthur interrupted.

'Not quite,' she said. 'I was telling the truth when I told you that our parents are in Greece. They wouldn't like my investigating you, but I knew I was on to something the moment I saw you.'

'Why?'

'It all started last October. I must have seen your face on the TV, on a news report about the World Serpent. Then, a few weeks ago I saw you on TV again. Rescuing

Ash from the frozen lake. And I remembered that your face was very important, only I couldn't recall why. So I started looking over my records and notes, hoping to jog my memory. And wouldn't you know it – there was a gap: 22 October, the day nothing happened. That's when it clicked. A part of me just knew that you had something to do with the missing day. When Loki hypnotised everyone I forgot about you just like everyone else. But I still remembered your face. It stayed in my mind somewhere, locked away for safekeeping where Loki couldn't get at it. Photographic memory.' She tapped her temple to emphasise the point. 'Things go in but never go out. With my parents away, it was pretty easy to track you down and enrol in your school. Ex does a great impression of our dad on the phone. And we investigated you. I acted non-threatening, sweet, coy–'

'Coy? To be honest, Ellie, you were coming across more lonely than anything else,' Arthur interrupted.

Ellie turned away. 'That part … wasn't necessarily an act. Anyway, when you weren't very forthcoming with information, and after the events at the museum, I realised something serious was going on. So we had to take drastic measures – interrogating you here.'

'This is nuts,' Arthur said, mulling it over in his head.

'I know,' Ellie agreed. 'But, Arthur, there's more.'

She sat back down and faced him head-on.

'This wolf from your dreams – I've heard of it before,' she said. 'Our parents loved reading us all the old myths. The Fenris Wolf was Loki's second child. And he had one task before the gods trapped him – to make an army. An army of wolves for Loki to enslave the world.'

'But in my last dream Fenrir escaped,' Arthur said, 'and came to our world.'

He stood up suddenly.

'Where are you going?' asked Ellie.

'To get Ash, to work out how to stop Loki.'

'Let us help.'

'Now you want to help?' he said disbelievingly. 'After kidnapping me on top of lying to me from the moment we met, you expect me to trust you? To believe that you're some sort of eleven-year-old Sherlock Holmes? Do you have any idea how crazy you sound?'

'More crazy than a boy defeating a Viking god with the help of a band of dead Viking warriors?' she replied, angry now.

'I've had enough of this. I don't have time to stay here arguing with you. I'm leaving and you're not going to stop me.'

He pushed past them and headed towards the door. Ex stood back, letting him go. As Arthur reached the exit, a shrill beeping sounded behind him and Ellie gasped. In spite of himself, Arthur turned back to see her studying a computer tablet. She looked up at him and her expression made his blood run cold.

'What is it?' he asked.

'When we started investigating, I set up a system to alert me if anything strange happened at your or Ash's house.'

'And?'

She held up the tablet for him to see. 'The Gardaí have just been called to the Barry house.'

'What? I need to get there now!'

She stood up. 'Arthur, please let us help you.' As he hesitated, Ellie continued, 'You don't need to trust us completely, Arthur. Just let us get you home.'

He didn't have time to argue. He could almost hear the seconds ticking past. Something was wrong at Ash's house and he needed to go. Damn Ellie, he thought, for putting me in this position.

Arthur looked at the girl who'd just kidnapped him. 'I don't really have a choice, do I?'

Ash had lost all sense of time in the darkness of the hood. She knew that they were travelling by road and assumed that, by the amount of space she had to move around, they were in a van. But that was the extent of her knowledge. They could have been moving for less than ten minutes or longer than ten hours; it was impossible to judge. Finally, some hands dragged her to her feet and out of the vehicle. She could hear the lapping of water but was still surprised when they forced her into a wooden boat. She felt slightly nauseous as she was rowed across the mostly still water. When they reached their destination, someone lifted her out and slung her over their shoulder. After a few minutes of jostling she was dropped. She yelped in pain as her shoulder hit a hard floor. A hand pulled the bag off her head roughly. She'd become so accustomed to the dark that she had to shut her eyes against the light, even though the room she was in wasn't particularly bright. She waited until she heard her kidnappers' footsteps recede into the distance before attempting to open her eyes again.

Rapidly taking in her surroundings, she could see that she was in a gloomy room – all dusty stone floor and walls – with a single flaming torch flickering on the wall opposite her. She noted three walls: one was rounded, the other two were straight. There was a heavy-looking wooden door in one of the straight walls. The room was full of dusty clutter: tools and building materials were stacked in one corner and in the other were piles of Celtic artefacts, the bronze and gold reflecting the dancing light from the torch. Everything that had been stolen from the museum, she presumed.

Ash tried to stand up, but bumped her head on something just as she started to straighten her legs. She looked up to see a fine iron grille just above her head. Then she realised with growing awareness that there was a similar grille in front of her, on both sides and a solid wooden floor below.

She was in a cage. A dog cage, by the looks of it.

'No point in wasting your energy,' said a voice. She turned around for the first time to see that there was another cage directly behind hers. Its occupant was a grown man and the cage was far too small for him; he was crammed in so tightly that he had to bend his head at an awkward angle. He was sideways on to her so she could not seem him properly, but what she could see was that he had a long black beard and wavy hair, both greasy from lack of washing. He was wearing a pin-striped suit that was covered in dust, presumably from the cellar itself. The back of the jacket had been scorched away and she could see that the exposed skin was red and blistered. The back of his hair had been burned away too, and some of the skin on his neck. But despite all this, what drew Ash's attention most was the sight of the eyes that now turned to her. They were a golden colour that she had never seen before and they were sad and tired.

'Just rest, child,' he said in a deep voice. 'You'll only frustrate yourself trying to escape.'

'But–'

'Trust me. It's not worth the effort. I've tried everything already. What's your name anyway, child?'

'Ash. And I'm not a child.'

'It's nice to meet you, Ash. I meant no offence, calling you child, but when you're my age almost everyone could be considered a child. I'd shake your hand but I'm trapped in a dog cage.'

What a strange man, thought Ash. 'And what's your name? Who are you?'

'My name? My name is Fenrir.'

'Fenrir? Like the Fenris Wolf?'

'Hmm.' The man smiled to himself as if it was funny. 'It's a long time since anyone called me that.'

CHAPTER NINETEEN

'Where are we exactly?' Arthur asked as they strode down the dark corridor that led away from the room he'd been interrogated in. Ancient flocked wallpaper was peeling off the walls and the dusty floorboards creaked loudly underneath their feet. Ellie was walking along with him but Ex had run ahead.

'Just some abandoned house a ten-minute drive from yours,' she answered him. 'We live on the other side of the city so we had to find somewhere closer to bring you.'

'Is it true that your grandfather's taking care of you?' he asked. After Ellie's revelations, he'd have to rethink everything she'd told him previously.

'Yup, that's true,' she said. 'Like I said before, we're usually home schooled. If my parents go away, they just leave us loads of work to do and Granddad supervises.

But he's pretty blind and nearly deaf now. He sleeps so much that it's easy to sneak out without him knowing.'

'Hold on a second!' Arthur said as something popped into his mind. 'You said we were a ten-minute drive from mine. But I was unconscious. How did you get me here?'

'Ex drove.' She bounded down a set of stairs ahead of him.

'What! Isn't he a little young?'

'Of course,' she said cheerily, heading for the front door. 'But he doesn't look that young so no one ever questions it.'

Sure enough, Ex was waiting in a running car when they came out, seated behind the wheel with one elbow casually propped on the open window. It was a 1960s Volkswagen Beetle with a pastel-blue paint job. Ellie climbed into the passenger seat but Arthur hesitated.

'Come on!' she urged through the open door.

'Whose car is this?'

'It's our parents'. Granddad used to drive it too, but he doesn't use it much any more.'

'Are you sure it's safe?'

'Of course it is. Ex has been driving since he was old enough to reach the pedals.'

Arthur got into the back seat, trying to shake off the distinct feeling that he was taking his life in his hands.

The Beetle arrived outside Ash's house safely. Arthur hated to admit it but, even though Ex had driven quite fast, he was clearly a very competent driver. This night was proving to be full of surprises. And by the looks of Max's expression at the open front door, not all of them would be so pleasant.

'What's happened?' Arthur asked, getting out of the car. Inside, he could see Stace talking to a couple of Gardaí, while Max was sitting on the low porch wall.

'Someone took Ash, Arthur,' Max blurted out.

'What?' Ellie exclaimed as she and Ex came up behind Arthur.

'I was at a friend's house,' Max said. 'And when his brother dropped me home the door was open like this. I went into the living-room and …' He trailed off but Arthur didn't notice as he burst past him to get a look for himself. The glass coffee table had been smashed; shards were scattered all over the thick carpet. There'd clearly been some kind of struggle. Ice's collar lay by the door, but there was no sign of the dog herself.

'I knew I couldn't trust that dog,' Arthur muttered to Ellie, who was standing behind him.

'I tried calling her and couldn't get through,' Max told them. 'Stace told me to ring the Gardaí and Mom and Dad wouldn't answer because they were at the parent–teacher meeting. They're on their way now, though.'

'Let me see,' Ellie said, shoving past Arthur into the room.

'Hold on,' he said, glancing at the men taking Stace's statement. 'Shouldn't we let the Gardaí look first?'

'And risk them wrecking my crime scene? Not a chance.' Ellie took a large magnifying glass out of an inner coat pocket, dropped to her knees and started examining the broken shards under the magnification.

'Is it him, Arthur?' Max asked quietly so the Lavenders wouldn't hear. 'Is it Loki?'

Arthur bowed his head. 'It has to be. Who else would want to kidnap Ash? I'm sorry, Max.'

The boy nodded slowly, despair written all over his face.

'Weird …' Ellie murmured as she scrutinised the carpet around the broken table.

'What is?' Arthur asked, kneeling down next to her.

'There's some kind of dust here.' She didn't look up at him as she spoke, just concentrated on her find. 'See here – where the carpet fibres are flattened down?' Arthur could just about make out the indentation she meant. 'That's a footprint. And there in the footprint are all these little flakes of dust. Hold on …' She touched her fingertip off the carpet, pushing hard, and then magnified her finger under the glass. Motes of bright-red dust clung to her skin.

'I've never seen anything like this,' she said. 'Have you?'

Arthur closed his eyes, remembering the vivid colour, seeing the dust and then–

'Yes!' he exclaimed loudly. 'The lake! All around the lake where we found Ice the shore was covered in mud this colour.' He even remembered Ash telling him that the lake was the only place in the country the mud turned that rich shade of scarlet.

'Then let's go!' Ellie said, standing upright. 'That is, if you'll let us help.'

'You want to help?'

'Of course we do. We're part of this now. Granted, this is the first case I've ever taken on, but still. If we hadn't been holding you, you might have been here to help Ash, to stop her being taken.'

Arthur realised he needed all the help he could get, even if he was still wary of Ellie and Ex. If they were working for Loki he would deal with them when the time came. Right now he had no other way of reaching Mullingar quickly. He made an executive decision. 'All right, let's go. We need to move if we're going to save Ash.'

Without letting another second pass, he ran out the door towards the idling car.

'I'm coming too!' Max cried.

Arthur looked back at Stace inside the house. As she spoke to the Gardaí, she was pacing up and down nervously, describing her sister in minute detail.

'No, you're not,' he told Max.

'But–'

'You're staying here with Stace. She needs you now, and imagine how she'd feel if you suddenly disappeared too.'

'But–'

'We'll get Ash back, Max. I promise.'

Arthur hopped into the back seat, with Ex behind the wheel and Ellie next to him, and before Max could plead with another 'but', they sped off.

303

Ash and the man who called himself Fenrir didn't say much to each other for the next while. She thought about engaging him in conversation but didn't trust him. Even though he was locked up like she was, if he was one of Loki's children it would be crazy to put her faith in him. It could be some sort of trick – Loki could be trying to win her over. Although she wasn't sure what for.

At one stage she remembered her phone and reached into her pocket only to find that the raiders who'd kidnapped her had taken it. However, they had missed the little webcam she'd swiped from Arthur's room, which was jammed in the inner corner of her pocket. She pulled it out and was turning it in her hands, trying to work out a way to use it to her advantage, when the door to the room creaked open.

Two men walked in and positioned themselves on either side of the entrance. They stood stock-still with crossbows across their backs. They were followed into the room by a girl in a wheelchair. She looked about Ash's age, with her black hair tied back in a tight, constricting bun. She was wearing an old-fashioned dress with frilly lace edging and matching white tights. Her expression was blank, neither pleased nor upset. The wheelchair itself was constructed from wicker – long, thin interwoven strips of wood – while the wheels and handles were black iron. The man pushing the chair into the room was tall, with a head of platinum-blond hair and intelligent eyes. His beard was cropped close to his strong jawline and he wore a long black coat over a similarly old-fashioned suit. Ash gasped audibly as she recognised Loki, quickly hiding the camera in her pocket.

'Hello, Ash,' he said, pushing the girl in the wheelchair forward. 'It's simply wonderful to see you again. I do hope you're comfortable.' He chuckled to himself momentarily, then looked around the cellar. 'Where's Arthur?'

'He's, uh …' the girl in the wheelchair started, looking down as if ashamed.

'Where is he?' Loki demanded, his tone dangerously low.

'I'm not sure, Wolf-father. I'm sorry. We got Ash first but when we went to grab Arthur he was missing.'

'Missing?'

'He should have been in his house. He'd been there minutes beforehand.'

Loki stepped away from the girl, took a deep breath to calm himself, then turned back.

'OK,' he said. 'Well, I was hoping that we'd have both little troublemakers out of the way tonight, but no matter.

At least Ash will get to see my greatest triumph, and no one, not even Arthur, can escape what I have planned.' He laid a tender hand on the girl's head. 'You've done well, Drysi.'

Loki swivelled on one foot, then marched quickly out of the cellar. The girl started to turn the wheelchair by herself.

'Wait!' Ash pleaded, rattling her cage. 'Let me out. Please. You don't know what you've done!'

The girl turned slowly towards Ash. She tilted her head with faux pity. 'I know exactly what I've done, Ash,' she said and began to wheel towards the door.

'Please,' begged Ash once more. 'I don't know who you are, but please let me out.'

The girl stopped and without turning said, 'I'm hurt, Ash. After all we've been through together I thought you'd know me. After all, you did risk your life to save mine.'

'Ice?' gasped Ash. 'It can't be.'

The girl Drysi looked back over her shoulder, smirked sadistically and said simply, 'Woof, woof!'

They were on the road to Mullingar in minutes, with Ex manoeuvring skilfully between other vehicles but being cautious to avoid any Garda squad cars. They'd stopped the car at the edge of the estate, giving Arthur a chance to run into the shrubbery – where, frustratingly, there was no sign of Eirik anywhere – and into his house. Thankfully, Joe still wasn't home from the parent–teacher meeting so Arthur didn't have to explain himself as he raced upstairs, pulled out the hammer from under his bed and legged it back to the waiting car. The hammer was now next to him on the back seat.

In the front, Ellie had taken her iPad out of her coat pocket – she must have everything in there but the kitchen sink, Arthur thought when she pulled it out – and was currently flicking through high-resolution photographs on the touchscreen.

Arthur took a break from Garda-watch and leaned forward to look at the pictures on the tablet. An image of the hammer filled the screen. By the looks of it, Ellie had taken the photo on the floor of his bedroom. She flicked her finger across the iPad to display another image – this time a close-up of the rune lettering on the hammer itself.

'So you did take photos of my hammer,' Arthur said.

'Hmm?' she asked, lost in thought, not looking up.

'Oh, yeah. The hammer. Thor's hammer.'

'Thor's hammer?' he replied, surprised.

'Clearly.' She flicked to another view of the war-hammer. 'It's said that Thor died battling the World Serpent. And according to you, this happened right here in Dublin. With that and what you've told me about it, I think this must be Thor's hammer.'

'Wow,' Arthur muttered. It had never occurred to him before, but it seemed so obvious now Ellie had pointed it out.

'According to legend,' Ellie went on, 'it's a powerful weapon. When you need it most it will always come to you.'

'Like in the lake.'

'Exactly. And it probably only works for you.'

'Why?'

'I don't know. From what you told me it looks like it chose you. The same way the pendant chose you.' She looked him straight in the eye. Headlights from passing cars moved across her serious face. 'You're clearly very important, Arthur.'

He blushed and looked away. I can't be important, he told himself. I'm just a boy who fell into this whole thing by mistake. And dragged my friends down with me.

'Hmm …' he heard Ellie muse, once again staring at her screen.

'What is it?' he asked, looking back at the iPad. The screen was filled with a photograph of a Celtic chalice taken in the National Museum before the raiders had arrived.

'These are all the items Loki and his raiders stole from the museum,' she told him, flicking to an image of some Bronze Age jewellery. 'The full list was in the newspapers so I looked them all up. I'm trying to work out why he took them. What was so special that he needed it so badly?'

'You're right!' he exclaimed. 'Loki wouldn't have gone to all that effort for money. It's too normal, too human. He must have been after something in particular. Can I have a look?'

'Go wild,' she said and handed him the iPad. As they moved ever closer to Lough Faol and Ash, Arthur started to scan through the images himself, searching for a clue.

'You know Drysi?' Fenrir asked when the girl and the guards had left.

'I thought I did,' answered Ash, watching the closed door with awe. 'At least, I knew her differently. I think ... this is going to sound stupid, but she used to be my pet dog.'

'She wasn't a dog. She was a wolf.'

'That's what Arthur said.'

'Arthur?'

'He's a friend of mine. A good friend. I should have listened to him. How do you know her?'

'She's like a daughter to me.'

'A daughter?' She turned to look at the man in the next cage.

'I raised her as my own, anyway.' He smiled at Ash. 'Although she didn't turn out quite as I'd expected. I hope she didn't cause you any harm.'

Ash was taken aback by how unthreatening Fenrir seemed to be. 'Well, I almost drowned the first time we met and now I'm locked in a cage,' she said wryly. She had expected Loki's second child to be just like the first: a monstrous and wicked thing. But Fenrir simply looked tired.

'How did she turn out like this? So ...'

'Bad?' Fenrir prompted sadly. 'Evil? Wicked?'

'Well ...'

'She wasn't always this way. It's a long story.'

Ash waved her hand at the deserted cellar. 'By the looks of it, we have the time.'

'All right, then.' Fenrir shuffled around in the cage so that he was facing Ash. 'My story starts a thousand years ago,' he said. 'A millennium. It's a long time in anyone's understanding. I was just an ordinary wolf in Asgard, the land of the gods. Then one night Loki found me. I'd been wounded but he had charms to fix that. Using old and powerful magic, the speaking of runes, he harnessed his power into a moonstone – a piece of rock that fell from the moon itself. He called it Hati's Bite and its power would only come into effect when the moon was full in the sky. Then he cast a spell on me, turning me into something huge and powerful. I could speak and I could change from beast to man at will. He gave me my name and, in return for my new gifts, he tasked me with an important mission. I was to take Hati's Bite and make him an army. An army of wolves for him to control.

'But before I even began my great undertaking, the gods of Asgard found and captured me. I thought I would never be free. Then my sister – the third of Loki's children – helped me escape. But, in doing so, she fell into an impossibly deep sleep. Taking her with me, I fled to the world of man, to Dubh Linn. Dublin.

'As soon as we arrived, I saw a young Celtic girl playing in a field. She was alone, running through the high grass on a warm summer's night, laughing and talking to herself. The moon was full that night also. So I hid my sister safely in the high grass and called to the girl ...' He looked up at the ceiling, wistfully recalling the encounter.

'She wasn't frightened of me at all. I remember thinking that she was the perfect candidate to start the army. I had her lie down, basking in the white glow of the moon. And then I spoke the rune magic that Loki had taught me, holding Hati's Bite over her. And she changed then. She had my powers also, including the ability to transform into a wolf. She was the first. And I loved her as a daughter. Drysi. We left that place together – the father and his new daughter – taking my sister. I told Drysi about Loki and his plan, and together we worked to fulfil his charge.

'As the years passed and I waited for Loki's return, I changed more men, women and children into wolves. The army grew and grew. I had hundreds at one stage – all powerful beasts that could not age. An army ready for world domination, just waiting for our leader to appear. But he never did.

'At first I was contemptuous of the humans around me, seeing them as weak, pitiful creatures that I could devour in an instant. I thought I was doing those I changed a great service, making them strong, powerful, immortal. But living amongst humans for such a long time forced me to change my mind. I saw their compassion, their kindness and the love they held for each other, and I slowly began to respect them.

'Eventually I stopped changing people. It seemed pointless. I became convinced that Loki would never return. Centuries passed and we learned to live peacefully alongside man, always careful to hide our true nature. Humans didn't know what we were and we tried never to reveal it to anyone. Unfortunately, some of the wolves weren't as restrained as I would have liked and occasionally attacked the humans. That's when the legends of the beast you humans call a werewolf started to spread.

'Like this nation of Ireland herself, everything changed in 1916. Many of us were living in Dublin at the time – we had to move towns regularly over the years before our lack of aging aroused suspicion. Drysi had never given up hope of Loki's return and one day, while walking through the narrow streets next to the River Liffey, she sensed him. She could hear him crying out in agonising pain under the city itself, the sound echoing up through some dried-up drains. It was so faint that no human would have heard it. She told me all about it but I wouldn't believe her. Or, rather, I didn't want to believe her. I forbade her to go near the place again.

'Easter rolled around a couple of weeks later and the Irish started to fight for their independence. I'd fought in many battles against many foes over the centuries and wanted to fight alongside the Irish again. I believed strongly in their cause. They'd been my constant companions for a thousand years and I yearned to see them achieve their freedom. But as I prepared to go and join the fighting, I noticed that Drysi was missing. I knew instantly where she'd gone.

'I ran to the place where she said she'd sensed Loki. In the distance, I could hear that the fighting had begun; gunshots and mortar bombs were going off all over the city centre. As I got closer, I could sense him too. I could even feel his anguish coursing through my veins. I knew, then, that she was right. Loki was bound under the city, somewhere nearby.

'I saw Drysi in an abandoned shop. I saw her walking past a window, her eyes fixed on the floor. She was concentrating so much that she didn't see that the fighting had spread. She didn't hear the Irish rebels on the second floor of the building. Some of the British forces … they …'

He closed his eyes, squeezing a pair of tears out that rolled down his cheeks.

'I don't know what happened. I don't know if it was a bomb or a shell or a grenade. Or if the foundations were weak to begin with. But either way, the ceiling fell in on Drysi before I could reach her.'

He stopped and turned away. Ash could picture the scene. She'd read about the Easter Rising in history the year before and had seen photographs of the aftermath of the fighting.

'I raced into the wrecked building,' Fenrir continued. 'It was difficult to see. There was smoke and dust and rubble everywhere. I could hear the rebels calling out in pain but I didn't have the time to save them. I just had to get Drysi out of there. I found her under some debris. I could tell from the awkward angle her back was twisted at that her spine was broken. Her legs were limp and lifeless. I knew instantly she would never walk again. But her heart was still beating and she was alive.

'And then I heard him again. Louder this time. Screaming in anguish under the wreckage of the building. Under the ground. Loki.

'I brought Drysi to safety and made a decision that day. A couple of weeks later, I gathered all the remaining wolf-people. I knew that if Loki ever escaped, then he'd expect his army to help him conquer the earth. But I no longer believed in his cause and realised that I had to get my people away from there, hide them somewhere he wouldn't find us. So we moved here. And we've lived here since then, underground, hiding.' He broke off for a moment and sighed. 'As you can see, my plan failed. I should have known you can't hide from a god.' His voice trailed off and for a moment there was silence.

'What is this place anyway?' Ash asked, looking around her, unwilling to let Fenrir lapse into despairing silence again.

'It's an old round tower. The Vikings killed all the monks who lived around it centuries ago, so we took it for ourselves. We had strength and a bit of magic on our side so we were able to turn it into what we needed. We built great halls – similar to the ones the gods have in Asgard – right underneath the tower. We lived here for a couple of centuries before moving to the city. When we needed a hideaway, this island was the perfect spot to return to. We even put in our own additions as we needed them, like a clockwork elevator for Drysi. This is our home. We've lived here largely peacefully since 1916 – that is, until Loki returned.

'Of course, many of the wolves were angry about having to live in hiding and I think secretly half of them had been hoping Loki would return. The others, like me, hoped he wouldn't. Drysi always prayed most fervently for his homecoming. She believed that the god would heal her of her disability. And then, a few weeks ago, Loki finally found us. He was furious when he saw the small size of the army waiting for him and had me thrown in here. Since then, I've only heard whisperings of what has happened. Drysi has been helping him. And half the wolves have pledged their allegiance to him. The others are held captive in other cells. That's it. That's all I know.'

※※※※※

Arthur was focused on one photo on Ellie's iPad. No matter how many images he viewed, he kept coming back to this one, studying it intently.

'What do you make of this?' he asked Ellie, showing her the photograph.

'It's just a green overcoat,' she said. 'Nothing special. What about it?'

'When Loki escaped the museum, he was wearing this coat.'

'So?'

'When I saw him first he was wearing a long black coat, so he must have changed into this one afterwards.'

He zoomed out of the image and all the pictures in the album appeared as thumbnails. 'Everything they took was old. Really old and priceless. Except that coat. According to the notes with the image, it was part of a small exhibition of items from 1916.'

'So you're wondering why he'd take a coat that wasn't worth anything?'

'Exactly. What's so special about this coat? Maybe this is what he was really after. It's the one really odd item in the list.'

'But why would he steal the rest of the stuff?'

'I don't know. To throw us and the Gardaí off the scent, maybe?'

'That's possible, I guess,' she agreed. 'Think about your dreams. Is there anything you remember from them that might help?'

'I don't know,' he said, looking back down at the iPad screen. 'I just keep thinking about the wolf and the ...'

'The what?'

Arthur was staring at the reflection of the full moon in the iPad glass. 'The moon,' he finished.

Suddenly Arthur gasped and pounded on the screen of the iPad, choosing the image of the coat again and zooming right in. The pixels blurred, then sharpened every time he went in closer.

'I don't believe it,' he uttered.

'What is it, Arthur?' Now all eyes in the car were on him. Even Ex was watching him through the rear-view mirror.

'In my dream, Loki had a piece of glass – a chunk of the moon itself. He needed it to transform the Fenris Wolf.'

'And?' Ellie urged him.

He pointed to the top button on the coat. It was a smooth and round chunk of glass.

'That's it,' he said grimly. 'That button there.'

'Which means that–'

Arthur interrupted, finishing her sentence for her. 'That was what Loki was looking for in the museum. All the rest of the stuff they took *was* just to throw us off the scent. At some point the Fenris Wolf and Hati's Bite must have been separated. But now Loki has it again and with it he can complete his army.'

Ash leaned back in her cage, letting it all sink in. Then she thought of something.

'If Loki wants to make a bigger army, he'll need Hati's Bite, right? And you have it?'

'Well, yes and no,' he said.

'What do you mean?'

'He will need Hati's Bite. But I don't have it. From the day he gave it to me, I carried it with me everywhere. When we lived in Dublin I used it as a button on my greatcoat. Hidden in plain sight so that none of the other wolves would recognise it. There were quite a few that I never trusted. But that day when Drysi was trapped, I was so crazed with grief that when the coat caught in the rubble, hindering her rescue, I tore it off and flung it away from me. It was only when I got home that I realised what I had done. I should have gone back to get it there and then, but all my attention was focused on my daughter. When I finally did go back after the fighting had ended there was no trace of the coat or of Hati's Bite. I have no idea where it is now.'

'Could Loki have found it?'

'I hope not,' Fenrir said fearfully, 'for all of our sakes.'

CHAPTER TWENTY

'So that's it,' Arthur said, admiring the round tower on the island. The great moon reflected in the still waters – now long defrosted. A few minutes beforehand, they'd arrived at the lake and parked the car in a lay-by off the main road, then warily crossed over the train track and onto the red shore. The first thing that had caught Arthur's attention was the flames burning in some of the narrow tower windows. There was no doubt that this was the place they were looking for.

'What's it?' asked Ellie, who was standing next to him along with Ex, taking in their new surroundings.

'The tower.'

'What tower?'

'That tower!' He pointed at the island.

Both Ellie and Ex looked confused. She raised an

eyebrow at Arthur. 'There's nothing out there except an overgrown island.'

'You mean ...' Arthur stuttered, 'you don't see it?' He looked again. There it was. Right in the middle of the island. His eyes couldn't be lying to him, could they?

Just then, he had an epiphany. He pulled the pendant over his head, and as soon as he did the tower and the torches disappeared from sight. He smiled to himself then handed the pendant to Ellie. Still confused, she took it and put it on. Her eyes nearly popped out of her head when the tower blinked into her own vision.

'Yup,' she said, 'that's definitely where we should be headed. But how will we get out there?'

They searched around the shore, looking for a way across. Finally, Ex emerged from some nearby trees carrying a row boat over his shoulders. It covered the top half of his body and made it look like his head had been transformed into the little vessel. They watched silently as he dropped the boat into the water with a splash. He smiled at them, pleased with his find.

'Look,' Arthur said before they all boarded, 'we'll go across quietly. We just need to find Ash and get her out. Any sign of danger and we're back on the boat. Got it?'

'Of course,' Ellie said cheerfully. 'Let's go.' They

climbed into the boat, with Ex getting in last and sitting at the stern. He took an oar in each strong hand. Arthur could tell from the way the paint had worn off the hull that it was an old vessel, but it felt sturdy enough as the boy started to paddle across the quiet lake. None of them said anything as they made their way towards the island. The atmosphere in the boat was tense. They didn't know what awaited them on the island, but they did know that it was down to them to save Ash. No one else would have believed them. Arthur watched the silent tower and clutched the pendant on his chest.

As they got closer, he could make out the beams of some flashlights glinting through the thick bushes that surrounded the edge of the island. He quietly attracted the others' attention, simultaneously putting his finger to his lips, and pointed at the shafts of light. They nodded in understanding and sat absolutely still, breathing as quietly as possible so as not to alert the people on the island to their presence. Ex rowed the boat carefully, breaking the surface as gently as he could so there would be no splashing sounds.

The closer they got to the island, the more each of them wanted to turn back. It was more than intuition: there was a building sense of dread with each stroke of the oar.

'Do you feel that?' Arthur said quietly after a while. The others silently nodded at him, both of them pale in the blue moonlight.

'We should go back,' murmured Ellie, staring at the island. 'We could just get in the car and drive home, snuggle into bed and shut our eyes.'

Ex's rowing had slowed down now and Arthur looked from one Lavender to the other. They were right, of course. It would be so much nicer to go home. He could see Joe and they could go to the cinema. They could even bring Max and–

'Ash,' Arthur whispered. He shook his head defiantly. 'No. We have to go on. The island is trying to push us away.'

'You're right …' Ellie shook the cobwebs from her own mind. 'It must be an enchantment of some kind. Anyone else would just turn back, but we can't.'

'We have to keep going,' added Ex with a grunt.

He rowed in a wide arc around the island, taking care to avoid the area where they'd spotted the lights, and eventually ran the boat aground. They found themselves in some thick and wiry bushes on the south shore of the island. They helped each other out of the boat and Ex hid the vessel securely in the dense bush. Arthur grabbed his

– or rather Thor's – hammer and looked up at the tower. Both Lavender siblings were also staring up at it.

'We can see the tower now,' Ellie whispered to him. 'Whatever magic is hiding it must be disabled once you're on the island.'

'That feeling of dread is gone, too,' Arthur murmured. 'You were right. It must have been some sort of intruder trap.'

He peered over the top of the scrub at the tower. It soared straight up to the sky, reaching for the moon, and was much larger than it had appeared from the shore – at least two hundred feet high. The torches flickered in the narrow windows peppering the sides of the building. These had been used in olden times for spotting approaching enemies. He hoped no one had spotted their approach.

Ex tapped Arthur on the shoulder and pointed to a door at the base of the tower. It was the only entrance that they could see: a small archway with a simple wooden door. There was a single man standing guard in front of it. Just then a pair of wolves padded from around the far side of the tower, their ears pricked, their eyes watchful. Arthur watched in awe as the man nodded a greeting at the canines and the wolves nodded back. When they were gone, Arthur crouched back down and faced the others.

'Those were wolves, right?' The Lavenders simply nodded, as surprised as he was. 'I was hoping there'd only be one wolf. Did you see the way they nodded back to the guard? Who knows how many there are!'

'What now?' Ellie whispered urgently, as the pair of wolves circled around again on another slow circuit of the island.

Arthur waited until they were gone to answer. 'I'm thinking this is too dangerous for us. We need to go back and get proper help.'

'Arthur,' Ellie said seriously, 'Ash is probably in there.'

'I know. Don't you think I know that! But what can we do?'

They fell silent, weighing up their limited options. Ex just kept watching as the wolves came around for a third time. His eyes never left the beasts, narrowing. His fingers felt along the ground, running over different sized rocks. Finally, he picked up a stone about the size of a tennis ball.

Ellie noticed the movement. 'Ex?'

Arthur turned, too, just as the wolves prowled out of sight again.

Ex swung back his closed fist. Arthur tried to stop him. But it was too late.

He launched the rock at the tower and Arthur felt like he was watching everything in slow motion.

The stone hit off the high wall, several metres over the sentry's head. The guard stepped away from the tower and turned to look at where he'd heard the knock.

Ex was on his feet with an oar gripped between two strong hands.

'Ex, no,' hissed Ellie, but he ignored her and ran towards the tower.

The sentry heard the boy's footsteps crunch on the gravelly terrain and turned, but Ex was already swinging the oar. It connected with the guard's head with a painful-sounding thunk and the man collapsed to the ground. Ex turned and beckoned urgently to them. Ellie was on her feet almost immediately.

'Wait!' Arthur reached out and grabbed her arm.

'No, Arthur,' she said snatching her arm away. 'We need to move now. Before the wolves come back.'

'It's dangero–'

'I know it is. But no matter what we do now the wolves are going to find us. Ex has left us with no choice.'

'We could go back to the boat–'

Before he could go any further she cut him off. 'I won't leave my brother.' With that she ran towards Ex, reaching into her trench coat pocket as she went.

For a second Arthur stayed in the undergrowth, conflicted. The situation was spiralling quickly out of his control. Why would Ex do something so rash? Could he really trust the Lavenders or was this a ploy to force him into entering the tower? Yet he was sure that their surprise had been genuine when he had pointed out the tower to them and Ellie had seemed as taken aback by Ex's actions as he had been. Whatever he was going to do, he would have to do it now, as the wolves would be back any minute. He still needed to find Ash and that tower was their only lead.

He made up his mind, grabbed his hammer and sprinted to join the others. The guard was out cold. Ex was tightening some cable ties from Ellie's pocket around the man's wrists and ankles, while she planted a strip of black tape across his mouth. Arthur put his ear to the tower door. All he could hear was the beating of his own heart. He pushed the door open a fraction and peered inside. The coast appeared to be clear. Together the three of them dragged the unconscious guard into the tower. Then they quickly shut the door and leaned the sentry against it as an added barrier to anyone trying to come in from outside.

After taking a minute to catch their breaths, they looked around them for the first time. There wasn't much to see. It was just a round, bare room, with a low wooden ceiling and a couple of lit torches in iron brackets on the walls. There was a cast-iron spiral staircase running up the centre of the tower. From its design and construction, Arthur guessed it was a twentieth-century addition to the medieval tower. The steps ran around a wide central iron column, complete with a door in one side. Arthur tried the door only to find it locked. He looked at the stairs leading both up and down into more gloom.

'What now?' asked Ellie, still panting.

'We don't have much time,' said Arthur. 'Those wolves will notice the guard missing and will raise the alarm if they can't find him.' He turned on Ex. 'What were you thinking pulling a stunt like that?'

Ex stared stolidly back. 'We needed to get inside. Here we are.'

Arthur reached for the pendant around his neck. He could feel a distinct warmth from it, but when he pulled it out it was only glowing faintly. He took this as a good sign – it meant he wasn't in immediate danger. He looked back at the staircase. He was overwhelmed by a strong feeling that he should go up the stairs. He didn't understand why but he sensed that it was important.

'OK, I need to go upstairs. You two wait here.'

'But–'

'Please, Ellie. You've both done enough. Just wait here, keep an eye on him,' he indicated the still unconscious guard, 'and yell if anything happens.'

As Arthur cautiously disappeared upwards, Ellie turned to her brother.

'I don't care what Arthur says,' she whispered, 'someone should check downstairs.'

'Naturally,' he said.

And with that, they descended quietly to the basement of the tower.

Ash was trying to think of an escape plan, turning the little webcam over and over in her hand to help her concentrate. Fenrir was hunched silently in his own cage, quiet again now that he had finished his story. Ash could hardly believe all that he'd told her. Part of her wondered if it had been a lie, one of Loki's tricks maybe. But she doubted it. It all seemed so plausible. And Fenrir really had given her the impression that he was genuine. After all, he'd saved Drysi from that collapsing building. And he'd saved his—

'Wait a second,' she said out loud, thinking as she spoke. 'You said you brought your sister here. Do you mean Loki's third child?'

'Yes, of course.'

'Well, where is she now?'

'Ah,' he said. 'I've hidden her.'

Suddenly there was a noise outside the door, which sounded suspiciously like a cry of triumph.

The door swung open to reveal Drysi. She wheeled forward into the room and right up to Fenrir. Ash put the webcam back in her pocket before the gloating girl spotted it.

'I knew it!' Drysi crowed. 'I knew she was alive all along! And I knew you'd eventually confess, Father!'

'Drysi,' Fenrir muttered weakly, 'please don't.'

'Don't what? Tell the Wolf-father? I'm sorry, but that's *exactly* what I'm about to do!'

And with that, she pivoted her chair and wheeled back out the entrance. But she failed to close the door properly and Ash had a clear view of what she did next. Drysi went straight for a central column in the adjoining room. Steps wound up around the iron pillar, but she ignored them and opened a warped wooden door in the column. She wheeled herself inside, shut the door behind her and, shortly afterwards, Ash heard the sound of grinding, ancient clockwork gears. That must be the elevator Fenrir mentioned, she realised, as the sound receded upwards.

Ellie and Ex were surprised to find that the stairwell went down further than they'd thought at first glance. Ellie had been counting in her head as they went and reached seventy-eight by the time they arrived at the first lower level. This was essentially just a small landing with a single door in the stone wall. She put her ear to it and listened to the chattering from within. By the sounds of murmuring and general hustle and bustle, there was a large crowd inside. She really hoped Ash wasn't in there. She shook her head at Ex and the pair of them continued further down the stairs. Eventually the steps came to an end. The room they found themselves in was similar to the one they'd started in – a circular stone area with torches flickering on the walls. There were two aged wooden doors here, though, opposite each other – and one of them was open.

Torchlight flickered through the door, but it wasn't bright enough to make out anything beyond, apart from shifting shadows. Ellie started to move towards the door but Ex held her back. He shook his head, held up his hand to tell her to wait, then proceeded cautiously himself. She followed, keeping two steps behind her older brother at all times and peering around his bulky frame.

'Ex?' she heard a startled voice say from the room. Ash!

'We found you!' Ellie exclaimed, racing into the gloomy little cellar then stopping in surprise when she saw two cages. Ash was on the ground, sitting in what looked like an old dog cage. There was a hefty man hunched in another cage next to her, gazing up with surprise at the Lavender siblings. She looked at Ash's face, expecting to see gratitude, but was met with pure distaste.

'I knew you two couldn't be trusted as soon as I saw you snooping round Arthur's room. Don't tell me – you're another of Loki's little pets, aren't you,' sneered Ash, turning her head away.

'Not at all,' Ellie said coldly, stung by Ash's accusation. 'We're here with Arthur. We came to rescue you.'

'Arthur's here?' Ash turned back. She felt like whooping but kept her composure. 'And the Viking army too, right?'

'Uh no … no army this time.'

'What? So it's just you?'

'Just us.'

'You mean to tell me that you two and Arthur came here to rescue me from an army of crazed wolves led by a Viking god and you didn't think it would be sensible to bring along some help?' cried Ash, her voice rising in pitch with every word.

'Look, I don't think you're in any position to object to your rescue party. Arthur was frantic with worry and thought the sooner we could get to you the better.'

Ash drew in a breath, secretly pleased that Arthur was so worried about her and aware that now was probably not the time to be quibbling over their rescue plan.

'OK, so where is he?'

'He went upstairs while we came down.'

Ash's momentary euphoria vanished. 'He shouldn't have gone off on his own like that. If Loki finds him … get me out of here, quickly!'

'We will if you tell us where the keys are.'

'They're in the room opposite,' the man in the cage said. 'We keep them in a cabinet there. But be warned,

334

there are other prisoners in there as well and there may be guards.'

'OK, thanks.' Ellie turned and took a step towards the door, then suddenly turned back to the man. 'Wait, what do you mean *we*? Who are you?'

'It's a long story, but we don't have time to go into it now.' Ash rattled the bars of her cage impatiently. 'Just hurry!'

Ellie left the cellar and crept across to the opposite door, with Ex on her heels. She put her ear to the door and could hear faint whispers but nothing too loud. Shaking, she swung the door open slightly and peered in. This was a much larger room, except it was long as opposed to round. It was full of tired, frightened-looking people all locked up in one big cage. Their eyes widened with apprehension when they saw her, but when they realised she was not one of Loki's servants they started calling to her, pleading for help. There was nothing else in the room apart from a small wooden cabinet fixed to one wall. She opened the doors, but in her haste used too much force and managed to yank the cabinet off the wall completely. About thirty keys – all identical – clattered onto the floor. Frantically, she flung them all back into the cabinet and carried the whole lot back to the little cellar.

'I had an accident,' she said apologetically, holding up the cabinet for all to see. When Ash saw the mess of keys she groaned loudly and turned to the man.

'Any idea which is the right one?'

'Haven't a clue, sorry.'

'All hope may not be lost,' Ellie said, falling to her knees by Ash's cage. 'Ex, will you go and listen by the stairs to make sure no one is coming?' As he did as she asked, Ellie pulled two hair clips from her bob. Using her teeth, she straightened them out and pushed them both into the padlock on the cage at right angles to each other.

'You can pick a lock?' Ash asked.

'I hope so.' Ellie's face was tight with concentration. 'I've never actually tried it before, but I've read enough about how it's done. This looks like a pin and tumbler lock so if I just push this in here …' she twisted the upper clip slightly, 'and raise the tension with this one …' she jammed the other clip in tighter, 'and I think I'm at the last pin *now* …' With one final screw, the lock clicked open.

She stood up triumphantly, lifted the lid and helped Ash step out of the cage.

'Do you think you can open the other cage?' asked Ash.

'No problem!' Ellie crouched down by the man's cage

and jammed the clips in his padlock. 'It was actually much easier than I expected. I should be able to do this one qui–' There was a loud snap as one of the clips broke off inside the lock mechanism.

'Can you get it out?' Ash leaned over her shoulder to get a view of the lock.

Ellie's fingernails clawed at the broken clip but she couldn't get a good grip on it. She looked up at Ash.

'I'm sorry …'

'You go!' said the man in the cage. 'Quickly, children. Get to safety.'

'No,' Ash said resolutely. 'We're not leaving you here.' She turned to the pile of tools. 'If we can just find a pliers or something to pull the clip out …' Suddenly, Ex pushed past her and picked something up from the pile. He took a firm stance by the cage and started swinging at the broken lock with the hammer he'd just picked up. The clang of metal on metal rang around the room. On the first blow, the lock bounced around but held fast. With the second, there was a distinct *kerrunking* sound. The third strike sent the lock clattering to the stone floor.

Fenrir stood up inside the cage to his full height, knocking the lid to the ground. Even though he was clearly malnourished, with black bags under his eyes and ripped clothes, he was still a sight to behold. He took the hammer from Ex and stepped out of his prison.

'Thank you,' he said to them. 'But you need to go. Get out.'

'But what about the others? We can't just leave them there,' Ash said, heading towards the door.

'I'll free the others.' He held up the hammer to demonstrate how he intended to do so. 'Just get out! This place is too dangerous for you, especially tonight.'

They didn't need to be told again and the three of them bounded back up the steps together. They had just reached the next landing when they heard footsteps clattering down the stairs towards them.

They must have found the guard, Ellie thought.

The footsteps were just above them and approaching rapidly. They looked around desperately for somewhere to hide. Suddenly, Ash bounded forward a couple of steps.

'In here!' she whispered. Before Ellie or Ex could stop her, Ash was pulling open the door on the midway landing, only to find herself facing a room full of men, women and wolves. One by one they stopped what they were doing and turned to look at Ash, who was taking in the room before her. It was more of a hall really, she thought – circular-shaped, with time-ravaged tapestries hanging from every wall. Fires roared in hearths encircling the room and candlelight shone brightly from a priceless-looking chandelier. There were long banquet tables set for dinner but no one was dining right now. Some of the people were tending to their weapons: tightening or replacing old strings in their crossbows, oiling the workings, and sharpening daggers and swords on whetstones. Others were working out: weight-lifting or doing push-ups or giving some punching bags a seeing to. The rest were poring over huge maps of Ireland and the world. Ash took a wild guess at what they were doing: planning a war. Or, more correctly, they *had been* planning a war. Now they were all staring right at her.

✳✳✳✳✳

Unaware of what was going on below, Arthur made his way slowly up the tower. He was halfway up when he heard the sound of rattling and rusty gears grinding. It started below him, then rose slowly past him and upwards, coming from inside the central column. He guessed that it was an elevator of some sort, but hadn't a clue who could be inside.

He proceeded up the stairs, taking care to keep his

footsteps light on the metal. Every time he passed one of the narrow windows, he looked out at the island. He could see a few watchmen on the ground below, walking the perimeter with their flashlights, along with even more wolves. This is a mistake, he thought. But it was too late to turn back now, and that strange sense persisted that he needed to continue upwards.

As he got closer to the apex of the tower, the spiral stairwell narrowed slightly. He could hear voices now, echoing back to him from the floor above. He made sure to be extra quiet, holding his breath as he neared the top.

He could see moonlight glinting off the metal of the top steps and he could feel a cold breeze now. He crawled up the last few steps on his hands and knees. Keeping low, he raised his head slowly over the top of the stairwell and peered onto the top floor.

He'd reached the open roof of the tower. A low stone parapet encircled the floor, above which was nothing but the wide, black sky. A single iron pole rose out of the floor. It was about ten feet high. The top of the pole was carved into a crooked claw, with fingers made for gripping. A series of small steps spiralled around the pole, also of iron. He could see a girl in a wheelchair whom he didn't recognise and a man he did – Loki. He was wearing the green coat that he'd stolen from the museum over a pin-striped suit and he was in the middle of saying something to the girl. Arthur kept low in the stairwell so they wouldn't see him.

'–cellent help, Drysi, just excellent, but time is moving fast.'

'Thank you, Wolf-father. Now please listen to me. I have important info–'

Loki turned on the girl. He was smiling sweetly although Arthur could read the anger in his beetroot face. 'Don't interrupt me when I'm pontificating, Drysi dearest. It's rude.' He moved away from her and continued speaking.

'We're so close now,' he said looking at the moon, the white disc reflecting in his eyes. 'Mere minutes until the moon's power is at its strongest. Midnight. The witching hour, when the real mischief begins.'

Suddenly, Loki burst into flames. His arms were outstretched and he just stood there calmly on fire. Arthur could see his grinning features through the blaze. The coat burned off and fell around him in snowflake-like ashes. He was now burning so brightly and so quickly that Arthur and the girl had to squint against the glare. As suddenly as it had come, the fire was gone. The god's skin was a horrid, deep red, with creamy pus bursting out of blisters and sores all over. His clothes had been almost totally destroyed and his hair was all gone, leaving a scarred, bare skull behind. Loki, who seemed utterly unperturbed by his changed appearance, cracked his neck as if he'd just woken up. For a second his green aura enveloped him. When it was gone, he was whole again, as good as new and wearing a fashionable grey suit. He bent down to the ashes of the coat at his feet and picked up all that was left: a single glass-like stone. Hati's Bite. He rubbed it between his fingers before climbing up the little steps and placing it in the claw at the top of the pole.

'When I first got here,' he said, descending again, 'I was almost overwhelmed by my disappointment in your father, Drysi. He hadn't created an army like I'd ordered. But then I saw the great possibilities. This tower – so close to the centre of Ireland – and home to all of you for almost a century ...' He paced around the floor, gazing over the edge of the parapet. 'This tower would prove so useful. Then you told me where Hati's Bite had ended up.'

'Father thought he was so clever, hiding it as a button on his coat.' The girl Drysi smiled. 'But I always recognised it for what it was.'

'That's because you take after me, Drysi. You're wily. You will get your reward.'

'Truly? Because I hate being cooped up here, Wolf-father,' she said, looking around her at the sky, at the tower. 'All those years, I hated being cut off from the outside world in this tower. My only glimpse of civilisation was when some of the hunting wolves would bring back newspapers and books for me.'

'But those newspapers led you to the coat, my dear.'

'True. I remember the day, last year, when I read about a new exhibition in the museum and I recognised a certain coat.'

'And getting it was so easy. So much fun, too! Which brings us here, to this point. So very close to the moon being ready and to me enacting my greatest plan.'

'And what's that, Wolf-father?' Drysi asked.

Without warning, Loki spun around, walked to the stairwell and looked straight down at Arthur. 'Why, hello, Arthur. Did you really think I wouldn't sense you there wearing that blasted pendant? I'm so glad you're here, though, just in time to see my triumph.' Loki turned back to the girl and continued in the same even tone. 'In answer to your question, Drysi, I intend to do what Fenrir failed to. I'll create the perfect army.'

Chapter Twenty-One

'Won't you join us, Arthur?' invited Loki, gesturing towards Drysi.

'I'm fine where I am, thanks,' Arthur said from the stairwell.

'I really must insist, Arthur. The pendant lets you stop me from inflicting any serious harm on you, but I'm sure I could manage to drag you up here without too much trouble.'

He's right, Arthur realised, and he reluctantly climbed the last few steps, stepping onto the rooftop. So high up the wind was biting, cutting through his clothing and slicing into his flesh. The girl in the wheelchair glared at him with deep distaste. Her eyes burned with a hatred he had never experienced before.

'Have you met Drysi?' Loki waved a hand lazily in the

girl's direction. 'She's my granddaughter. I'm very proud of her.'

'Oh, he's met me, Wolf-father,' Drysi told him, keeping her eyes fixed on Arthur, 'except he knows me as Ice.'

'Of course!' Loki exclaimed, smirking. 'How could I forget? Drysi tells me you were suspicious of her from very early on, Arthur.'

Arthur simply glared at the girl in response. He'd known that Ice couldn't be trusted and wished now that he'd done more to force Ash to believe him, whatever it took.

'So you took advantage of Ash?' he demanded of the girl. 'Even after she tried to save you?'

'I wasn't in any danger to begin with. I'd never have broken the ice as a cub. You two were supposed to fall in and drown. But even when that didn't go according to plan, there was a light at the end of the tunnel. That *stupid* girl insisted on taking me home with her,' Drysi spat. 'It gave me the chance to spy on you and look for another opportunity to get rid of you both. Although having to play nicey-nice around her simpleton family made me want to throw up.'

'Why did you do all this?' Arthur asked her angrily.

She looked down at her legs. 'I'm broken,' she said,

'and now that he has the moonstone back the Wolf-father will fix me.'

'Exactly,' Loki said. But as he said this Arthur noticed that the god avoided looking at the girl and he suspected that Loki was lying.

'You've never been very susceptible to my tricks, Arthur,' Loki was saying, clearly eager to change the subject. 'And you always seem to miraculously turn up just when I don't want you to. I wonder why that is …' He looked over the edge of the roof, staring into the middle distance as if contemplating the answer to this question. 'No matter,' he broke off suddenly, his lips turned up in a grin again. 'Because this will be my final great trick. And this time, even you can't stop me.'

'You thought that last time and I still managed to defeat you, Loki. I'll do whatever it takes.' Arthur tightened his grip on the hammer by his side.

'Whatever it takes?' Loki looked at Drysi. 'Whatever it takes, he says! Arthur, please, don't say stuff like that or you'll have me in hysterics. Besides, there is nothing you can do to stop me this time. The moon is rapidly approaching midnight, I have Hati's Bite and I'm in the perfect position to use it.'

'What do you mean?'

346

The Father of Lies walked over to the tall pole. 'Hati's Bite magnifies the power of the moon and can be used to turn a human into a wolf. But up here, it's so much more. We're high up, close to the centre of the country – a place brimming with ancient magic. From here the spell won't just affect one person: it will spread over all the land. Every man, woman and child in Ireland will transform into a wolf. And they'll all bow to me, their Wolf-father. I'll have an army of millions to enslave humanity. When I created Fenrir I gave him humanity, and when he created the rest of his pitiful army, they also retained a sense of their humanity – I realise now that this was a mistake. It let them think, make up their own minds about what they were doing. But ...' he spread out his arms, palms up, 'I am humble and never let it be said I don't learn from my mistakes, so I won't let it happen this time. My new warriors will be mindless beasts. The only thing they'll understand is to obey me.

'You're lucky, you know, Arthur, to be here to witness the dawn of this new world. It will be something to tell the grandkids about – no, wait, you won't be able to because you'll be a mindless wolf too.' Loki grinned at Arthur. 'This is going to be such fun. Especially for me. In fact, only for me. It's not an easy process, the transformation,

347

and you'll be in quite a lot of pain.'

He paused and looked upwards at the night sky. 'The moon will be in alignment in just over a min–' Loki was cut off suddenly by a commotion from below. Shouts, growls and feet pounding across the stony ground were creating a cacophony of sound.

Loki glanced over the edge of the tower, then turned to the girl, exasperated. 'Drysi, be a sweetheart and see what's going on down there, will you? And tell them to *shut up*: they're ruining my big moment.'

'Of course, Wolf-father.' Drysi wheeled towards the central column.

'And, Drysi?'

'Yes, Wolf-father?'

'Please relieve our guest of that monstrosity in his hand. I'd do it, but I'm sure I'd get quite a shock.'

Arthur tensed and held the hammer close to his chest with both hands. There was no way he was letting the girl take it from him. He knew it was his one really effective weapon against Loki. He turned to run, but as he did something knocked painfully into the back of his legs – Drysi's wheelchair. He went hurtling forward and landed agonisingly on his knees, but managed to keep a tight grip on the hammer. Then the girl reached forward and in one impossibly swift and strong motion, she wrapped her fingers around the handle and yanked the hammer from his grip. Arthur just couldn't keep hold of it. With a twisted smile, she opened the little door to the elevator and left them alone.

Ash, Ellie and Ex took a step backwards from the watching army and bumped into the guards who'd been racing down the stairs and were now right behind them. There were four of them – all men, all huge and all terrifying.

'Well, well, well,' said the guard in front. 'It looks like we've got some intruders.'

'That's the little blighter there,' grunted another guard, rubbing the side of his head tenderly and pointing at Ex. 'That's the one who knocked me out.'

The first guard looked at the injured one with a wicked smirk. 'Fancy repaying the favour?'

'Yeah,' he said, grinning back, 'I might just do that.' The four guards advanced slowly on Ash, Ellie and Ex, forcing them backwards into the room. Ash turned around to see that all the occupants who had been poring over maps and plans were now on their feet and also advancing. They were completely surrounded, with no escape.

'You can't do this!' Ash shouted to them over the sound of grinding gears. The majority of the approaching raiders laughed – a sound that was part chuckle, part bark. The distant ticking noise of the gears grew louder until it ceased suddenly with a metallic clang. The guards at the door turned to the sound, then moved aside to let Drysi through. Arthur's hammer was clenched in one fist.

'So, you managed to get out of your cage, Ash. You didn't make it very far, though, did you?' she sneered, moving forward. The raiders stopped as they watched her, waiting for her command, no doubt. Ash was speechless. If Drysi had Arthur's hammer, then it could only mean one thing. He was in serious trouble.

'What should we do with them?' one of the guards at the door asked Drysi.

She considered the question for a minute, keeping her eyes fixed on the three children.

'I don't think Wolf-father Loki would miss three young cubs in his army, do you?' She looked around at the waiting crowd. 'Kill them.'

Without any more hesitation, every man, woman

and wolf turned towards Ash, Ellie and Ex. The children looked around desperately for a way out, but found none. It seemed like their time was well and truly up. Ellie smiled sadly to Ex as he took her hand. Ash simply shut her eyes, waiting for the inevitable.

As she anticipated the first stroke of pain, she felt a rush of air by her face and heard an ear-bursting roar. She opened her eyes to see a wolf as tall as her standing next to them, baring his razor-sharp teeth at the others. His fur was pure black, bristling along his back as the muscles in his shoulders rippled, tensed for a fight. Half of the fur and flesh on his back was completely burnt away, showing only blistered redness in patches. It's Fenrir, Ash realised.

'Do not harm these children!' the wolf spoke in a voice that boomed around the entire room. 'Let them and us go peacefully and no one will be hurt.'

All eyes turned to Drysi. She had hers fixed firmly on the great wolf.

Finally, she spoke to her troops. 'Why are you all still standing there? I gave you an order. Kill them. All of them.'

At that, all hell broke loose as several things happened at once.

Loki's supporters charged, some of them transforming mid-run into wolves, their clothes falling in heaps on the floor.

Even more wolves stormed through the door and started attacking whoever they could reach. They must be the freed prisoners, Ash guessed.

Before any of Loki's army could reach the children, Fenrir snapped his massive jaws at them, throwing wolves and men aside as if they were rag dolls.

And all the while, Ash, Ellie and Ex were rooted to the spot. They were too frightened to move and, even if they had found the courage, they wouldn't have known where to run.

'Under the table!' Fenrir roared at them, mid-battle. His gruff voice managed to break them out of their stupor. Ash saw the table he meant – a long bench full of maps behind a row of men cranking crossbows. '*Run!*' Fenrir urged them again, bounding forward himself to bowl over a couple of the men, giving the children the space to dive under the wooden table.

Ash shut her eyes again. The noise was terrible: barks and growls, yells and moans of pain, the whishing sound of arrows cutting through the air, the thud as they hit flesh. Somebody or something landed heavily on the tabletop. The force of it shook the very floor underneath them and caused a deep split to crack halfway through the dense timber of the tabletop.

A wolf appeared at one end of the table, thrusting its bared teeth towards them with spittle foaming around the edges of its mouth as it snarled. The three of them shuffled backwards, trembling as they went. The wolf was too large to fit into the tight space but that didn't stop it from trying. It kept pushing forward, lifting the bench with its back muscles as it squeezed towards them.

The animal snapped at Ash. Its teeth were stained yellow and brown, with spots of fresh blood dripping down its snout, and she could smell its rancid, hot breath. It had almost reached her. Close. Too close. She pushed back further into Ellie and Ex and, while doing so, kicked out with her right foot. Her heel collided with the beast's snout, sending its head reeling sideways. But the beast just shook away the pain and kept coming for her.

'Come on!' Ex yelled over the noise of the battle. He had crawled out the far end of the table, was on his feet and was helping Ellie to hers. Ash could see now that most of the fighting had moved to the opposite end of the hall, giving them a mostly free run to the exit. She didn't particularly cherish the idea of running headfirst into a battle zone, but it was definitely preferable to being eaten alive by this wolf.

The Lavenders were already running by the time Ash struggled to her feet. She sprinted after them, her legs and chest aching with the effort. But all her focus was on the door. The door, the door, the door. The way out. To safety. To Arthur. Just get out, Ash, get out.

The others were through the door already, on the spiral steps, taking them two at a time.

Suddenly something knocked into the back of Ash's calves and her legs collapsed underneath her, sending her toppling backwards.

Ellie and Ex were gone. In their race to be free, they hadn't noticed she wasn't behind them any more.

Ash prepared to hit the ground hard, but instead she landed on somebody's lap. A pair of strong arms coiled around her and she twisted her head to see that it was Drysi who had knocked into her and was now holding her in an iron grip. She could feel Arthur's hammer between them on the girl's lap.

'Let me go!' Ash struggled to get away, but the wolf-girl was far too strong.

'You're going nowhere, Ash!'

Suddenly, two hands were on top of Drysi's, pulling

her arms away from Ash. Both girls looked back to see Fenrir standing there – back in his human form and naked save for a pair of too-small black trousers that had been discarded in the battle. 'Drysi my daughter, let Ash go,' he said calmly. 'She has done you no harm.'

'Perhaps not,' she replied, trying to resist his grasp. 'But you did, though. When you wouldn't let me help Wolf-father Loki all those years ago. You made me this way: damaged.'

'Don't do this, Drysi,' he said. 'The best part of you, of me, of all of us, is our humanity. Don't forget that.'

Drysi stopped struggling and slumped in her chair, as if in defeat. Fenrir let go of her arms. Suddenly her face contorted with rage and hatred and she shoved Ash to the ground. As Fenrir helped Ash to her feet, Drysi wheeled herself out the door and into the elevator. They could hear the crank of the gears as it started to rise. Ash looked up at Fenrir.

'Thank y–'

'Get out, Ash, now,' Fenrir cut her off urgently. 'Run!'

She did as she was told, finally racing through the exit. Ellie and Ex met her on the steps, both of them running back down to see where she'd gotten to. As they turned and bounded back up the stairs, Ellie took one last, fleeting glance into the hall. The battle was still raging, but the numbers seemed to be decreasing. Many of the fighters seemed to be escaping through tunnels hidden behind tapestries, while others were lying dead and broken on the ground. And Fenrir, in the middle of it all, was picking something up from the floor – it looked like a small black ball – which he placed in his pocket.

Arthur had never felt more alone than he did at that moment, standing on the top of the tower with Loki. He could hear the fighting and carnage from deep below as the wind swirled around him, chilling him to the bone. And he was here, with the god of mischief, about to face who knew what. He could run and try to get help, but what was the point? Time was running out and he had to stop Loki while he could. Or at least try. He stared at Hati's Bite glinting in the moonlight, desperately trying to come up with a plan.

'Come along, Arthur,' said Loki. 'You've got the best seat in the house for the show of a lifetime. You may as well enjoy it.'

Arthur spun towards him. 'You can't do this!' he

bellowed, then, grabbing his pendant from his neck and holding it in his outstretched hand, ran at him. Loki sidestepped and thrust out a hand, knocking Arthur backwards with a lazy swing that had all the force of a god behind it. Arthur hurtled across the roof on his back then slammed into the perimeter wall, where he lay dazed. The pendant, which had flown from his hand on impact, skittered across the roof. Loki was now standing between Arthur and his last defence against the god and his magic.

'*I* can do what I want, Arthur,' sneered Loki, spittle flying out of his lips as he enunciated every syllable. 'After tonight, the people of this world will truly know fear. They'll truly know pain. And destruction. And mayhem. And death. And mischief. Midgard will be mine. And then I'll take Asgard.' He threw back his head and screamed, 'And then I'll destroy it all!'

Suddenly, a tiny flicker of green lightning shot out of Hati's Bite behind him. Loki turned and watched, seemingly transfixed, as another bolt burst forth; it lit his face with a sickly green colour momentarily and the corners of his lips turned upwards.

'It's starting,' he murmured, mostly to himself. He swivelled back towards Arthur, his arms raised triumphantly.

'It's starting!' He dashed to the edge of the roof and surveyed the land before him, roaring, 'My future army! Relish the pain. Drink it up!'

He started chanting something then, at the top of his voice, that Arthur couldn't understand. It was an ancient and dead language he'd only heard in his dreams of Asgard. The same three words over and over.

'*Fenreiq bjorlam disldo, fenreiq bjorlam disldo, fenreiq bjorlam disldo!*'

Besides producing the miniature bolts of lightning, Hati's Bite was starting to glow with the same mysterious green aura that always surrounded Arthur's pendant and preceded one of Loki's transformations. More and more lightning exploded and the green glow started to flow from the stone, spreading slowly outwards, carrying its evil curse with it.

Arthur was the closest and so the first to experience the transformation as the light washed over him. It began with an unusual sensation of every fibre in his body constricting and tightening. It wasn't exactly painful but was hugely uncomfortable. If that was all that had been involved, it would have been bad enough. But as that sensation quickly wore off, Arthur discovered it was all about to get a whole lot worse.

His jaw started to expand forward, jutting outwards into a canine snout. He wanted to shriek with the agony, but couldn't get a sound out of his transforming mouth. He put his hand to his face and felt fur sprouting all over his cheeks as the muzzle continued to grow. Then his legs shortened, folding in on themselves with joints realigning to create a wolf's hindquarters. He could hear bones snap and scratch off each other inside the limbs as they continued to reshape.

The pain was unbearable.

This had to be a dream.

The whole thing.

There was no way this could be happening to him now.

There was no way that he could withstand this level of pain. A sound that was part howl, part scream tore from his chest and filled the night.

If only I would black out, he thought as the joints in his arms loosened then tensed and restructured themselves. If I black out, I won't notice the pain. I'll wake up a wolf and it'll all be over. Anything to stop this agony.

And then his back broke.

359

Ash was the first to start convulsing.

Drysi was watching as the green light swept out and down from the tower. After escaping from the battle, she hadn't been sure what to do next, but knew it was best not to bring the hammer back to the roof. So, when she saw Ash, Ellie and Ex emerge from the tower moments later, she smiled to herself. She watched with glee as Ash told the Lavenders to get to safety while she turned to re-enter the tower and help Arthur. But before she could take a single step the green light enveloped her and she fell to the ground in agony, followed seconds later by Ellie and Ex.

Meanwhile, Fenrir had run upstairs. He glanced through the open door to see the children on the ground and he knew instantly what was happening. The green light was spreading ever outward, floating eerily across the still water. Upwards, he thought. I have to go upwards.

Arthur was hunched over on the roof when a man he didn't know stepped up next to him. The bones in his spine were rearranging themselves, crunching and grinding as they did. Somehow, as if through a distant fog of pain, he noticed that the light didn't seem to be affecting the man.

Loki turned when he heard the scuffle of feet on stone.

'So,' he said, 'the Prodigal Son returns. Come to join me finally, Fenrir?'

'I've come to stop you!' With one great stride, he was next to the pole and reaching a hand out to Hati's Bite. But before he could touch it, Loki was beside him, standing on the steps. The god picked up the topless man by the neck and slammed him back down on the cold stone floor, shaking the very foundations of the tower.

'You're too late, Fenrir,' Loki said, walking around the man who was struggling to his feet, clutching his side. 'You should have destroyed the Bite centuries ago, when you had your little change of heart. But you didn't because deep down you were afraid of what I'd do to you when I came back if you did. Pitiful!'

Fenrir suddenly pounced, wrestling Loki to the ground. He held his arms and pinned his legs.

'You don't control me any more, Loki,' he said, with a notable shake in his voice.

'Is that right, Fenrir? Then why are you so scared of me?'

With a burst of green light, Loki was gone, replaced

by a golden wolf. The sudden transformation sent Fenrir rolling across the rooftop.

'I'm scared because I have something to live for,' Fenrir answered him, back on his feet, hunched over and ready for another onslaught.

'What?' spat the Loki-wolf. 'The daughter who hates you?'

'Drysi is one thing,' said Fenrir. As he spoke, they started to circle each other in tight arcs around the pole, keeping their eyes fixed on each other. 'She's good, deep inside. I know she is. And I think I can reach her. But there's more.'

'What else is there? I'm curious.'

'My humanity.'

'Ha!'

Arthur was rapidly losing consciousness. He could no longer concentrate on the proceedings; he couldn't even feel the pain. His sole thoughts were of the hunt, of meat, of flesh, of obeying Wolf-father Loki.

'You gave me all this power to make you an army,' Fenrir continued, 'but you never thought of how powerful being human could be.'

'A human is a flea compared to a wolf or a god,' Loki said with bile. 'Transform now and fight me.'

'No, Loki. I won't. I won't transform any more.'

'Pathetic! You always were a useless wolf!'

And, with that, the Loki-wolf attacked.

The spell was spreading. Drysi could feel it, she could sense the dark magic radiating out from the tower. It was over the water now and soon it would reach land, transforming every last wretched human. She was looking down at the contorted bodies of Ash, Ellie and Ex, gloating, when the hammer stirred in her lap. At first it gave the smallest of tremors, so slight that she wasn't even certain she'd felt it. But as she took a tighter grip on the handle, she could feel it start to pull upwards. Eventually, it was struggling in her fingers as the entire hammer strained to get free, to fly upwards. But Drysi's fingers were strong and weren't letting go any time soon.

Ash, like Arthur, was forgetting who she was. Her mind was erasing memories and emotions at a frightening speed. The hunt, she thought. Obey Wolf-father Loki, she thought.

The hammer, another part of her shouted. The hammer! Her eyes had been fully transformed into a wolf's and the vision through them was beyond anything she had ever experienced – crystal clear, everything sharply defined, the darkness suddenly bright. And through those eyes, she could see the hammer clearly from where she was. The girl – Drysi? Wasn't that her name? – was clutching the hammer. Holding it back from … from someone. But who? And why?

Move, a part of Ash screamed. Move, move, move.

She didn't know why, but she did. She crawled along the rough ground, a twisted mutation halfway between being a girl and becoming a wolf. Fur grew in patches along her skin, her face was long, her hands were part paws. But she kept moving, stumbling forward on uncertain and new legs.

Drysi never saw her coming. She was too focused on holding onto the hammer.

Ash reached her and sank her sparkling new fangs into the girl's right shin. Of course Drysi didn't feel it, but as Ash jerked backwards, unbalancing the girl, the sudden surprise loosened her fingers. The hammer soared skywards before Drysi could catch it again.

The boy on the roof could no longer remember his name. He could no longer remember his age, his family, his friends or where he grew up. He could no longer remember that he was a boy. If he could think at all, he would think of himself as a wolf being born. And he was midway there – a terrible halfling, part boy and part wolf.

Suddenly something landed on the roof next to him. It looked heavy, with a long handle and an iron head. He knew what it was; he knew it was important. He just couldn't remember why.

And then–

A hammer! It was the hammer. It was his hammer. His: Arthur Quinn's. *That's who I am: I'm Arthur Quinn.* He reached out an arm only to find that grey fur had budded from the back of what had once been his hand and what had once been fingers had transformed into claws. He scratched the sharp claws against the handle of the hammer, struggling to get any sort of grip. But without a thumb or any proper fingers, it was impossible. Yet even the touch of it against his skin helped him clear his head.

A snarl rumbled out of his throat as he looked up at the other occupants of the rooftop. The golden wolf Loki was on top of the man Fenrir. His jaws were snapping at the man's jugular, but Fenrir had grasped handfuls of fur on either side of the Loki-wolf's face and was just managing to hold him off. However, Arthur could tell from the strain on his face that the man wouldn't last much longer. The green light was still spreading from Hati's Bite, the ceremony well underway.

I can't let this happen, Arthur told himself determinedly as more spasms ricocheted across his spine. I have to ignore the pain. I have to concentrate. If I can just get my right hand back …

He shut his eyes, trying to block out the agony. He stopped listening to Loki or the cries of pain from Fenrir and the people on the ground below. He looked into the darkness inside his eyelids, focusing on the blackness, willing his body to return to human form. Then he thought of his dad. He could picture Joe making a Saturday-morning fry-up for the two of them. He imagined Ash coming to join them for breakfast, with Max and Ellie and even Ex. In his mind's eye, he saw them all sitting around the kitchen table, chomping down on sausages and runny eggs and buttery toast. And then someone else joined them. His mother. She sat across the table from him, simply smiling.

Arthur smiled back, then opened his eyes and looked at the ribbon around his right wrist. The attached paw had changed back into a hand and the fingers were already coiled around the handle of the hammer. The whole right side of his body – from the shoulder to the foot – had become human again. Now he really was half boy, half wolf.

He struggled up onto his one good leg; his left one was still canine and awkward to stand on, but it allowed him just enough balance to hobble across the roof towards the pole. Out of the corner of his eye, Fenrir saw the boy moving. With a renewed burst of strength, he reached up and grabbed the back of Loki-wolf's head and pulled as hard as he could, snapping its neck back painfully. Loki screeched in agony and transformed back to his godly form. As he did, Arthur reached the pole and the steps that led up to it. This part would be more difficult.

Another wave of pain hit him as the magic fought to continue his transformation. He drew a deep breath trying to summon the strength he needed to climb the steps. As he did he became aware that he was standing on something cold and metallic. He moved his foot and looked down. Just below him lay his pendant, glowing fiercely. He bent awkwardly and picked it up, looping it around his neck. Instantly he felt stronger, the pain of the transformation reduced, and he faced the steps with a new resolve.

Loki still had Fenrir pinned underneath him.

'Transform!' he commanded. 'Transform, damn you!'

Suddenly flames burst from each hand. He pushed them into either side of Fenrir's face and the man screamed in agony. But despite the inferno encasing his face, he shook his head over and back, refusing to become a wolf.

Arthur slowly hopped up the first step on his human leg, keeping his shaky balance by placing his wolf arm on the steps ahead. There were five steps to the top and he stumbled on the second one, his paw slipping.

Loki turned when he heard the claws scratch against the iron. His eyes widened when he saw Arthur on his feet, the hammer in his firm grip, balancing himself on the pole with his left front paw.

'*No!*' screamed the god, starting to race forward. But before he had got more than a step, two arms wrapped around his legs and he toppled to the roof. Fenrir grunted, using the last of his strength to hold on to the struggling god while Arthur hopped up to the next step and the next, without even taking the time to keep his balance.

But he was weak and Loki was now truly enraged. The god writhed in Fenrir's grip and blasted him in the face with a burst of green fire that threw Fenrir backwards, finally beaten.

Loki turned back just in time to see Arthur, on the final step, raise the hammer above his head and bring it down hard, right on top of Hati's Bite. The whole thing exploded instantly, sending Arthur, the god and the man flying from the tower.

Chapter Twenty-Two

Arthur's right eye fluttered open to the sight of a gleaming white hospital bedroom. He was lying in a bed with a couple of too-soft pillows propping up his head and a blanket tucked tightly around him and under the hard mattress. He couldn't see out of his left eye and when he touched the bandage that had been wrapped around his face there, he found that the left side was numb. There was no other bed in the room and Joe was the only other occupant, staring out the window at an overcast day. From the view outside, Arthur guessed that they were on a high storey.

'Dad?' Arthur croaked. His throat was sore and dry.

Joe whipped around quickly, then ran to his son's bedside. He took his hand and brushed some stray hairs out of his face. His eyes were puffy and bloodshot; either he hadn't gotten much sleep or he'd been crying.

'You're awake!'

'What …?' He couldn't manage to finish the question and broke into a fit of raspy coughing.

'Shh, son. Here, have some water.' He offered a small flask with a straw to Arthur, who sipped gratefully.

'What happened?' he asked – his voice still gravelly – when he was done drinking.

'You were in an accident last night,' Joe said, sitting down on the hard-backed chair next to the bed. 'Your right shoulder was dislocated, but it's been set, and your right leg was sprained. And …'

Arthur's fingers instinctively went to the bandaged side of his face again. Although it was still mostly numb, he could feel the faint echo of pain there.

'There was some shrapnel,' Joe went on. 'It scratched your cornea. Your left eye is … uh …'

He turned away, struggling to finish.

'Blind,' Arthur completed the sentence for him.

'Yes. Yes, Arthur. I'm so sorry.'

'It's OK,' Arthur said. He didn't know how to feel or what to think. Part of him was devastated, the part that wanted to scream and cry and mourn his loss. The other part of him was just relieved he hadn't turned into a wolf

371

– that part of him figured that an eye was a small price to pay.

'Are my friends OK?'

'They're fine, they're outside. I'll just get them.' Joe went to leave but stopped before going through the door. 'I'm really happy you're safe,' he said, then went out.

'Me too,' muttered Arthur.

A moment later, Ash, Max, Ellie and Ex entered the room. They rushed to the side of his bed.

'How are you feeling?' Ash inquired.

'I've lost the sight in my left eye.'

'We heard.'

'Apart from that, I'm not too bad. So what happened?'

'There was an explosion,' Ellie told him. 'You destroyed Hati's Bite.'

'I remember that,' he said. 'What happened next?'

'We saw you, Loki and Fenrir thrown from the tower by the force of the blast,' said Ash. 'Even unconscious you still somehow kept a grip on the hammer as you fell and it lowered you safely to the ground like it did when it saved us from the lake. By the time we had finished checking on you, all of Loki's army and Fenrir's supporters had disappeared. When the tower blew up, most of them must have escaped down the hidden tunnels under the island. After we had a quick look around, we got you in the boat. You were unconscious and your eye was scratched but not bleeding too heavily. Your arm was, well … anyway, we knew we had to get back to Dublin as quickly as possible.'

'Luckily Ex is a great driver,' interrupted Ellie.

'Right,' Ash continued. 'We brought you straight here to the hospital.'

'And my hammer?'

'I've got it safely hidden in my room right now.'

'But what did you tell everyone?'

'We pretended that I came home to find Ice missing again,' said Ash. 'I was so frantic looking around for her that I accidentally knocked over the coffee table, which smashed, and left the door open when I ran out. Eventually I discovered some older kids had taken her to that abandoned house nearby.'

'The one we interrogated you in,' Ellie interrupted again.

'I said that these kids had been hassling us lately,' Ash went on. 'Anyway, you guys followed me and we watched as the bullies set up all these fireworks and bottle-bombs to throw at Ice. But you went in and saved her, Arthur – just as one of the bottle-bombs went off, injuring you.'

'But what about Ice? I mean if she's Drysi ...' he trailed off.

'Easy. We told everyone that the fireworks spooked Ice so much that she ran off when you got blown backwards and we haven't been able to find her since.'

'And they bought all that?'

'They did when they saw the fireworks that Ex set off after we dropped you here!' Ellie said proudly.

'Mom and Dad could see why Stace and Max called the Gardaí. They were still pretty paranoid after the museum raid,' Ash added.

'What else happened?' Arthur asked.

'Well, we called in a private tip to Detective Morrissey to tell him where he'd find the stolen artefacts.'

'In a magically hidden tower?'

'It's not hidden any more,' Ellie told him. 'The spell must have been destroyed when the wolves fled. Guess they'll be wondering where it came from, but at least they can't trace it back to us.'

'So what happened to Loki? And Drysi? And Fenrir?'

'They all went missing after the explosion,' Ash explained. 'We don't know where Loki or Fenrir fell and we couldn't find any trace of either of them afterwards, so we have to assume they both survived and got away.'

'And after I destroyed the Bite, we turned back into humans,' Arthur said.

'That's right,' said Ellie. 'And luckily, the magic never actually reached past the lake.'

'What about the other wolves? Did they turn back?'

'No. We saw some of them running off through the forest. Destroying the Bite had no effect on them, probably because they'd been turned fully already.'

'So they're all still out there?'

'But scattered and injured, with no one to lead them.'

'We won, though?' Arthur said.

'We won.'

'And Ash learned some interesting facts,' Ellie said.

Ash told him all she'd heard from Fenrir: how he'd turned good over the years and how Loki's third child was still hidden somewhere out there.

Ash finished, 'If we find Fenrir, he could tell us where to find the girl.'

'How will we ever manage that?' Arthur sank down further into the mattress, feeling disillusioned.

'We actually might have a lead on that,' said Ellie. 'Ash lost her webcam during the battle in the hall and I saw Fenrir put it in his pocket. I'm not sure if we can use it, but it might help.'

'It's GPS-enabled so if he still has it we should be able to track him down,' added Ash.

'What do we know about this third child?'

'The legends don't say much about her,' said Ellie. 'She's known as Hell's Keeper and it's said that she has the power to unleash Hell on Earth.'

'Great!' Arthur said sarcastically. 'Will we ever be done saving the world?' The five of them laughed – grateful that they were still alive but also to mask the fear they all felt.

※※※※※

The doctors kept Arthur in the hospital for the next week. They ran various tests on him, changed his bandages every couple of hours and gave him strong painkillers to numb the throbbing ache in his left eye. He only got to see the damage for himself on the third day. A nurse was changing his bandages and he asked for a mirror. Reluctant at first, she eventually conceded and got him a small one. A deep red scar ran across his left eye, starting just over his eyebrow and ending on his cheekbone. It was held together with black thread and was starting to scab already. A black line traced straight across the eyeball itself, slicing through the cornea. The rest of the eye was red, flushed with blood.

'All right,' he said steadily to the nurse, 'thank you.' But as she rewrapped the bandages, he kept picturing the injured eye in his head.

⚒⚒⚒⚒

Life became more normal over the next few days. The others went to school daily and visited him often. They spoke little of their recent adventure; it frightened them to think about what had almost happened to their friends and families. When they did talk about it – usually in hushed tones – they spoke of Ash's attempts to track down Fenrir with the GPS-cam. The camera was a lost blip, constantly 'out of range'. They tried to work out other ways to find Fenrir, but to no avail.

Arthur was released on a bright Wednesday morning. The cut across his face was mostly healed by then, although a slick line of scar tissue was forming in its place. His attending doctor had fitted him with a leather eye-patch. He'd told Arthur that he could look at getting a glass prosthetic, but that he would have to wear the patch for a few months until the tenderness was gone. Arthur spent the next few days resting at home and trying not to scratch at the forming scabs. Then, on the following Sunday, Arthur and Joe Quinn moved out.

Arthur hadn't mentioned the exact day to Ash and the others. Ever since his mother had passed, he'd never been a fan of goodbyes. But of course Ash had realised what was happening as soon as Joe started packing the car. Joe was trying to squeeze the last boxes in and Arthur was sitting in the passenger seat, his iPod earphones plugged in, when his friends walked up the drive. He popped the earphones out and let them hang around his neck, the music still playing faintly.

'I'll just be a minute,' Joe said to him, eyeing his son's approaching pals. 'I have to check we haven't forgotten anything inside.' He left them to it.

Arthur shut his good eye momentarily, then climbed out of the car to face them: Ash, Max, Ellie and Ex.

'Hi guys,' he said.

'So this is it,' stated Ash, looking at the stuffed car.

'Yup. I didn't know how to …'

'It's OK,' said Ellie, taking a step towards him. She embraced him in a firm hug. 'I haven't known you that long, but I'll still miss you.'

'Me too.'

When he pulled away, he found that Ex was standing

in front of him. He clasped Arthur's right hand and shook it surprisingly tenderly.

'You're not too bad, Arthur,' he muttered.

Arthur leant closer so the others wouldn't hear. 'Take care of them, Ex,' he whispered.

Max ran forward and wrapped his arms around Arthur's waist, squeezing tightly. 'I'll miss you, Arthur! And I'll miss our games!'

'Well, you just keep practising, Max. And when I come to visit you'd better be great!'

'I will,' he promised, stepping back from Arthur. He pointed at the wooded area on the green. 'Someone else over there wants to wave goodbye.'

Arthur had to squint to make out the forms of Eirik and Bjorn hiding in the trees. While Eirik seemed quite fond of using the make-up now, Arthur was surprised to see that Bjorn had also painted his face (although even from this distance it was clear that the effect wasn't as subtle as Eirik's). They were waving and Arthur waved back. Finally, he turned to face Ash.

Her upper lip quivered slightly as she moved towards him and her eyes were glistening, although she was managing to hold back the tears. He could feel his right eye watering as he looked at her and he half-wondered if he'd be able to cry from his damaged left one.

'Arthur–'

'Ash–' They spoke simultaneously, then Ash continued.

'I'm worried about you,' she said. 'What if Loki … you know.'

'That won't happen,' he interrupted her. 'We'll find him. We'll stop him.'

'That'll be harder with you in Kerry. And I'll never get to see you.'

'I'll visit.'

'I know. You're my–'

'All set?' Joe asked, coming back out of the house.

'Yup,' Ash said. 'All set. Stay in touch, Arthur.'

With that, she turned away from him. The others followed her back across the estate. Arthur watched them go, sadly.

'You OK, Arthur?'

He looked up at his dad and tried to smile.

'Yeah, I'm OK. Let's go home.'

Epilogue

Drysi was sleeping in the small bedroom as Loki studied the calendar in the kitchen.

After being thrown from the tower top, he'd landed on a boulder, snapping his spine in two. The fall would have killed a mortal, but Loki had simply healed himself. Then, in the confusion of the mass exodus from the island, he'd discovered the girl on her side, barely conscious. She'd been pitched from the chair with the force of the explosion. He was about to walk off when he heard her voice.

'Wolf-father.' It was weak, barely audible. 'Wolf-father, Hel is alive. Fenrir hid her.'

He turned back, picked her up and strode away.

After a night of wandering the countryside, he came across the empty holiday home. It was a pretty, modern bungalow overlooking a hillside. Family photos of the owners covered the walls. They obviously only lived at the property during the warmer summer months. Loki broke in with little difficulty and that's where they'd been ever since.

Loki – all alone in the kitchen – never slept. He didn't need to. He spent the days and nights looking at the calendar he'd pulled off the wall, staring at the date he'd circled with his own blood.

If what Drysi had said about his daughter being alive was true, then Arthur had defeated him for the last time. He would find his daughter. But first he had to find Fenrir. His son had gone missing in the mêlée and only he knew the location of Hell's Keeper.

Loki smirked. He knew that with Drysi's help he would find Fenrir. They just had to wait. Until the next full moon …

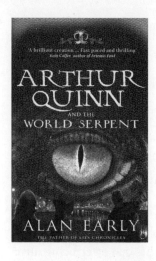